BOOK ONE

CITY
LOVE

SUSANE COLASANTI

 KATHERINE TEGEN BOOKS
An Imprint of HarperCollins Publishers

Katherine Tegen Books is an imprint of HarperCollins Publishers.

City Love
Copyright © 2015 by Susane Colasanti
All rights reserved. Printed in the United States of America.
No part of this book may be used or reproduced in any manner whatsoever
without written permission except in the case of brief quotations embodied
in critical articles and reviews. For information address HarperCollins
Children's Books, a division of HarperCollins Publishers, 195 Broadway,
New York, NY 10007.
www.epicreads.com

Library of Congress Cataloging-in-Publication Data
Colasanti, Susane.
City love / Susane Colasanti. — First edition.
pages   cm
Summary: "Told from alternating points of view, *City Love* is the
story of three very different girls living together in NYC as they struggle
to find the balance between their dreams, their pasts, and their complicated
hearts"— Provided by publisher.
ISBN 978-0-06-230768-2 (hardback)
[1. Love—Fiction. 2. Friendship—Fiction. 3. Roommates—
Fiction. 4. New York (N.Y.)—Fiction.] I. Title.
PZ7.C6699Ci 2015   2014028440
[Fic]—dc23   CIP
                                                                    AC

Typography by Erin Fitzsimmons
15 16 17 18 19   PC/RRDH   10 9 8 7 6 5 4 3 2 1
❖
First Edition

For Matt,
the love of my life

ONE

SADIE

THE ENORMITY OF THE SITUATION hits me at the most random time. Setting up my teapot in my new room, I'm suddenly so excited I actually bust out a dorky happy dance. I am not above busting out a dorky happy dance, particularly at random times.

I have officially left for college.

This is my new apartment for the summer. I might even stay here freshman year with the same two roommates. I'm stoked to get to know them. Rosanna moved in today. Darcy moves in tomorrow. My older brother is cool, but I've always wondered what it would be like to have a sister. Now I sort of get to find out . . . without the irritations of living at home.

No parents constantly hovering with their relentless interrogations and antiquated opinions and when-I-was-your-age rants.

No curfew. No boundaries.

No rules except for the ones I want to make.

How awesome is that?

I cannot freaking *wait* for college to start. High school wasn't that bad for me, but it made me sad to see how horrible it was for a lot of other kids. I did what I could to reach out to the kids who needed it the most. Random acts of kindness is my jam.

Rosanna appears in my open doorway. Actually I hear her before I see her. The light *snap-snap-snapping* sound I heard when we met this morning is back. Now I see that her fingernails are snapping together as she flicks her thumb against her middle finger. She seemed nervous when we met. Maybe she's still nervous? But she said she was okay when I asked before. I think she just needs some time to adjust.

"Hey," I say. "All unpacked?"

"For now."

"Are you hungry?"

She nods.

"I'm not going to have the energy to unpack kitchen stuff after I tackle this suitcase. Do you want to go out for dinner? I know a place nearby that's good and cheap."

"Perfect," Rosanna says.

I unzip my ginormous suitcase. How I'm going to figure out where everything goes in my new tiny closet is beyond me. And I thought our closets back home were small. How weird is it that I went away to college and I'm less than a mile from home? I even stayed in the same neighborhood. The thing is,

I'll probably never see my parents until I intentionally go back home to see them. That's the thing about New York City. Each neighborhood is like its own town. The West Village isn't that big, but you can pretty much avoid anyone else who lives here for as long as you want. Thank you, population density.

I couldn't wait to leave home. So when this housing opportunity came up with the University of New York, I jumped on it. They offer summer housing for students enrolled in the fall semester who are doing summer internships on campus or at companies affiliated with UNY. Rosanna has one of those summer jobs. The same opportunity is offered to students who are taking summer session classes, like Darcy. Darcy hooked us up with a video chat right after we got our housing assignments a few weeks ago. So the three of us have virtually met already. Darcy said she couldn't wait to see our beautiful faces. I can already tell she's going to be a lot of fun.

Even more fun? My internship at the Department of City Planning. Urban design is something I became passionate about a few months ago. My best friend, Brooke, wants to be an urban planner. The ironic thing is that I helped her figure that out. The more Brooke realized urban planning was perfect for her, the more I realized urban design is a career that fits in perfectly with who I am. New York City is my boyfriend. I'm constantly geeking out over his architecture and parks. Spaces specifically designed for people to gather in positive ways that inspire relaxation, happiness, and connection have always intrigued me. New green spaces and repurposed streets (like Summer

Streets, when major avenues are closed to cars for a few hours, or these little plazas in Times Square with lounge chairs) make me giddy. But I never really gave much thought to the planning behind these spaces until I took a guided tour of the High Line with this couple from Seattle who were visiting my parents. That's when enlightenment struck in the form of a career goal. I was like, *Dude. I could be one of the designers behind the coolest new structures in New York City.* Designing the spaces in which people rejuvenate and connect with one another would be like the hugest warm fuzzy ever.

Urban design wasn't always my future career choice. I wanted to be an elementary school teacher before. Peer tutoring in high school was awesome. I loved challenging myself to explain things in the simplest ways I could without disrespecting the kids I was tutoring. The best days were when they laughed at my corny jokes. A lot of the kids I tutored were failing English. They just didn't get what all those authors from back in the day were talking about. Schools should update their required reading lists with books that students from this century can relate to. Then maybe more kids would actually like to read. I loved tutoring and I loved the internship I had last semester at Hunter College. Their School of Education is launching an antibullying program this fall called Starting Now that was inspired by initiatives like It Gets Better and Born This Way. Everyone at my internship worked with elementary education majors to develop activities that focused on increasing awareness of the consequences of bullying. Kids who understand how strongly their words and actions can affect others are the ones who will be more likely to take action against bullying when they see it. Starting Now will be run in twenty-three schools. It makes me happy to imagine kids doing activities that I designed when they go back to school.

My teaching goal was more of an expected track. I love kids and I love tutoring, so it made total sense. But I could spread the love on a much larger scale as an urban designer. I could reach thousands more people in countless positive ways, maybe even millions, than I could as a teacher. I'm excited to see what my new internship brings this summer.

Rosanna watches me unpack my suitcase. I can't believe she's already unpacked. Her boxes arrived right after she did. We both moved in this morning, but she got here after me. I hope she's not mad that I took the bigger room. My mom said that when an apartment is vacant and everyone's moving in around the same time, the person who gets there first can pick which room they want. Rosanna didn't have that much stuff: only the two bags she took on the plane and a few boxes. You would think the girl who moved from Chicago would have way more stuff than the girl who moved less than a mile from home.

"Do you know which drugstore is the least expensive?" Rosanna asks.

"Try CVS or Rite Aid. But you might have to go to a few different places to get everything you want."

"I almost died when I saw how much toothpaste cost at Duane Reade."

"Yeah, you'll want to avoid Duane Reade. They're outrageous."

"How does anyone afford to live here?"

"It's not easy."

"Sorry to bother you with all these questions. I feel so out of place." *Snap-snap-snap.*

I look up from my suitcase. Rosanna's been emitting her unsettled vibe since the second we met this morning. She has that nervous/shaky/adrenaline thing going where you're in a new place and you're scrambling to get settled, but you don't know where anything is. I want to do everything I can to make her feel more comfortable.

"You're not bothering me at all," I reassure her. "I'm happy to be your tour guide. Oh, and I know where the best gelato is. One less thing for you to worry about. We can go there after dinner if you want."

"Cool. Um, do you want me to help you unpack some of those Target bags?"

"That's okay. It looks like more than it is." My mom took me to Target to get a bunch of stuff for the apartment. I had no idea I'd need so much for a furnished apartment. Mom insisted on some new kitchen things. And I'll need sheets and towels and other basic stuff for college anyway. Before I knew it, we were pushing an overflowing cart down the school supplies aisle, attempting to cram in a few packs of pens between a bright orange pasta pot with a built-in colander and my new comforter.

After working a miracle by finding room in my closet for most of my clothes, I walk with Rosanna to Joy Burger Bar for dinner. They have the best veggie burger ever. This is important. Ever since I became a vegetarian last year, I've been on the prowl for the best veggie burger in New York. My prowl has turned out to be a more difficult search than you'd expect. Most veggie burgers fall apart when you take your first bite. It's so disappointing when the satisfying meal you were anticipating quickly becomes reduced to crumbled bits of carrot and sprout all over your plate. But Joy Burger Bar knows what they're doing. Their veggie burgers are not only delicious, they're cohesive. And they have the most refreshing iced tea served with the perfect amount of sweetness, not too much ice, and sprigs of fresh mint. Rosanna will love JBB.

Being outside after unpacking and rearranging furniture all day is a double shot of cheer. Summer is in the air. People on the street are smiling and laughing with groups of friends. I love it when the energy is really up like this.

"Let's cut through the park," I say.

"Which park?" Rosanna asks.

"This one right here. Washington Square Park."

"That's the one with the arch, right?"

"Yeah. We'll walk back this way so you can see the arch all lit up. The fountain lights up, too." This is Rosanna's first time in New York. It blows my mind that someone my age has never seen these cultural icons before. I'm happy for Rosanna that she gets to experience all of this glitz and glamour for the first time. "The park was renovated so that the fountain is perfectly framed by the arch. They spent some ridiculous amount of money to move the fountain like twenty feet."

"Really?"

"It's entirely possible that I'm exaggerating. But the fountain is epic. See how everyone congregates around it? This is the kind of place you could come to if you're having a bad day and immediately feel better, you know?"

"Yeah." Rosanna looks around with wide eyes, taking in all the action.

A street performer is doing an elaborate magic trick near the fountain. Lots of colored scarves are involved. We stop behind the deep circle of people surrounding him to watch. Rosanna is a few inches taller than me and can see everything. I have to stand on my tiptoes to see what's happening.

The crowd is dazzled by how quickly the plethora of scarves is changing colors. They burst into enthusiastic applause. The magician bends down and smiles at a little boy at the front of the circle. He holds a blue scarf out to the boy. The boy is reluctant to take the scarf. He probably thinks it will be snatched away as part of another trick. But then he sticks a tentative hand into the space between them. The magician dangles the scarf. The boy grasps it. His laughter rings out, making other people in the circle smile at how adorable he is.

"How cute is that little boy?" Rosanna says.

"I know. I love how sweet this guy is with him." Part of the reason the street performer has attracted such a huge crowd is his positive energy. He scanned the crowd while he was performing, taking the time to make eye contact with as many people as possible. He paid extra attention to an old lady up front wearing a denim jacket with about ten million buttons. The man radiates goodness. Even his collection bucket is yellow with a big smiley face. HAVE A MAGICAL DAY! is stenciled on with glossy red paint.

"Thanks for swinging by, folks," he tells the crowd. "You're the reason I have the opportunity to do what I love every single day. Except when it's raining. But even when I'm stuck at home instead of shooting Silly String at unsuspecting tourists, I'm still the luckiest man alive because of your support. Thanks so much." He busts out a final trick where shiny Silly String goes flying above the crowd. More enthusiastic applause.

Street performers fascinate me. I always wonder about the chain of events that led them to where they are now. Did they always want to be street performers? Are bigger dreams burning in their hearts? Or is it all about interacting with an audience for them? Whatever their dreams are, they know they're in the right place to make those dreams reality.

New York City is for dreamers. New York City will always be where I belong.

TWO
DARCY

IF I CAN MAKE IT here, I can make it anywhere.

As long as I can avoid getting mangled by one of these crazy bikers.

A bike messenger just zoomed past me so quickly a paper bag actually flew up from the sidewalk, sucked into the vortex he left behind. Another flashed by so close to me I had to check to make sure my nose was still attached. The flavor of crack they're on has yet to be determined.

Mental note: Beware of bike lanes.

Making my way to the building I'll be calling home this summer while hefting a gigantic backpack would be easier back in Santa Monica. The streets of New York City are fierce. New Yorkers walk like they have to be somewhere right now. Like every single person on the street has to be somewhere *right this second*. A family of German tourists was nearly taken out by an impatient businessman bursting through their group a few blocks ago. He was running to cross the street before the light changed. The guy had zero awareness that he had almost knocked over a little girl. Perhaps he'd like a side of social skills with his oblivion.

Don't get me wrong. I absolutely love the frenetic energy of cities. Especially this city, which I believe to be the greatest city in the world. I'm just having a cranky morning on top of hardly sleeping on the plane. Someone should really tell the guy who was sitting next to me that snoring so loudly you make your whole row of seats vibrate is not normal. Underneath my stank mood, I'm appreciating everything (including the bike messengers on crack and strung-out race walkers). These New York sensations are unparalleled: the rush of pounding the pavement in the summer heat, the sound of cabs honking and music blaring from an apartment window, the sight of vintage mopeds in colors like powder pink, and the smell of bacon wafting from a restaurant as I walk by. So much is happening. This is the place where dreams become reality. This is the place where anything is possible. This is the city that never sleeps and I intend to be wide awake for every breathtaking second. Operation Summer Fun Darcy is a go.

I unload my backpack in front of my new building. This building is so New York. Crumbling brick, ancient fire escapes, and a stoop that has clearly seen its share of drama.

I love it.

My backpack has somehow gained fifty pounds since I flew

into JFK way too early this morning. Unpacking this monster will be a rigorous endeavor. I dig around in one of the outside pockets for my set of keys. Then I hoist the backpack back on, unlock the heavy front door, unlock the second door after the row of mailboxes, and begin the trek up to 4A. A fourth-floor walkup wasn't my first choice for a summer share. I only enjoy walking in a mostly horizontal direction. People usually assume I'm athletic by the way I look. But sports (or any kind of working out) is not my thing. I just inherited some good genes. Anyway, this is what UNY's housing office gave me. My dad refused to spring for a decent apartment. He wanted me to see how average people in the real world live. As if scoring any kind of apartment in downtown Manhattan is average. Dad says I need discipline. I say discipline is confinement in disguise.

By the time I get to the apartment door, I'm sweating. I dump my backpack on the floor. Fortunately I like to layer. I start stripping off my oversize retro tank down to the fitted cami underneath as I turn the key to let myself in.

Sadie and Rosanna are already here. I love that we've talked online so I can recognize who's who. We only had a few minutes, but it was enough to get a general idea of their personalities. Sadie (midlength copper hair with gold highlights, brown eyes, petite, ready for her internship in a pretty floral top and black pencil skirt) is unpacking kitchen stuff with all the cabinets open. Rosanna (long wavy light brown hair, brown eyes, taller, ready for camp in a basic tee and shorts) is turning the kitchen table around. They stop what they're doing when I burst into the apartment. I don't mean to burst. It's just kind of how I roll.

"Hey, ladies," I say, whipping the tank over my head and flinging it on the nearest chair. Then I lug my bag in and drop it near the couch. "This place is fantastic. Look at those windows!" We were graced with the good fortune of scoring a prewar apartment with huge French windows. Almost makes up for the Everestesque climb. "Don't you want to open them?"

"We have the AC on," Rosanna says. "It's so hot out."

"Tell me about it. Since when is it such a sweltering hot mess this early in the morning? What time is it, eight?" I flop onto the couch. "Sorry, I'm disgusting. Navigating the subway system with backpacker gear is even harder than backpacking through Europe. I'll try not to sweat all over the cushions."

Sadie laughs. She comes out of the kitchen. The kitchen isn't one of those typical microscopic cubbies. This one opens up into the living room, separated by a small breakfast bar. I like the layout.

"When did you guys get here?" I ask Sadie.

"We moved in yesterday. We actually have to leave soon, but we wanted to get up early and work on the place some more. The cabinets are kind of gross." Sadie glances at the kitchen. "I'm making progress, though."

"You don't have to do that. We could just hire someone."

The girls give me blank looks.

"To clean? We could hire a cleaning lady to get the place in shape. Easier than doing it ourselves, right?"

"Um . . . I don't mind cleaning," Rosanna says. "I already started on the bathroom."

"Wasn't the apartment supposed to be cleaned before we moved in?" Sadie asks. "That's standard for New York."

"Guess the rules don't apply to lowly student housing," I say. Then I sigh like I will never ever drag my sprawled exhausted butt off the couch. "This couch feels incredible."

"You must be tired from your flight," Sadie says. "And from hauling your bag around. It looks really heavy."

"Oh, I'm used to it."

"Did you really backpack through Europe?" Rosanna asks.

"Best year of my life. It was the most enlightening experience a girl could hope for. I took a year off after high school to explore. That's why I'm almost nineteen. You guys are eighteen, right?"

They nod.

"Have you ever been?" I ask Rosanna.

"To Europe?"

"Yeah."

"Not so much."

"Not so much or not at all?"

Rosanna blushes. "Not at all."

"Better to save it for when you're older anyway. You'll get more out of it. At least, that's what my dad said when he tried convincing me not to go. Luckily my mom won that battle."

"I can't wait to go to Europe," Sadie says. "Not that I'm going anytime soon."

"You're already super lucky. Growing up in New York City? That's so cool. What neighborhood?"

"Right here in the West Village. I'm hoping to avoid running into my parents."

"What a drag. You move away to college and it's like, *What up, parental unit. Thanks for still being all up in my face.*"

"They're not that bad. It's just . . . whatever." Sadie turns to Rosanna. "What's Chicago like?"

"Not as exciting as New York," Rosanna says. "There's so much to do here. I don't even know where to start."

"We start by asking the locals for hot tips." I look at Sadie. "Where do you like to hang out?"

"There are some gorgeous outdoor spaces around here. I'm kind of obsessed with green spaces and architecture in general. Just a heads-up that I might spontaneously start geeking out over a window or something while we're walking down the street. Have you heard of the High Line?"

"That park that was built on an elevated railway?" Rosanna asks.

"Yes, and it is beyond impressive. We have to go."

"I read about it in the *New Yorker*. I'm dying to see it."

"We're there." Sadie looks at me expectantly. "You in?"

"Totally. But I meant . . . like bars and clubs."

"Oh. I haven't really gotten into them yet."

"Just let me know where you want to go. I can get you in anywhere."

"I don't have a fake ID," Rosanna says.

"Fake IDs are for amateurs. I've been crashing bars since I was fifteen. Trust me. I know how to work a bouncer."

Rosanna is not impressed. Maybe she doesn't believe me. Or maybe clubs aren't her scene. She's clearly not the kind of girl who whips her top off at Mardi Gras. But I'm hoping there's a wild side percolating underneath her reserved exterior.

"We're going to have a blast this summer," I promise them. "You'll see."

Rosanna goes back to the table and starts fussing with it again.

"Why do you keep turning the table?" I ask.

"I'm trying to figure out which way it should go. Long way? Wide way? I can't decide. What do you think?"

"Does it matter?" I snap.

The girls stop what they're doing. They look at me.

"Oh my god," I say. "I am so sorry. I've been . . . it's been a hard time for me. You probably think I'm a monster. Please know that I'm not a monster. I'm just carrying some heavy baggage." I tip my head toward my enormous backpack in an attempt to lighten the mood.

Mental note: Take it easy. The last person I want to be is the girl who becomes all bitter and cynical and an emotionally stripped skeleton of her former self because of some boy. No boy will ever have that kind of power over me again. I need to leave that drama behind. This up in here is all about Summer Fun Darcy.

"No worries," Sadie says. "We're all adjusting. Meeting new roommates is awkward."

"Especially when you act like a dumbass the second you arrive." I propel myself off the couch. "Long way," I tell Rosanna. "Definitely."

My backpack is so overpacked it might spontaneously burst right here in apartment 4A. Unpacking will help ease my mortification. I can't believe I got off on the wrong foot with Rosanna. That's not me. Meeting new people is my thing. And here I thought being a sweaty mess was as gross as I was going to get today.

I'm declaring a state of emergency. Attitude adjustment starts now.

I topple my backpack over on the floor, unzip the long side zipper, and start unpacking. This will be a fun summer for all of us. These girls have no idea what they're in for.

THREE
ROSANNA

DARCY ARRIVED WITH A BANG.

She whipped her tank top over her head when she walked in the door. She threw it on a communal chair. Does she intend to pick it up?

We do not know.

She could turn out to be one of those nightmare roommates I've heard about who tosses her stuff everywhere and expects you to deal with it. As in, if you don't like living in a disaster area, you're more than welcome to clean it up yourself. Darcy flopped on the couch with her feet up on the armrest. Her shoes were still on. Who puts their shoes on furniture? Doesn't she care that the couch will get dirty? Then she bit my head off for no reason. Now she's unpacking her bag right here on the couch instead of in her room where you're supposed to unpack.

Fortunately Sadie and I have a few things in common. We both love New York City. We're both dreamers. Although she's a lot more optimistic than I am. It's not that I'm a pessimist. More like a realist. You can't help being cynical if you've experienced and witnessed a lot of crap. That's why I'm going to be a social worker. I want to help make the world a better place. I don't care how much money I make. Doing what I'm passionate about is all that matters.

Part of me is also an idealist. I expect the world to operate in ways a lot of people insist are impossible. I want an end to war. I want people to treat one another like human beings with equal rights. I want everyone to contribute to society in meaningful ways.

I want happy endings to always come true.

That said, I don't expect to be served my own happy ending on a silver platter. Hard work and dedication are essential. I fully intend to earn the happy ending I deserve. Until that day arrives, I will carry happy ending hope in my heart.

Darcy thinks the kitchen table should go the long way. I'm not about to question her taste. First of all, she's gorgeous without even trying. She has the kind of interesting blue-green eyes I've always wanted. Brown eyes are so boring. Her dark brown hair looks cute in a choppy cut that's effortless but trendy. She's shorter than me but taller than Sadie. Darcy is rocking a fitted cami that was under the flowy tank she whipped off when she came in, several trendy chains of various lengths and colors, cherry-red shorts, and platform flip-flops. Compared to the ancient tee I've been marginally getting away with for too many years and my fairly new but somehow already outdated maxi skirt. Just being in the same room with her is making me wish I could afford to overhaul my entire wardrobe. But that would be impossible.

Money is really tight back home. I'm the middle of five kids. My parents have been scraping by for as long as I can remember. They can't afford to support me now that I'm out of the house. My mother wishes she could send all of her kids to college. She gets so sad that she can't support us the way she originally planned that sometimes she breaks down and cries. But my older brother and sister are both managing on their own. They took out student loans and received federal financial aid. They work twenty hours a week on top of their full course schedules. I'll be doing the same thing. I'm determined to make this work just like they are. I want to show my mom that it's okay for her kids to make their own way in the world. She should be proud of dedicating her life to nonprofit outreach with Planned Parenthood. Just like my dad should be proud of teaching at-risk kids on the South Side.

I arrange the kitchen table the long way and push in the four chairs around it. This summer is going to be the most challenging time of my life. Just buying groceries will be nearly impossible to pull off. But I refuse to be defeated by circumstances I can't control. So what if I have nothing saved? Living in New York City has been my big dream ever since I was little. Whenever I read books that took place here, I'd get this warm tingly feeling that this is where I was meant to be. And now I'm here.

Finding this summer housing deal was the only thing that made it possible to move here before the semester started. A day camp on the Lower East Side hired me as a counselor, thanks to the University of New York's career planning center. Then UNY told me about apartment shares. My job will cover the rent this summer, but I won't have much left over to pay for everything else. Despite this horrific realization, I refuse to be afraid. Figuring out how to pay for everything is a skill I've honed to perfection. I'm all about budgeting, sales, and coupons.

This will work out.

It has to work out.

Failure is not an option.

Darcy is yammering away. Asking us questions. Telling us how awesome Santa Monica is. Unpacking the entire contents of her massive bag on the couch. She hasn't even seen her room yet. That's the first thing I wanted to see when I got here. Doesn't Darcy want to see her room? She must know the two best ones are taken. Isn't she worried her window might be on an air shaft or looking directly into a bedroom next door or something? It's like she doesn't even care. All I know is if she leaves those piles of clothes on the couch, I am not cleaning them up. Who unpacks her stuff in the living room? When she just met the two girls she'll be roommates with all summer?

Not that I would ever ask Darcy any of this. She's way too intimidating.

FOUR
SADIE

RIGHT AROUND THE CORNER . . .

That's what the sign over my bed says. I hung it there to remind me that my soul mate could be anywhere. We could run into each other when we least expect it. Or right when we're hoping our paths will finally cross. I don't know where I'll find him. But I will definitely know it when I do. As Brooke would say, I will have the Knowing. We share the motto over my bed. I've been repeating it every day for two years, building up to this moment when I have more freedom than ever.

Sometimes I'll be walking down the street and an epic feeling will come over me. That's the best way I can describe it. An epic feeling is when all of my wishing and hoping and dreaming about the boy I'm meant to be with comes rushing at me full force. The epic feeling reminds me that he could be anywhere. I really believe he's here somewhere. Maybe he's thinking of me, too. Imagining what I'm like. Wondering how he'll finally meet me. Wanting to hold me in his arms and kiss me the way he's been dying to for so long.

The weird thing about the epic feeling is that anything can trigger it. Last night I was walking down 5th Avenue between 11th and 12th Streets and I looked up. Brooke is always trying to get me to look up more. I couldn't believe everything I'd been missing before I made an effort to look up instead of zipping around in my usual busy mode. Not only beautiful architectural details I somehow never saw before. But a different kind of energy with people I passed on the street. Anything is possible in this city. That possibility grows with every new detail I notice, every new interaction I have. So I looked up and saw the moon positioned right between a big tree and a building. A bunch of windows in the building were illuminated by the warm glow of lamps. And just like that, I could feel what it would be like if my soul mate lived in one of those apartments. He'd live there by himself. No parents. No roommates. I would love going over to his place and he would love it when I came over. Because being together would be the best part of our day. Being together would make everything else in our lives even more amazing.

"Sugar?"

I snap out of my daydream. The barista is waiting for my response.

"Oh, sorry. What?"

"Do you want sweetener?"

"Yes, please."

"Splenda, raw, agave, simple syrup?"

"Just regular sugar would be great. Thanks." This isn't my usual coffeehouse. This one mostly caters to high-strung, type A workaholics on some kind of permanent cutthroat deadline. My usual place serves coffee old-school style. They just have one kind of sugar. Actual sugar. But this place is on the way to my internship. What can I say? New Yorkers are suckers for proximity. Walking two blocks out of our way can be a major detour.

As my coffee is being sweetened, I glance toward the door. My soul mate could walk in that door any second. When he sees me, he'll know we're meant to be together. It will be magic, just like in *Sleepless in Seattle* when Tom Hanks sees Meg Ryan for the first time. She's watching him from across the street. Something makes him turn around to look at her. A light of recognition sparks in his eyes, even though he's never seen her before. But it doesn't matter. Their instant connection is obvious even from across the street.

I want to know that magic. I want to feel what it's like to meet the love of my life. My heart tells me that it will feel the same exact way I've been imagining it will.

After I pay for my coffee and leave, I see a college boy heaving his overloaded laundry bag down the sidewalk, reminding me that I have to do laundry when I get back to the apartment. I knew I should have done my laundry before I moved out. I was so anxious to leave as soon as possible I made the stupid decision to cram my dirty clothes into the new wheely hamper that was part of our Target haul. One more second of my mom's pity glances and whispered worried chats with my dad and I would have lost it.

Today is the first day of internship for incoming freshmen and sophomores. Juniors and seniors started yesterday to prepare ten-minute presentations about their fields of study under the urban planning umbrella. The idea is for those of us starting out to be exposed to different areas of urban planning so we can learn more about our options. I already know urban design is my jam. But hey, I'm always open to new ideas. Maybe someone's presentation will dazzle me.

My internship is in a beautiful building on Bond Street. As I approach the building, I instantly fall in love with it: polished steel and glass, sleek awning with light strips along the sides, impressive lobby done in Italian marble. The street number is raised metal in a simple, round font. I can't help smiling as I push my way around the revolving door.

A bunch of people huddle into the elevator with me. Some of them are probably other interns. Some of them are older professional types. Most of them watch the elevator numbers light up as we ascend. I feel very grown-up with my coffee cup and sleek new Kate Spade tote. My worn-out ginormous bag simply would not do.

The elevator opens to the third floor with a bright *ding*. I get out with a few other probable interns. The open-plan office is all white with pops of color. The entire space is flooded with natural light. The two far office walls are dotted with massive round porthole-style windows. I've never seen round windows that big. Cubicles are gathered in sections separated by architects' tables, glossy white filing cabinets, and walls sprayed with whiteboard or blackboard paint. The cubicles have personal enhancements like bamboo plants, stuffed animals, and Koosh balls sitting along the top of their walls. This is clearly going to be a fun place to work.

"Welcome, interns!" the cheerful receptionist says. I was so sucked in by the main office floor that I didn't even notice her desk across from the elevators. "Please make your way to conference room one, first door on your left."

I hustle around the corner. The big round clock above her desk said it was 8:58. There's no way I'm going to be late on my first day.

Conference room one is just as gorgeous as the main floor. Long glass conference table. White leather desk chairs. More porthole windows. Oversize screen for presentations on the wall at one end of the table. There's even a counter with packaged snacks and a sink. A sign above the faucet says that the water is triple-filtered and we can help ourselves to a reusable bottle. But then I notice that there's a bottle on the table in front of every chair, along with glossy white folders and pens in rainbow colors. Baskets of Sharpies, Post-its, and highlighters sit at the center of the table. I grab the closest empty chair.

"Welcome to the best internship of your life!" a guy in his mid-20s declares as we sign in. He's Parker, our internship supervisor. I recognize him from my online interview. Same tousled wavy brown hair. Same John Lennon glasses. But now I can see more of his Brooklyn hipster style. Parker is rocking a plaid button-down and rust-colored skinny cords. "Or at least what I hope will be. Good to see all of you in person. We have an outstanding group of talented, intelligent, creative people at this table. I hope you're as excited to be here as I am to work with you."

Parker goes on to explain what we already know from the email he sent us: juniors and seniors majoring in urban planning will be giving us ten-minute presentations on their fields of study. First up is a guy studying structural engineering. A girl who wants to be a natural resources planner goes after him.

Then he walks in.

I've never seen him before. But he's exactly my type. My heart skips a beat.

"Hey, everyone," he says, "I'm Austin. I'm a senior planning to pursue a masters in urban design. Urban designers combine aspects of planning with architecture . . ." He looks at me. And kind of forgets what he was saying.

Our eyes lock.

"I'm particularly interested," Austin continues, ripping his eyes off mine, "in the ways in which design relates to environmental science and holistic wellness. Let me show you some examples." Austin dims the lights. The first slide is of a beautiful living room labeled DELOS BUILDING WELL-NESS. "Delos Living places health and wellness at the center of design decisions. This is one of their residences at Sixty-Six East Eleventh Street. They also design libraries, schools, and other indoor public environments with improved living conditions. Better water, better air, better light . . . everything a building can do to provide healthier living standards for its workers and residents."

He looks at me again.

He keeps looking at me.

As Austin goes to the next slide to discuss LEED-certified new construction, I am in total and complete awe of him. Not just because he's the most gorgeous boy I've ever seen. He's about six feet tall, average build. I watch his arm muscles flex as he gestures toward a LEED rating systems chart. His toned arms tell me that he works out, but he doesn't hit the weights too hard. Love that. It's such a turnoff when guys are huge. Austin has brown hair that's short on the sides and a bit longer on top. The most gorgeous thing about him is his eyes. Austin's eyes are the perfect shade of sky blue. Even sexier? His eye color changes with the light. When he dimmed the lights, his eyes looked almost violet. But when light from the computer screen hit his eyes, they were more like a baby blue.

This boy is beyond adorbs.

I'm not only riveted by the way he looks. Everything he's saying is resonating with me so strongly I swear everyone in the room can see me vibrating. I practically jump out of my seat when he gives a shout-out to the High Line.

Austin finishes his presentation and turns the lights back up.

His eyes lighten from twilight to early afternoon.

"We have"—he checks the time—"one minute for a quick question. Anyone?"

No one has a quick question.

"Okay, well I'm upstairs on five if you want to find me." He smiles right at me with such genuine warmth, butterflies bust out flapping like crazy in my stomach. Is love at first sight a real thing?

The rest of the day goes by in a blur of paperwork and ID cards and getting-to-know-you activities and cubicle assignments. I keep looking around for Austin, but I don't see him anywhere. He must have to stay up on the fifth floor. I'm emotionally exhausted by the end of the day. But in a good way.

A second wind strikes me when I get back to the apartment. I grab my packed wheely hamper, detergent, and the card that operates the washers and dryers in the laundry room. Then I begin the long haul down four steep flights of stairs to the basement. I knew I was lucky growing up in a second-floor walk-up on the corner of Grove and Bedford—a sweet configuration with a sweeter location. Some of my friends from high school lived in crazy walk-ups with superhigh ceilings, rickety staircases, and halls that would be broiling in the summer. From the way I'm already sweating, I can tell our halls will be merciless by August.

Arriving at the laundry room is a huge relief. It will take an unprecedented feat of strength for me to haul my laundry back upstairs. But it could be worse. At least we have laundry in the building. This is way better than maneuvering a heavy laundry bag outside when it's raining or freezing or a hundred degrees. I find two washing machines next to each other: one for lights and one for darks. A cute boy in a UNY tee comes in carrying an Ikea bag filled with rumpled clothes while I'm loading a washer.

He smiles at me. I smile back.

Right around the corner . . .

"Hey," he says. "You here for summer session?"

"I have an internship. What about you?"

"Full course load." He extends his hand for me to shake. "Glutton for Punishment. Nice to meet you."

"Laundry Procrastinator. A pleasure." We shake.

"Are you new?"

"I moved in yesterday."

"Welcome. This is my third summer in the building."

"Did you get to have the same apartment?"

"Let's just say I'm lucky to *not* have the same apartment. Wildlife should be restricted to the great outdoors. Not under my bed like last summer."

"Ew. What was—no, don't tell me. I don't want to know."

"Don't worry. They fumigated last summer. The exterminator comes once a month now. You should be good."

I shudder as I bend down to take more clothes out of my hamper. I pull out a fistful of panties. Glutton for Punishment looks at them. I fling them in the washing machine so hard a wayward one with flowers and peace signs flies onto the floor.

Right in front of the washing machine he's using.

My panties have landed at his feet. And I don't even know his real name.

He picks up my panties. He holds them out to me. "You should probably take me to dinner first," he jokes.

My face gets hot. I try to laugh. The laugh sounds more like I'm choking. This is one for the Of Course file. Of course I threw my panties at a cute boy I just met. Why wasn't I more aware that I was grabbing up panties? Why didn't I wrap a shirt around them before I took them out of the hamper? And why is this so freaking embarrassing?

I snatch the panties and throw them in the machine. Maybe if I pretend this never happened, he'll forget that my panties came flying at him by the next time we run into each other.

"My girlfriend has ones like those," he says. "With little peace signs? They're cute."

The Of Course file is seeing some serious action today. Of course he has a girlfriend. Boys that cute are rarely single. Or if they are, they're usually single for a reason. Of course he felt the need to bring her up. There's no way anything could ever happen between us after the Mortifying Panties Incident.

"So what floor are you on?" he asks.

"We're in 4A. I'm dreading the walk back up with all this laundry."

"Let me know if you need any help. I'm in 3A."

"Thanks."

We stuff the rest of our clothes in the machines in agonizing silence. After he's gone, I realize I never got his name. Not that it matters. New York City social interactions work in mysterious ways. You could live in the same building with someone for years and never see them. Or you could run into the same person twice in one week. There's a good chance I won't ever see him again, even though he lives below me.

By the time Darcy swings by my room when Rosanna's ready to go out, my laundry is all neatly folded and put away. The Mortifying Panties Incident has faded from critical intensity to moderate embarrassment. The boy in 3A is cute, but there's no way he compares to Austin. I haven't stopped thinking about Austin since the second I first saw him. I'm still trying to get a grip on my initial reaction to him. What was that? It wasn't just the heart-skipping-a-beat thing. My whole body reacted the second I saw him. I felt flushed. There wasn't enough air in the room. Every time he looked at me my heart pounded so hard I could hear blood rushing in my head. Who has a reaction like that to someone they don't even know? And what does it mean?

Right around the corner . . .

FIVE
DARCY

"BLEECKER STREET HAS CHANGED SO much," Sadie says. "That overpriced chain tea store we just passed? Used to be an herb shop. My parents remember it from back in the day when they moved here after college. It was a West Village institution. But rents keep getting more and more outrageous. The mom-and-pop stores can't afford to compete against all these obnoxious chains." Sadie stops in front of an ice cream parlor called Cones to look around. "At least Cones is still here. I don't recognize half of these other stores. And I've lived here my whole life. Really with that tea store? There's an amazing teahouse around the corner on Morton Street that's empty most of the time. But this store always has customers. How is that fair?"

Rosanna and I nod compassionately. It can't be easy to watch your hippie neighborhood become a suburban mall.

"Sorry," Sadie says. She breaks into a smile. "End of rant. Onward and upward, roomies! What's next on the agenda?"

We're looking for things to brighten up the apartment. Sadie wants plants. Rosanna wants a new pillow. I don't blame her. The one on her bed is disgusting. I ordered a bunch of cute stuff for our place already, so I'm not looking for anything in particular. Window shopping is super fun. I hear what Sadie's saying about how the neighborhood's changing. And yeah, I feel bad that the flavor of this historic district is being spoiled by chain stores and pretentious boutiques. But I would be lying if I said the new Bleecker Street isn't fabulous in its own way. Because it totally is.

A clump of tourists is crawling along at a glacial pace in front of us. Sadie motors off the sidewalk and skitters around them in the bike lane. I'm both horrified and impressed by her dexterity in navigating the bike lane. Rosanna and I follow her lead. Sadie is such a New Yorker. She tries so hard to stay positive that I know she's not going to grumble about the meandering tourists the way she probably wants to.

A girl who looks a couple years younger than me passes us. I turn to admire her fun DIY style. She's rocking pink Hello Kitty knee socks over black leggings, a distressed Pink tank shredded across the back, vintage white Nikes with a purple swoosh, huge turquoise glasses, and long ponytails with retro ribbons dangling in the breeze behind her. New Yorkers are known for their unique style. I'm having a blast getting to see it all up close and personal.

"Gross," Rosanna says. "Did you guys see that?"

I twirl back around. At first I think she's talking about Hello Kitty Girl. But she's looking ahead of us.

"What did I miss?" I ask.

"A guy went into that deli and didn't even hold the door for the old lady behind him. Hello, she has a walker! Rude much?"

We watch the old lady attempt to maneuver her walker so she can push open the door. Sadie runs ahead of us. She pushes open the door and holds it while the lady lurches in.

"Bless you," the lady says.

Sadie comes back to us. Rosanna is staring at her.

"What?" Sadie asks Rosanna.

"That was awesome," Rosanna proclaims.

"Not really."

"Yes really. You freaking rule."

"Just a random act of kindness."

"Can I be you when I grow up?"

Sadie laughs. "I'm pretty sure you know how to hold a door open."

"But you have the confidence to actually do it."

"I'll let you do it next time."

"Okay. Anything I can do to reduce the amount of rude in the world. Seriously, did he not see her? People are way too caught up in their own worlds."

"I know!" I say. "I saw a guy practically run down a family of German tourists this morning. All because he was racing to catch the light. Is knocking people over really worth gaining an extra minute? Oh, and stay clear of the bike lanes. Just saying."

We approach a boutique with beautiful bags in the window. I stop to admire the view. I'm a sucker for beautiful bags. One in particular catches my eye, calls out to me, and gives me a seductive wink. High-end accessories know how to play me like a fine-tuned string instrument.

"That bag is exquisite," I announce, pointing out the one that looks like it was made for me. There's no way I can resist going in. I open the door and step aside to let them in. "Ladies?"

Sadie and Rosanna browse while I chat with the cute guy who comes over to help me. I would so be hitting on him if he wasn't gay. He tells me all about the bag: how it's one-of-a-kind, how it's imported from Italy, how its classic lines will never go out of style. Sold. I pay for the bag while Sadie holds a dress up against herself for Rosanna to see. Rosanna smiles halfheartedly. Her gaze shifts around the boutique. She's tottering by a rack of summer scarves, one leg crossed in front of the other, arms nervously wrapped around herself. She clearly does not want to be here.

Back outside, I hold the bag up for their approval. "What do you think?"

"It's gorgeous!" Sadie gushes. She tentatively touches the satin piping. "How could you even think about carrying any other bag when you have this?"

"A girl can never have too many bags." I look at Rosanna for her reaction.

"Wasn't it really expensive?" she asks.

"Oh, no worries there. My dad gave me a credit card with a ridiculous limit. His attempt at erasing the travesty of never being around while I was growing up. It's like, *Hi, I'm a workaholic who can't be interested enough to raise my daughter, but I can throw money at her when she's older to make up for it.* I don't think so."

Rosanna is agog. They both are.

"TMI?" I inquire.

"No, it's . . . that's amazing. I wish I could see anything I want in a window and just go in and buy it. You're so lucky."

Sadie glances at Rosanna, then smiles at me. "We basically want to be you."

"Trust me. You don't." A woman who's attracting a lot of attention is walking toward us. People she just passed on the sidewalk are staring. They're taking pictures of her from behind. I recognize her under the big black sunglasses and shiny hair pulled back into a relaxed pony. "That's Claire Danes."

"Where?" Rosanna says. Then she sees her. "No. Way. That's totally Claire Danes."

Claire breezes by. The air is suddenly charged. She has an electric magnetism that affects everything around her. It must be amazing to have that kind of power over people. I want to be that powerful one day.

We turn to watch Claire saunter down the street. More people turn and stare as she passes. Everyone is transfixed as she majestically swishes by them. Girl power to the max.

"Let's follow her," I say.

"You can do that?" Rosanna asks.

"People do it all the time around here," Sadie says. "The West Village is flooded with celebs. I don't know how many people actually follow them down the street. But we wouldn't be the first."

We start following Claire. Not in an obvious way. We're super casual like we're three friends strolling around the Village on a Tuesday evening who just happen to be going this way. Okay, we were going the other way, but no one has to know.

Rosanna giggles. The giggles erupt into a snort, which makes Sadie crack up. This is far from an undercover operation.

"Be cool," I tell them. "She's going to know we're following her."

The girls try to compose themselves. Rosanna smooths her hair down, clears her throat, and straightens up. Sadie is shaking her head like she can't believe we're such tourists.

Claire goes into an upscale gift shop. Her dark sunglasses make it hard to tell for sure, but I swear as we're loitering outside the window gawking at her, she's looking right at us and recognizing us as the fools she passed a few minutes ago. She'll know we're following her unless we act normal. Claire Danes cannot know we are the crazy fangirl stalkers we are.

"Let's keep going," I mutter. "That way it'll look like we were just checking out the dipped candles."

We walk on by like we didn't even recognize her, playing it off super casual. We allow ourselves to stop and squee two blocks later.

"I can't believe we saw Claire Danes!" Rosanna shrieks. "I love her!"

"Not that we stalked her or anything," Sadie clarifies.

"Of course we didn't stalk her," I say. "We're not creepers. We were just on our way to . . . somewhere over there."

"Right." Sadie nods. "That place."

"You guys," Rosanna says. "She was *right there.* We could have reached out and touched her."

"That wouldn't have been creepy at all," I say.

Rosanna is freaking out. "Did you see her skin? It was like porcelain. She looks incredible. I hope I look half as hot when I'm that old." She whips around to see if Claire left the shop. "Can we walk back? I have to see her one more time."

"Let's go," I say. Rosanna is exuding a whole different energy than when I met her this morning. She's not a reserved girl fussing over the kitchen table anymore. She's an excited girl who's opening up to the possibilities of this amazing city. Our wild and free summer is off to an excellent start.

One of the best things about being wild and free with a superhigh credit limit is being able to treat my friends. I'm thrilled when the girls accept my offer to buy them dinner. We find a bistro with a cute outdoor garden and settle in for what I hope will help build the foundation of a solid friendship. I don't want to blow it. Especially since I need to make up for being such a douche to Rosanna this morning.

"Should we do coffee and dessert?" I ask the girls when our dinner plates are cleared away.

"I'm okay," Sadie says.

"You've already been way too generous," Rosanna adds.

"Stop," I tell them. "We're doing coffee and dessert. End of discussion."

The girls beam at me. I love that they're so appreciative.

While we're waiting for dessert, I decide to share a secret about one of my biggest fangirl crushes.

"I have a confession to make," I start. "You might think this is too mainstream. But." I lean in conspiratorially. "It is my unwavering belief . . . that the musical sound of Ethan Cross rules."

"OMG you like him?" Sadie yells. At first I think she means it in a way like *How can you like him?* But then she says, "I've been obsessed with him since ninth grade!"

"Um, excuse me, he's been my husband since eighth grade," Rosanna interjects.

"Take a number, ladies," I say. "He's all mine."

Hardcore fangirling ensues. This sisterhood was meant to be.

SIX

ROSANNA

DARCY ISN'T AS BAD AS I thought. She might not even be bad at all. It was really generous of her to treat us to dinner last night. I peeked at the check while she was writing in the tip. There's no way I could have afforded to pay my share. Especially considering that the muffin and coffee I splurged on this morning practically required me to take out an additional student loan. I thought the cashier at the café was joking when she told me the total.

Back in high school, I was pressured by rich kids to spend money I didn't have in certain situations like group dinners. Group dinners are the worst. They always end up costing more than they should. Everyone should only pay for what they ordered, plus their portion of the tip. But it never turns out that way. You end up paying like twice as much as what you actually owe. And when everyone else agreed to split the bill however many ways, it was embarrassing to be the only one at the table disagreeing.

It's good to know that I could take out another student loan if I ran out of money. Not that I'm going to run out of money. And not that I want to be in debt until I'm eighty. But it's comforting that I could still cover housing if I had to resort to Plan D. Having a Plan D is part of my survival strategy. The thing about Plan D is, even though I know I won't need it, having it waiting to catch me like a trapeze safety net is reassuring. Plan D helps me breathe easier when I'm feeling anxious about the future. Like about how I'm going to pay for everything. Or about putting myself through four years of college in one of the most expensive cities in the world. When the anxiety becomes unbearable, I construct as many alternative backup plans as I need to. One particularly excruciating night I had to go all the way down to Plan Q before I could breathe again.

Darcy is a sweetheart. She seemed way more relaxed at dinner than she did when she burst into the apartment yesterday, wired and chucking her clothes all over the place. She could have just been delirious from her long flight. Or dealing with something completely unrelated. There's no reason to assume she snapped at me because of anything I did. I definitely judged her too harshly. My cynical side has been known to flare up. Trusting people more would probably be a good thing. I could start working on that right now with this trust activity we're doing.

"Trust that your fellow counselors will catch you," our camp orientation director tells us. "They will not let you fall. Your eyes will be closed when you let yourself fall back. You won't be able to see them. But trust that they will be there with their arms outstretched, ready to catch you and protect you."

This trust activity is one of the many activities we've done today. It's our first day of orientation as camp counselors. The campers don't start until next week, after public schools get out, but I love this day camp already. It's on the Lower East Side. This area is very 70s New York City. Or at least what I imagine 70s New York City was like. I saw some guys rocking tube socks and those vintage red short-shorts with the white racer stripes down the sides. One girl I passed on my walk from the subway had a huge 'fro. Adidas circa 1982 were spotted along with tremendous headphones. The Lower East Side is classic New York in the best possible way, as if time could be preserved here forever like in one of those amber bubbles on *Fringe*.

Mica is up next for the trust activity. We clicked right away over the best conversation at lunch. I was ranting about some lacking behavior I saw on the subway that morning.

"This guy lunged for the only empty seat," I was saying, "as if he didn't see the lady with a baby heading for the seat first. He just dove right into it."

"Unacceptable," Mica agreed.

"I know, right?"

"Why can't people be nicer to one another? Did he really need to sit down that bad?"

"He didn't look sick or anything. And all of his limbs were working."

"Did you give up your seat?"

"I would have, but I was standing. Another guy let her have his seat, though."

"We need more guys like him. Can you imagine how beautiful the world would be if everyone acted the way they're supposed to?"

"Seriously. How hard is it to treat others the way you want to be treated?"

"I'm saying."

It was the best first conversation I'd ever had with anyone. Mica totally gets me. We were obviously meant to be friends.

Mica stands with her back to us. We're gathered behind her in two lines, one on either side of her. I stretch my arms out with one crossed over the other and grasp hands with the boy across from me. This lattice structure we're making is strong enough to catch everyone as long as we work together. One counselor is standing at the far end to grab Mica's shoulders if she slides back too far. When we're ready, Mica crosses her arms over her chest, closes her eyes, and lets herself fall back while keeping her body as straight as possible. We catch her.

Mica will also be a freshman at UNY. I've heard that college is where you establish lifelong friendships. I can't wait to get started. My friends in high school weren't exactly the kind of friends I wanted to have. They were a decent group, but I didn't feel like any of them really got me. College is my chance to meet new people who will truly understand me.

On the subway ride home, I take out my book and lose

myself in another world. I left off at one of those really good parts where you don't want to stop reading but you have to because real life is demanding your attention. I'm so absorbed in the story that I don't realize the lady next to me is reading over my shoulder.

So. Freaking. Rude.

There are levels of inappropriate behavior. Throwing a plastic bottle in the regular garbage when a recycling bin is right there is bad. Not looking to see if someone is coming up behind you before you let the door swing shut is worse. Talking too loudly on your phone in a confined space with other people is straight-up offensive. But reading over someone's shoulder? That's borderline harassment. From the casual look on her face, I can tell the lady sitting next to me is completely oblivious.

Someone sat down on the other side of her at the last stop. Which she naturally took as an invitation to scrunch closer to me. Now she's all wedged up against me, invading my personal space.

I don't think so.

I lean away from her a tiny bit.

She leans in closer to me by the same amount.

I lean away some more.

She leans in some more.

When she's practically in my lap, I suddenly yank the book away. She almost falls flat on her face.

A grandma sitting across from us gives me a knowing smile.

I'm sure she's endured more than her share of subway offenses over the years.

People are looking at the lady next to me. She should be mortified. But she plays it off like nothing happened. She doesn't apologize for getting all up in my book. She doesn't even look at me.

When I get off at my stop and climb the subway station stairs into the summer evening light, my frustration melts away. I already feel like New York is my true home, which doesn't surprise me. Somehow I knew I belonged here way before I arrived.

I'm telling the annoying-lady subway story to Sadie and Darcy in my head as I walk home. They will think it's hilarious. I'm lucky that I get to go home to my people tonight. New York City may be home to millions of people, but without your people it's easy to feel alone.

SEVEN
SADIE

"EXCUSE ME," A GUY'S VOICE says from the entrance to my cubicle. "Have you seen Parker?"

I look up from the array of brightly colored Post-its spread out on my desk.

Oh my god. It's him.

"Not yet," I say. "Maybe he's in his office?"

"I already looked." He holds up a folder. "More paperwork on the checklist. I handed it in late last year and got the worst placement."

Is it possible to be starstruck by someone you just met yesterday? Not even *met*. Drooled over from across the room. *Get it together, Sadie. Help the boy figure out where Parker is.* "The checklist for . . . ?"

"Oh, sorry. Upperclassmen have field-study placements for the last four weeks of internship. We get to list our top three choices of where we want to be placed, but we have to write essays about why each agency is a good fit for us. Last year I got stuck at the housing authority. Let's just say their snack station didn't include triple-filtered water. Not that they had a snack station."

Austin has perfect arms.

"So what are your top three choices?" I ask.

"Delos Living is number one, of course. Ed Kopel also does a lot of LEED-certified construction. And BKSK Architects. They did Twenty-Five Bond Street. Have you heard of it?"

And those *eyes*.

"No," I say.

"Seven people purchased the property together. Then they worked with the architects to create an apartment building with lots of common areas. It was kind of conceived as a big house."

He's so hot I can't even look at him.

"Anyway," Austin says. "Sorry to bother you. Parker has to be around here somewhere." He turns like he's about to leave. Then he turns back. "You're a freshman, right?"

I nod.

"Do you have an area of interest yet?"

"Urban design. Same as you."

"Nice. I'm sure you'll love it."

"I wanted to thank you for your presentation. I'm really loving the environmental side of design now."

"Oh, good." Austin gestures toward the Post-its. "That looks interesting."

"Not sure how interesting, but definitely necessary. I can't believe everything I have to get done this week. The Post-it technique is a desperate attempt to salvage my sanity."

He takes a step inside my cubicle. "What are you working on?"

"Spires."

"Dude. I love spires."

"I know! How awesome is the rotating LED light on One World Trade?"

"The beacon of hope. Freaking amazing. Isn't it visible for like fifty miles?"

"That's what I heard."

We smile at each other. I don't know what it is. Something about this boy feels really familiar . . . almost like we've met before. But there's no way I would forget meeting him.

"I'm Austin." He extends his hand to me.

"I'm Sadie." We shake.

Austin looks around my cubicle at the bare walls and ancient filing cabinet. "Not too cozy, is it?"

"Yeah, it's a bit on the stark side now? But we'll be redecorating next week."

"Really?"

"No." I laugh. He laughs, too. "At least we're allowed to bring in whatever we want to brighten things up." I point at my replica of the *LOVE* sculpture I brought in today. It sits right above my keyboard to remind me of what's most important. As soon as I pulled it out of my bag, it was official. My cube had been personalized.

"The least they can do to offset the torture of endless paperwork." Austin taps his folder against his fingers.

A Post-it gets stuck to my arm. I must have been fidgeting without realizing it. "Paperwork is just a test of how bad you want it," I say, casually brushing off the Post-it and hoping Austin isn't picking up on how nervous I am.

"Judging from the amount of paperwork they're testing me with, I'd say I want it pretty bad."

"Then I have no doubt you'll get placed at Delos. You obviously belong there."

He scans my Post-its. "Can you show me your Post-it technique? I have a feeling I might need it one day."

"Sure." I roll my chair over to the side so he can stand at my desk. While I'm showing him how I organized the Post-its to represent each aspect of the project, our arms touch for a second. I yank my arm away like I was just burned. My mind is only half on what I'm explaining. The other half is wondering when our arms might touch again. Or our legs. Or our hands. Okay, I guess my attention discrepancy is more like 20% explaining, 80% physical contact.

Out of the corner of my eye, I see Parker pass by. He scoots back and leans in.

"There you are," he says to Austin. "I was looking for you up on five."

"I was down here looking for you," Austin says.

"You have that paperwork?"

Austin holds up his folder. "Right here." A paper slides out of his folder onto the floor. We both reach for it at the same time. I grab the paper and whip back up. My head bangs against his chin.

"Sorry!" I say. "Are you okay?"

Austin rubs his chin. "I think I'll live." He turns to me as he's leaving. "Thanks for the tips. I feel more organized already."

I smile at him, but inside I'm crushed. Why did Parker have to show up like that? I could have talked to Austin all day. Assuming he'd want to keep talking to me. What if he doesn't even like me? What if he's just being nice because I'm new? What if the attraction is all on my side? But what if he *does* like me? Why would he linger in my cubicle like that if he didn't like me? And why would he keep looking at me during his presentation yesterday? This running commentary plays on a mental loop while I'm working. By the time it's my lunch hour, there's no way I can eat. My stomach is twisted in anxious knots. Uncertainty is the worst.

I roll out of the office at five as a jittery ball of anticipation. What if I run into Austin in the elevator? Everyone leaves at the same time. It's totally possible that I'll see him. I fluff my hair with a shaky hand and try to smooth down some random wrinkles on the side of my sundress. Why is my sundress wrinkly like that? Was it folded under while I was sitting? Okay. I really need to calm down. If I do run into Austin, I doubt he'll even notice.

The down button of the elevator has already been pressed. A few people are waiting for it. When the elevator bell *dings* and the doors slide open, a rush of adrenaline hits me so hard I see dark fuzzy spots for a second. My heart hammers until I realize Austin's not in the elevator. I get in, the doors slide closed, and my pulse returns to normal.

But then I see Austin through the lobby windows. He's outside talking to some guy. Seeing him is all it takes for my nerves to start twanging so hard I'm actually shaking. I attempt some deep breathing. Is there another way out of the building? Probably some back exit with an alarm I would set off. I have no choice but to leave the normal way.

I glance outside again before pushing through the revolving door. The guy Austin was talking to is gone, but Austin's still there. Why would he be just standing there alone? Could he be waiting for me?

"Hey," Austin says when I come out.

Right around the corner . . .

"Hey." He looks even cuter than he did before. How is that possible?

"How was the rest of your day? Did the Post-it technique work out for you?"

"Not exactly." If he only knew how distracted I've been from the second he left. "I'll figure it out tomorrow."

"You definitely will." He flashes me a smile so bright I'm temporarily blinded. No boy has ever made me this nervous and exhilarated and happy all at once.

"Well . . . see you tomorrow."

"Hey, um . . . do you have plans tonight?"

I shake my head.

"Do you . . . I mean, I know this is late notice, but would you maybe want to do something? It's so gorgeous out. We could walk around for a while and see what we feel like doing. If you want."

"Yeah," I say in a tone that I hope comes off as casual instead of exposing how hard I am freaking out right now. "Like you said, it's gorgeous out."

"Are you hungry?"

"Not yet. Are you?"

"Nope. But dinner can be part of the outdoor funtivities."

"Did you just say 'funtivities'?"

"I wanted to snatch it back the second it left my mouth."

"No, it's cute."

"Not too dorky?"

"Just dorky enough." No boy has ever asked me out this quickly. I didn't even know this kind of thing happened in real life. There's a very good chance my chin has hit the floor. I might need a forklift to scrape it up.

"So . . . is that a yes to dinner outside?"

"Absolutely. I love eating outside."

"Of course you do." He looks around. "Which way should we go?"

Austin asked me to dinner and I said yes. That's officially a date, right? When you eat together? Holy crap. We're about to have our first date. We could just stand here all night and it would be the best first date ever. But what if this isn't actually a date? What if it's just hanging out as friends? I mean, who asks out someone they just met? He'll probably be at a bar with his friends tomorrow night, laughing about how easily he got a girl to say yes.

"Come on," I say. "We'll do my favorite walk."

We walk west toward the Hudson River. There's something about walking downtown along the water that always gives me an epic feeling. Whenever I'm agitated or sad, I'll walk along the water and automatically feel better. Walking restores my hope that everything will be okay. Especially at night. The city lights soothe me. The city energy makes me feel like anything is possible. Like all of my dreams will come true if I keep dreaming big. I want to share that energy with Austin. Or at least try to. Making another person feel exactly what you feel is hard. But I think he'll understand. I can't wait for it to get dark so the city lights can work their magic on him.

"Have you ever noticed how many blue doors there are around here?" Austin says.

"Um, and red doors. I thought I was the only one who noticed stuff like that."

"No way. Counting colored doors is my jam."

"It's *my* jam."

"We can share a jam." Austin smiles, looking all around. I love that he looks up when he walks. I love that he notices the little things that make this city so beautiful. I love that we're walking down Perry Street, a street I've walked down a million times before, and he's making it feel new. The landmarks I'm so familiar with feel completely different now. In a good way.

We cross the West Side Highway to the walking path along the river. Something else I've done a million times before. But when I turn left this time with Austin by my side, every cell in my body is buzzing with excitement.

"Where do you live?" I ask. What if Austin has been here this whole time? What if he lived near me and I didn't even know it?

"Jersey City."

"Have you been there a long time?"

"Two years. I was in a dorm freshman year. Then I wanted to find an apartment near UNY, but the city's crazy expensive. So I got a place in JC with two other guys."

"Do you still have the same roommates?"

"Nope. I'm solo now. Trying to be a grownup and all that. I found a one-bedroom near my old place. What about you?"

"I just moved to an apartment near UNY, but it's student housing. I have two roommates who appear to be awesome. The crazy thing is I grew up in the West Village not far from my new place."

"Way to pull off going away to college without going away."

"Tell me about it. I really need to explore. I've never been to Jersey City."

"You grew up here and you've never ventured across the water?"

"There was no reason to go." Until now. "I'd like to see it sometime."

I'm hoping Austin will say that he'll take me. But he doesn't say anything. He just looks across the water at the Jersey City skyline. It's amazing how much the skyline has been developed over the past decade. When I was little, there were hardly any tall buildings to look at. Now I love looking at the stripy-light building on my night walks. It's this building with a slanted top that has stripes of light moving across it. Sometimes the top is lit up only white with no movement. Other nights stripes of different colors blink across the slanted top. Some nights the top is dark. I've always wondered what the colors mean.

"Do you know what that building is?" I point at it. "The one with the light stripes?"

"It's a financial center. A few different banks are in there."

"Wow."

"What?"

"I've been wondering what that building is for years. And you just *know*."

"I drive by it all the time."

"That's so weird."

"Driving by it?"

"In a car? Yeah."

Austin laughs. "You don't ride around much in cars, huh?"

"Try never. Except a few summers when my parents rented a car for weekend trips. But it's weird that I've been on this side of the river admiring that building for years and it's just some office building you pass on the way to Home Depot or wherever."

We look at the light stripes. Wide purple stripes and thin red stripes are blinking.

"It does look cool from over here," Austin says. "But it's just a regular building up close."

"That's so disappointing."

"Maybe we could find out what the colors mean. Would that make you feel better?"

"That would be amazing. I've always wondered what they mean."

"Unless they're randomly generated and have no significance whatsoever."

"At least we'd know. Better to know than not know. Even if it's bad news."

"I don't know about that. Sometimes the element of mystery adds to the allure."

True, surprises can be fun. Then there are other times when you'd give anything for answers. Like I'd love to know if Austin is going to hold my hand at some point tonight. I've been wondering our whole walk. Which is scary and thrilling at the same time. That thing where you want him to touch you and you're pretty sure he wants to touch you, but he can't touch you because it's too early or things are undefined or whatever. You want it so bad, but you can't have it yet. Like cinnamon buns fresh from the oven that are too hot to eat. You have to wait until they're cool. Except in this case, things with Austin are only getting hotter.

"Am I seeing what I think I'm seeing?" Austin asks. He's

looking out at Pier 25. The pier with the mini-golf course.

"Hells yeah," I confirm. "And can I just say that the waterfall hole is the most challenging one you'll ever play?"

"Are we about to have a mini-golf throwdown?"

"That depends."

"On?"

"Whether or not you can handle it."

Austin gives me such an adorable smirk it takes all the effort I can muster to not melt into a puddle. "Bring it," he says.

We decide to eat first, so we head over to the Shake Shack a few blocks down from mini golf. Austin scores us an outside table right as two girls are leaving. Snagging an outside table during the dinner rush on a gorgeous night is all about being in the right place at the right time. Or persistence, if you feel like lurking by the tables for the slightest sign that someone might be leaving soon.

"Did you know this Shake Shack is LEED Gold Certified?" Austin asks.

"Why am I not surprised?"

"Because I only take you to the best places?"

"That must be why."

Austin is a total gentleman. He pulls out my chair for me. He asks what I want so he can go in and order for us. He even brings extra napkins on our tray. How did he know I like extra napkins? When we go to mini golf after dinner and Austin is paying for our games, he asks for the purple golf club for me. How did he know I always get purple?

Being with someone who knows what you want without you having to tell them is paradise.

After Austin pays and we take our golf balls and clubs, he picks up a scorecard.

"Do we have to keep score?" I ask.

"How else will we know how majorly I kicked your butt?"

"What about playing for fun?"

"The fun part is when I majorly kick your butt."

"Competitive much?"

"Much, yes."

"Fine." I pull a mini pencil from the bin. "But don't say I didn't warn you."

"About what?"

"About how majorly I'm going to kick your butt."

"Oh, it's like that, is it?"

"Pretty much, yes."

"Let's do this."

Five holes later, Austin is up by two points.

"Hole in one!" he yells. He runs to the hole. He does a little dance, swinging his club over his head. "Majorly. Kicking. Butt."

"Very impressive," I say. "This one isn't easy. The green looks flat, but it's not. Lots of imperceptible slants are hiding."

"Yeah they are." He struts some more. "How you like me now?"

"Same as before."

Austin comes over to me. He puts his arm around my waist. "How much was that?" he asks.

Someone behind us lets out an exasperated sigh. I turn to see an angry tween chomping her gum so aggressively she's engulfed in a thick fog of grape Bubblicious.

"Sorry," I say. "Do you want to go ahead of us?"

"No, just go."

"Kids nowadays," Austin mutters under his breath.

I take my shots and hustle to the next hole. My heart is racing. Austin has already touched me on purpose. That means he can touch me again like it's what he does.

When will he touch me again?

Austin lines up his ball at the ninth hole. Before he takes his first swing, he gazes across the water at his town glittering in the distance. He just stands there, grounded, and absorbs the view. His moment of Zen inspires me to look up at my own city. It's the little things that make me the happiest. Streetlights around the pier illuminating the trees. The warm glow of hundreds of windows in the tall Tribeca buildings. A few bright points of light visible in the sky. The smell of hyacinths in the summer night air. At this moment, standing here with a boy I just met who already feels like home, I am overwhelmed with city love. City love is the kind of love that never dies. No matter how many boyfriends come and go, no matter how many heartbreaks I endure, this city will always be my true love.

"How awesome is it to be playing mini golf in downtown Manhattan?" Austin says.

"I know! I think about that every time I play here." I love that we're on the same wavelength. I love that one of my fave songs just came on the sound system. I love that Austin appreciates the little things like I do. Plus he's cute, funny, smart, and is dedicating his life to improving my city. He had me at holistic wellness.

Things begin turning around a few holes before the hardest one. The hardest hole involves a waterfall where most of the balls get trapped. You have to hit your ball over a skinny bridge in order to avoid the frustrating fate of waterfall limbo. I've watched several people hunkered down on the green trying to retrieve their swirling golf ball by patting at the water with their club. Eventually the balls that are trapped in the water filter out to the lower part of the green, where the hole is. Unless they don't. Some of the pink and purple smudges barely visible underwater have probably been there since the course was built.

If you asked me how exactly to hit a golf ball to guarantee it goes over the skinny bridge, I wouldn't know how to describe the technique. The way you have to hit it is just something I intuit. I can tell if the ball will go over the bridge in midswing. This time, I know I'm free and clear the second I swing my club back. Austin and I watch the ball roll smoothly down the center of the bridge and circle down to the lower green. And that's not all.

It's a hole in one.

"*Woooo!*" I jump around like a maniac. The group behind us cheers.

"How did you do that?" Austin wants to know.

"I can't reveal my secrets. Then they wouldn't be secrets anymore."

Austin places his ball where I put mine to take his shot. "Why does it feel like I'm being hustled?"

"You're not. That was pure luck. I have no idea what I'm doing. Except, um, I don't know . . . getting a hole in one on the hardest hole?"

Let's just say Austin isn't as lucky. His lead unravels from there. By the time we get to the last hole, I'm up by four points. I end up crushing him.

"You wanted to keep score?" I say. "Bring it."

Hole eighteen looks simple, but there's some tricky tilting involved. Austin takes his shot. His ball doesn't even come close to the hole.

"Now you're giving up," I tease. "You're just falling apart."

"You didn't tell me you had mad mini-golf skills. Anyone playing with you would crumble."

I like that even though Austin is competitive, he's not a sore loser.

He insists on celebrating my victory as we're walking down Leroy Street. It's late enough that there aren't any cars coming down this little street. We stand in the middle of the street, arms up in Vs for victory.

"Wow," Austin says.

"What?"

"I didn't think it was possible to meet someone as dorky as I am."

"There's a difference between being dorky and dorktastic."

"Which one am I?"

"Dorktastic."

"How can you tell?"

"Isn't it obvious?"

Austin lowers his arms. He comes right up to me. I lower my arms and try not to panic. Something is definitely about to happen.

He hugs me. Right here in the middle of Leroy Street. A street that I've walked down a million times before. If I had known even one of those times that this scenario would unfold in my future, Leroy Street would have acquired significance of extraordinary proportions way before tonight.

"Thank you for saying that," Austin says. "Achieving dorktastic status has been a goal of mine for a really long time."

"Keep dreaming big," I say against his shoulder. Could I just live here with his arms around me in the middle of the street forever?

Austin pulls away from me a little. "Nope, not done." He hugs me close to him again.

Could tonight be any more magical? No. No, it could not possibly be.

Eventually we break away from each other. I hate that he's walking me home because that means I have to go home. But I love that he's walking me home because it's the perfect opportunity for him to kiss me.

"This is me," I say when we get to my building.

"Thanks for destroying me at mini golf," Austin says.

"Thanks for treating."

"Thanks for being awesome."

"Thanks for being dorktastic."

We're smiling at each other like complete idiots when the front door of my building flings open. Darcy flies down the steps before she realizes I'm the one awkwardly lingering by the stoop with a boy.

"Hey!" Darcy says. One look at Austin and I can tell she's dying to know who he is.

"Hot date?" I joke. Because why would Darcy be leaving for a date when I'm getting home from one? It's after ten.

But Darcy says, "Absolutely," like she's serious. The girl is hardcore. I have a feeling I'm about to learn a lot from her.

"Have fun," I say.

"No doubt." Darcy takes a last look at Austin before diving into the night.

"That was my roommate," I tell Austin.

"She seems fun."

"She is." We're smiling at each other like complete idiots again.

"Do you want to go to a party with me tomorrow?" Austin asks. "It's at my friend Trey's place in Brooklyn."

"Totally." Austin doesn't need to know that it will only be like the second time I've gone to Brooklyn. I feel bad enough that I've never been to Jersey City. How far is Jersey City from the West Village? Two miles? Yet it feels like twenty.

"Okay, well . . . I better get going. Can we talk tomorrow about what time I'll pick you up?"

I'm so relieved that we're not meeting at the party. Attempting to navigate my way around Brooklyn would be an epic fail. "Yeah. Wait, did I give you my number?"

Austin whips out his phone. "Hit me."

After my number is securely stored in his phone, we linger awkwardly some more. Is he going to kiss me? Or does he think the first date is too soon?

"See you tomorrow," he says. Then he hugs me goodbye.

I can wait for our first kiss.

Our first kiss . . . which I'm pretty sure will be happening tomorrow night.

Tomorrow night . . . which I'm pretty sure will be even more magical than tonight.

EIGHT
DARCY

THAT BOY SADIE WAS WITH on our stoop is super cute. She didn't say anything about having a boyfriend. She doesn't seem like the casual dating type, but the way they were ogling each other when I came out made it clear that what they have is anything but casual. Sadie better be ready for me tomorrow. I'll be drilling her for all the hot details.

Even hotter than Sadie's boy? Is the boy I'm making out with right now on the subway. We're going at it like we don't care who sees. Not that the subway's crowded at two in the morning on a Wednesday night. But this weird old guy is leering at us from the other end of the car. Welcome to the late-night F train. PDA, anyone?

Zander pulls me onto his lap so I'm straddling him. He presses his hand against the back of my head to kiss me harder. Oh, did I mention that we met today? He came up to me when

I was walking to class. Asked me out on the spot. He was like, "Excuse me for bothering you, but you're too beautiful not to introduce myself." I didn't have time to talk. But we talked tonight at this East Village dive bar where we saw a show. The band was a trip. Some girl was doing improv artwork on butcher paper spread out on the floor in front of the stage. Her charcoal sticks scratched frantically every time the beat picked up. The lead singer was one of those angry girls who are here to tell you that nothing matters because we are all going to die. She was wearing a frilly shirt with tulle flowers while she screamed about our collective demise.

Good thing Zander and I talked at the show. We haven't done any talking on the ride home.

The subway makes a stop. No one gets on or off our car. Weird Old Guy is still leering at us.

"We're the next stop," Zander says.

"Now can you tell me where we're going?"

"Do you really want me to tell you?"

"No. I want you to kiss me some more."

He does. Then he pulls back and looks at me.

"This is one of the most romantic moments of my life," he says.

Normally I'd brush off such a faux-profound statement. But if the boy could kiss me for twenty minutes and still find me attractive after staring at my face under these harsh subway lights, I know he must really mean it.

We get off and walk over to Union Square. I heard this is

where street performers and skater kids hang. And that single twentysomethings gather on the stairs to the park like they're the Spanish Steps. The park is deserted right now. I def want to come back here during the day to scope out the scene.

Zander takes me to this cool diner called Coffee Shop. "It's open twenty-three hours a day," he advertises.

"Why not twenty-four?"

"They close between five and six in the morning to regroup."

As if the prospect of a cool diner being open twenty-three hours a day weren't sweet enough, the menu says breakfast is served anytime. I am *so* coming here with Sadie and Rosanna. But only if they agree that pancakes taste better in the middle of the night.

A thirtysomething woman passing by our table looks at me. "I love your dress," she says. "Where did you get it?"

"ModCloth." I fully admit to being a ModCloth addict. You know how some brands are so your style it's like they're in your head? That's how ModCloth is to me. They're retro in such a cute, fun way. Managing to be trendy and stylish but still unique is not easy to pull off.

Zander and I get into the kind of heavy discussion about life you can only have over late-night pancakes. Zander is a musician. He's all about going with the flow.

"What, I'm supposed to take after my dad?" he's ranting. "He has a miserable life with my mom in suburbia where the only thing to look forward to is poker night with the boys so he can hide out in his friend's garage and pretend he's not married for a few hours. Think I'll pass on the cookie-cutter lifestyle."

"Word. Everyone knows the best part of life is outside the lines."

Zander holds his coffee mug up to toast me. "Here's to living outside the lines."

We clunk mugs.

I already know this date is just for fun. Zander's fantastic, but no boy can tie me down this summer. Darcy Stewart is a boyfriend-free zone. I have the whole summer ahead of me to have as much fun as I want. As many boy adventures as I want. The possibilities this summer can bring are infinite. New York City is my drug of choice. It's like I don't even want to sleep because I might miss something. No matter what time it is, there are people creating and thriving and partying. There are late-night pancakes and making out with boys on subways and that twirly sensation of being dazzled by a million options. I want to do it all.

"Where to?" Zander says after we split the check. I wanted to pay, but he insisted on covering his half. My first class isn't until ten tomorrow morning. We could stay up all night. Dragging my tired ass to class on three hours' sleep is a familiar proclivity from my high school days.

"Any good raves going down at four?" I inquire.

"Not on a Wednesday. I mean, Thursday."

"So what do you like to do in the middle of the night?"

"Skydiving is always good. Or shark chasing."

"In the Hudson?"

"You'd be surprised."

"Any other suggestions?"

"That depends. Want to stay up all night?"

"Absolutely."

"I know the best place to watch the sunrise."

"Take me there."

Zander takes me to the East River Promenade. You can see across the river to whatever borough that is over there. How lame is it that I don't even know where I'm looking? Studying a map of my new city might be a good idea. It's weird how you can only go a few blocks in Manhattan and enter a completely different energy zone. The east side and west side aren't that far apart geographically. But they are vastly distinct. The west side has a hip/celeb/trendy bar/cobblestone street vibe. The east side is more of a classic/old money/ladies in fur coats/ elaborately uniformed doormen scene.

We watch the sky come to life as the city wakes up. Lights snap off. People appear and another day begins.

"When can I see you again?" Zander asks.

Never seeing each other again is the best thing for both of us. If I saw him again, things would move forward. Emotions would get complicated. Zander is into me. I can tell. It wouldn't be fair to string him along, make him hope for something I can never give him. The kindest thing is to say goodbye now. He can remember me whatever way he wants. That's the beauty of preserving time. I will never become a girl he falls out of love with. And the memory of him will remain like the memory of this night. Perfect.

I take a deep breath and begin to explain.

NINE
ROSANNA

A GIRL I'VE NEVER SEEN before locks eyes with me the second I enter the packed dorm lounge. She's over by the punch bowl, shooting me a look so nasty I'm surprised I don't die right on the spot. I look over my shoulder to see if the person she's glaring at is standing behind me. But no. She clearly hates me. Or she thinks she does. Because you kind of have to know who someone is before you can choose to hate them.

If you told me I'd be invited to a party my third day in New York, I would have told you (very politely because it was nice of you to suggest I'm on anyone's social radar) that you were crazy. People don't exactly invite the boring girl to parties. But this invitation was by default. A campus activity group is sponsoring my day camp on the Lower East Side and the affiliated camp on the Upper East Side. They're the group that's throwing the party. Counselors from both camps are here.

Parties make me nervous. I never know what to do with myself. Should I mingle? What is mingling, anyway? Going up to a bunch of people you don't know and engaging them in small talk? How is that fun? I'd much rather chill with people I already know. I recognize counselors from orientation, but most of their names are eluding me. Mentally playing the name game we did at camp this morning isn't helping me connect people's faces to their names like it did before. The only person I really know so far is Mica. I don't see her yet.

Okay. This is a good chance for me to expand my horizons. College is where I'm planning to reinvent myself. Reinventing yourself isn't possible in high school. Everyone knows you in high school. They label you and judge you so harshly you're boxed in until graduation. It's impossible to change your reputation unless you go to a huge school with thousands of kids, which I unfortunately did not. I spent most of high school wishing I could be a better version of myself. I couldn't wait for a fresh start in New York where I could be the person I was truly meant to be.

This is my chance. I take a deep breath. I can do this.

Right when I'm about to push my way into the crowd, someone bumps into me. She has a cup of red punch in her hand. Except her cup is empty now. I watch in horror as her punch spreads over the front of my shirt. Of course I had to wear my only decent going-out top, which is now completely ruined. Because of course it's white and this blood-red stain will never entirely come out.

"Oh, I'm *so sorry*," the girl who bumped into me says. She's the same girl who was giving me the evil eye when I got here. Her tone implies that she's not sorry at all.

"Do I know you?" I ask.

Nasty Girl has fire in her eyes. For a second I think she's going to hit me. She crumples her cup and drops it at my feet. Then she saunters over to a group of Upper East counselors and starts laughing at the top of her lungs.

A few people who saw the assault are throwing me pity looks. There's no way I'm going to stand here with a rude stain on my shirt getting pity looks. I make a hasty escape to the bathroom.

Luckily the bathroom is empty. Bending over the sink, I pump the soap dispenser and frantically paw at the punch on my shirt. I don't want anyone walking in on this. The stain is not coming out; it's only spreading. There aren't any paper towels. I bunch up some toilet paper, wet it, and wipe at the stain. Now I have a soaking wet shirt to go with my lovely stain, accessorized with toilet paper shreds stuck everywhere.

I try to swallow the pit in my throat. That girl hates me. And I don't even know who she is. See, this is why I hate parties. Unforeseen drama. Being the target of Nasty Girl's evil energy makes me want to leave, but I remind myself why this is good for me. I can ignore her. She made her point. She wants to intimidate me so I run out in tears. Sorry Nasty Girl, you don't win that easily. Rosanna Tranelli is a fighter. Rosanna Tranelli will not be bested by some punch-chucking lunatic. Do the kids on *Glee* shrivel up and cry when slushies are thrown in their face? No, they do not. They go and sing some badass mash-up that gives the rest of us chills.

Mascara is smudged under my eye. I wipe it away, brush myself off, and hold my shirt out under the hand dryer. The stubborn red stain taunts me. I ignore the taunting. When I go back to the party, I don't look her way. I don't even look around for Mica. I stalk over to the snack table. Tons of individually bagged chips, pretzels, and cookies are out. I sneak one of each into my bag. These can be lunch and dinner tomorrow. After everyone takes what they want, I'll sneak some more on my way out.

"Party at your place later?" a boy says.

I glance up at him. He looks a couple years older than me, but his confident vibe makes him seem even older. He's wearing a black suit, white shirt, and magenta tie. The aura of success surrounding him is unmistakable. What is a guy like him doing at a party like this?

"Snacks are my friend," I say. And I thought getting sloshed with punch was embarrassing. This guy saw me sneak food into my bag. What am I, some old lady on a coffee break at her macrame circle?

"You wouldn't know it." He looks me over appreciatively.

Really? Are lines like that really supposed to work on women?

"You wouldn't expect a guy in a suit to show up at a dorm party," I retaliate.

"Don't let the suit fool you. I've been known to rock a dorm party up at Columbia. My little sister is the one throwing this party and I'm funding her group. I came straight from my internship at Goldman. Hence the suit and tie." He smooths his tie down. "But enough about me. Tell me something interesting about yourself."

"Like how I'm rocking a punch-stained ensemble this evening?"

"Keeping it classy."

"I try."

"Drag about your shirt."

"Yeah."

"I saw the whole thing. She's nuts."

He saw? So he saw me get sloshed *and* he saw me sneaking snacks into my bag? I am *mortified*. Why is he even talking to me? I am a freak of astronomical proportions.

"She hates me for some reason, which is weird because I have no idea who she is."

"How do you know she hates you?"

"You saw the whole thing, remember?"

"You've never met her before?"

"No. She wasn't at the Lower East camp orientation, so I'm assuming she's a counselor at the Upper East camp. Or she could be someone's friend."

"My sister would know. Want me to ask her?"

"That's okay. I don't want to make things worse. Whatever her problem is, I'm hoping she'll get over it."

"Probably not. People like that don't change."

"Thanks for the support."

"Sorry. You're an optimist. That's an admirable feature. I've been swimming with the Wall Street sharks too long. First, growing up with my investment banker dad, then this internship for the second year. Cynicism rubs off on investment bankers pretty quickly."

"You want to be an investment banker?"

"I do."

"What do investment bankers do, exactly?"

"They manage other people's money. Help them get rich and stay rich. That's the basic idea, anyway."

Why would Wall Street Guy assume I need a basic explanation? I wanted to learn the details of the job description. Not hear something I've known since third grade.

"How exactly do they do that?" I ask.

"Oh, you wanted the long and boring story? We'll have to save that for next time."

"There's another party?"

"No, I meant . . . if you wanted to see me again."

I don't even know Wall Street Guy's name and he's asking me out? How pretentious is that? Like I would ever go out with him. He could never understand my life. He's an investment banking intern in a suit that probably cost more than my freshman year tuition and I'm a girl with punch spilled all over my only good going-out top. We are worlds apart.

"Did you want to know my name first?" I say.

He laughs. "Sorry. I told myself to be smooth when I was

psyching myself up to come talk to you. But I might be coming off as less smooth, more creeper. Can we start over?"

"Totally."

Wall Street Guy extends his hand to me. "I'm Donovan. But I go by D."

"I'm Rosanna."

"Nice to meet you, Rosanna."

"Why do you go by D?"

"The name Donovan never seemed like me. Too formal or uptight or something."

"I feel the same way about my hair. That it doesn't seem like me."

"Your hair is gorgeous. Long and wavy. What's not to like?"

"Thanks, but I've always felt like it should be straight. Straight hair seems more like me."

"You probably shouldn't trust someone who's known you for five minutes, but I disagree. You are definitely a wavy hair kind of girl. Makes you even more gorgeous."

Again with the compliments. Women must fall for his charming ways all the time. His smile is part of the package. He's actually a really good-looking guy. Sandy blond hair with a bit of a wave to it. Almond-shaped hazel eyes. He even has that classic handsome-man dimpled-chin thing. And I can't help noticing that he's taller than me. At five nine, it's not every day I can literally look up to a guy. He's about six three.

"Was I a creeper again?" D asks. "Sorry, I was just being honest."

"No, that's . . . I mean . . . thanks for the compliment," I sputter.

D smiles at me warmly. It's suddenly ten degrees hotter in here.

"So tell me something interesting about yourself for real," he says.

Why can't I think of anything? And why is he making me so flustered?

"There's not much to tell. I just moved here from Chicago two days ago. I'm a counselor at the Lower East Side camp. Which, yeah, I already said that."

"Have you been to New York before?"

I shake my head. "First time."

"You're going to love it here. New York has the best restaurants, museums, indie film festivals, every kind of live music you can imagine . . . and if you're a masochist like me, lots of bad karaoke." He smiles at me again. The lounge gets even hotter.

"What about you?" I say, attempting to divert the attention away from me. I can feel my face heating up. But not because I'm blushing. It's just so freaking hot in here. "Are you from New York?"

"Born and raised on the Upper West Side. My parents still live in the brownstone where I grew up."

"Do you still live up there?"

"No, I'm in Tribeca now. My parents bought me a loft last year. Still needs some work, but it's home."

"How old are you?" I blurt.

"Twenty-one. You?"

"Eighteen."

"So we're both legal," he jokes. At least I think he's joking.

Nasty Girl passes by. She makes sure I absorb her stink eye. Then she helps herself to some more punch. What is she going to do this time, pour it over my head?

"Yeah, she *really* doesn't like you," D observes. "Are you sure you don't know her from somewhere?"

"I'm telling you. I've never seen her before."

"What a weirdo. Watch out for weirdos in this city. New York is amazing, but it's a weirdo magnet."

"That's why I'm here."

"You seem kind of normal to me."

"Kind of?"

"Mostly. With a note of mystery."

He flashes me that smile again. It gets hot in here again.

My heart pounds. I hate that he's making my heart pound. I don't want to give him the satisfaction of knowing that his charming ways are working on me. Not that they're even working. I'm fully aware that we're the worst possible match.

"I have to go," I say.

"Already?"

"I have . . . stuff to do. For camp."

"Well, it was wonderful talking with you, Rosanna."

"Same with you."

"May I have your number? Just in case you'd give me the

pleasure of your company in joining me for dinner."

Dammit, Wall Street Guy. Stop being charming. Don't you realize we could never be together? You are evil. You represent everything that is wrong with this materialistic society. Greed. Corruption. The breakdown of our financial infrastructure. We aren't just on different wavelengths. We're on opposite ends of the electromagnetic spectrum. I know I shouldn't give him my number. What would be the point?

I give it to him anyway.

TEN

SADIE

THE SUMMER SOLSTICE SHOULD BE a happy day for me. What better way to welcome in the light than on the day with the longest daylight time all year? But for me, the summer solstice is an annual reminder of the one thing I never want to think about.

A large group of people have already gathered in Central Park by the time I arrive at our meeting place. I recognize a lot of the people here. They're regulars like me. We meet at the same place every year. There's a hill on the west side of the park near Strawberry Fields called Hernshead. A big weeping willow rests at the bottom of the hill, swooping out over the lake. Whoever decided this would be the best meeting spot for our group definitely understands our pain. Hernshead is a mournful, reflective place.

There's a table with a banner hanging from it that says CHECK-IN. Dakota is stationed behind the table. She's an older lady in her sixties who likes wearing long, flowy things with lots of scarves. There's a folding chair next to her that she won't use. Dakota is always too busy hugging people and greeting everyone with gusto to sit down.

I'll never forget how kind she was to me the first year I came. I was nervous. My mom had been telling me about this group for a while before I joined. She thought it would help. When I was thirteen, I felt ready to join. But I was still nervous about the group. Did everyone else already know each other? Would a lot of people be crying? Was I supposed to talk about what happened while we were walking? I really, really didn't want to talk about it. I hoped no one was going to force me to. Dakota smiled at me warmly. She had kind eyes.

"Welcome to our group," she had said the first time I came to the walk. "Are you registered to walk with us today?"

I nodded.

"What's your name, hon?"

"Sadie Hall."

Dakota checked her clipboard. Her clipboard had rainbow stickers all over the back.

"Here you are." She made a note on her list. Then she gave me a red rubber bracelet. There was blue printing on the bracelet that said CARRY THEM IN YOUR HEART.

Dakota gave me another warm smile. "There's someone I'd like you to meet." Dakota called Vienna over from where she was standing by the edge of the lake, trying to balance on a rock with one sneaker that kept slipping.

Vienna came over and looked at me.

"Vienna, this is Sadie," Dakota said. "Sadie, this is Vienna."

"Hey," Vienna said.

"Hey," I said.

"Want to walk together?"

I nodded.

That first day on our walk around the reservoir, I found out that Vienna was fourteen, lived way up at the top of Manhattan in Inwood, had two hamsters named Beaker and Dr. Honeydew, loved Spree except for the yellow ones, and lost her brother when she was ten. She wore an oversize tee with her brother's photo so everyone would know why she was walking.

"Who are you walking for?" she asked.

I didn't want to talk about it.

That was fine with Vienna. She had lots of other things to talk about. We immediately clicked that first day and have walked together every year since.

When I approach the check-in table, Dakota gives me her signature warm smile. Her familiar scent of sandalwood incense comforts me.

"Sadie," she says. "Welcome."

"Hi, Dakota."

"Happy solstice."

"Happy solstice. I love your scarf." Dakota is rocking a new orange and pink striped summer scarf over a flowy lime-green sundress. She clashes in the most rebellious ways. It's one of the many reasons I love her so much.

"Thanks, hon. You're starting college this fall, right?"

"Yeah, at UNY."

"Great school. I always knew you were a smart cookie." She sighs. "Amazing how time flies, isn't it? Seems like yesterday you were walking with us for the first time. How could that have been five years ago?"

"I don't know," I say. But I kind of do. Five years ago feels like five years ago. Older people tend to perceive time differently. They're always saying how quickly time passes. Dakota would have loved to trade places with me senior year. Time was taking its sweet time. It felt like forever until I could move out.

After I check in, I relax on the hill. The lake is peaceful today. As I've been feeling less than at peace lately, its calm serenity is a welcome respite. I lie back on the grass and gaze out at the water.

"Hey, Sadie," Vienna says, climbing up to me. She's wearing the same tee she wears every year for this. Same photo of her brother. Same dates below the photo.

"Hey, Vienna."

"Long time no see."

I laugh. The only time we ever see each other is once a year for this.

"How are you doing?" I ask.

"Taking it one day at a time. You?"

"About the same."

Vienna sits next to me. We watch more people arriving and greeting each other. Old friends reunite. Small cliques gather to catch up. Vienna takes off her rubber bracelet and plays with it, stretching it over and over. This year the bracelets are yellow with purple printing that says WE WILL NEVER FORGET.

Vienna looks the same way she did when we first met. Vulnerable. Lonely. Hungry for connection. "You look good," she says.

I snort.

"No, you do. Like, *really* good. Are you on a cleanse or something?"

"Um, no. Restricting my body to four hundred calories a day is not my idea of fun times."

"Are you still a vegetarian?"

"Of course."

"So it's not an iron-slash-protein rush that's making you glow."

I sit up and shove Vienna with my shoulder. She thinks being a vegetarian is making me weak. In Vienna's perfect world, everyone would eat meat like the proud omnivores we were meant to be.

"You think I'm glowing?" I say.

"There is a definite glow happening."

I smile shyly at the grass.

"Oh!" Vienna yells. "There's a guy! How could I not have known? Who is he?"

"He's . . . this boy I just met."

"And he's already making you glow? I'm impressed. What's his name?"

"Austin."

"We like Austin because . . ."

"He's amazing," I answer without thinking. Or maybe it's that I feel more amazing with him than I ever have before. There's just something about him that feels like home.

"How did you meet?"

"At my internship. We had the best time hanging out last night. It started out as a spontaneous thing, but totally turned into our first date. We're going out again tonight."

"Damn, girl. Sadie don't waste *no* time."

Dakota rings a chain of bells. That's the signal for everyone to gather by the check-in table. We'll start walking up to the reservoir in a few minutes. Vienna and I head down the hill.

"I'm so happy you're happy," she says. "You must be dying for tonight to get here."

"Totally."

"Does Austin have a cute friend? I could use some boy time later to take my mind off all this."

Even if he did, the four of us would never do anything together. Vienna and I would never be part of any group hang. It's not that I wouldn't want to be friends with her in real life. The bond we share is tight. The weird thing is, we never see each other except for once a year at the Remembrance Walk. Getting together other times would somehow dilute the intensity of our annual gathering. And I'm not sure how well our bond would hold up outside of Central Park. It's almost as if taking what we share outside of this context would blow every-thing up. My friends would ask how Vienna and I met. Then I would have to tell them about the walk. Then I would have to tell them *why* I walk, which is something I'm not ready for any of my friends to know about. Keeping that part of my life com-partmentalized is the only way I can stay optimistic. Vienna and I have bonded over our shared loss. Our bond grows stronger every year. Vienna told me that everyone in her life knows about her brother. But I need to restrict my loss to this time and space. This walk allows me to grieve one day a year. That's all I will allow myself. All the other days, I can pretend it never happened.

The walk begins. Vienna and I fall into step next to each other. I watch the other people around us. Some of them lost loved ones so long ago that the years have reduced their hurt to a dull ache. Others are struggling with the gaping raw pain of recent loss. Everyone deals with grief in their own way. Those coping mechanisms become apparent during the walk. Some people laugh and celebrate life. Others brush away tears, lost in their memories. Last year one woman was so consumed by grief she crumpled to the ground. The gut-wrenching sounds of her desperate sobs haunted me for weeks after.

There's a moment of silence when we get to the top of the reservoir. We all stand with our heads bowed. Some people put their hand over their heart. Others put their hands together in prayer. Vienna closes her eyes tightly. I know she's remember-ing her brother. This is the time I should be thinking of my loss. But even thinking about everything that happened would initiate a flood too powerful not to drown in.

We start walking again. The mood is reflective now. People are more subdued, speaking in quieter tones. I catch glimpses of buildings over the trees surrounding the park. What are people dealing with behind all those windows? How many hurting souls will remain broken forever? There's so much secret pain in this city. It's amazing how many of us are tied to one another by the things that hurt us the most. The most painful experiences bring us together in the most powerful ways. Walking with my people once a year is enough for me. I'm not ready to open up to anyone yet. If I ever will be.

"So . . . yeah," Vienna says. "I might be interested in someone, too."

"Ooh?"

"He might be a good friend of mine. Someone I want to be honest with. But I might not want to risk ruining our friendship."

"That's rough."

"This is all hypothetical, of course."

"Of course. It's hypothetically rough."

"The thing is . . . I can't stop thinking about him. It's like all of my brainpower is dedicated to imagining what it would be like if we were a couple."

"Do you think he might like you?"

"I don't know. It's hard to tell."

"You should definitely tell him how you feel. I know it's

scary, but you have to take a chance."

"But what if he doesn't like me that way? And then things become so awkward between us we stop hanging out? I'd rather have him this way than not have him at all."

I understand how conflicted Vienna feels. But she has to follow her heart to find the love she wants. Deep down, I know following your heart is the only way to create true happiness.

Then there's my cynical side. The side of me that I keep hidden from the world. I want to believe that the world is good and happiness is abundant. Except . . . there's a reason I do this walk every year. A reason that totally sucks. What happened was so unfair. And so random. It could have happened to anyone. Is it hypocritical to be an optimist when I'm disappointed with the world? My anger is always lingering. It's always there below the surface.

And I don't know how to make it go away.

ELEVEN
DARCY

CHILLING ON THE WASHINGTON SQUARE Park fountain after class will definitely be one of my fave low-key activities this summer. Tons of kids are sitting around the edge of the fountain kicking back with friends or soaking up some sun. The fountain is clearly a frequent origin point for hookups, but social perks aren't its only attribute. This whole park has a soothing energy that mellows me out. Balance is something I'm trying to be more aware of. My natural state is to be on 24-7. That might not be the healthiest thing in the long run. And I want a long run. What better way to be invincible?

Rosanna is meeting me here after camp. We seriously need to work on that girl's wardrobe. My heart goes out to her. She doesn't have a lot of money to spend on nonessentials. Although I would argue that a killer wardrobe *is* essential. Your daily ensemble selections are how you choose to present yourself to the world. Which, I get it, sometimes a sister needs to be dragging. There were mornings back in California I was so exhausted from some all-night private-beach party I could barely pull on leggings and a cami. I mean, I'd still accessorize, but yeah. So it's not like I expect Rosanna to be a fashion plate every single day—just most days. I want her to shine. I want her to show that fun and free side of herself I hope is hidden under her serious, critical shell. A complete wardrobe would reveal all the sides of her personality. Fortunately I can help her in that department. Soho has some of the most eclectic shops and I'm treating.

A cute boy with a UNY tee sits down next to me. "How's it going?" he asks.

Maybe if he didn't look so much like my ex he'd be my next boy adventure.

I ignore him. The last thing I need to be reminded of is the one thing I'm trying to forget.

He's not giving up. "Beautiful day, huh?" he tries again.

"Seriously?" I snap.

The smile is startled off his face. I immediately feel horrible for being such a bitch. I'm about to apologize when he gets up, moves to the next free spot on the fountain edge, and starts chatting up another girl. Not cool, Darcy. Not cool. How could I let myself become such a hot snapping mess?

I still feel horrible about snapping at Rosanna the day I moved in. My anger hasn't been the easiest emotion to tame lately, which sucks. It royally, epically, historically sucks. The last person you would describe as angry is this girl. Until some boy destroyed her happy streak. But I will not let a boy shape me into a person I don't want to be. Especially some asshole who had the audacity to dump me. An asshole I loved more than anyone.

You could say I'm a work in progress.

My ex ended us right before I left for New York. That's why I was lugging all that rage in my baggage when I moved in. We were so happy together. We were so in love. Or so I thought. Then everything fell apart overnight. Turns out that our thoughts about the relationship were diametrically opposed. I thought we were going to try the long-distance thing. I thought we were going to be together for a long time. Meanwhile, he thought dumping me so hard my heart would shatter into a zillion pieces was the best way to go. Because why wouldn't you want to devastate the girl you said you loved? Out of nowhere? With no advance warning?

Oh, and then? I saw him out the next night. He was at Urth Caffe with his friends, whooping it up at a big rowdy table. He was totally oblivious to the fallout of his actions. Urth Caffe was our place. That's where he took me on our first date. That's where we went for brunch the morning after we had sex for the first time. That's where he gazed into my eyes and swore that no girl could ever be more perfect for him than I was.

Urth Caffe was the last straw.

I darted over to his table. His friends immediately shut up. The sudden dip in volume caused people at other tables to look over, which was a good thing considering I wanted as many spectators as I could get.

"Hey, Darcy," he said, looking up at me with those big eyes I could never resist. "Why are you—"

There was no time to think. I picked up his soda and threw it in his face. Yeah, I'm that girl. The one who slings drinks in bad boys' faces with flair. My new motto could be Act Now, Think Later.

This summer I'm all about being spontaneous. I love being free and going with the flow. I want to forget about consequences for a while. Keep things light. Let my anger go. This summer is mine to play with and New York City is my playground.

Getting back to my normal happy self would be a lot easier without the jarring bursts of pain. Every time I think I'm done being hurt by him, a memory will flash in my mind so eidetic it's like I'm right back at square one all over again. We weren't done yet. Not even close. How could he not have seen that?

A street performer near the fountain is drawing a huge crowd. An impressive achievement anywhere, but especially here. New Yorkers hardly stop for anything. They walk quickly with purpose. They always have someplace to be and they needed to be there ten minutes ago. But this boy is making them stop and watch.

Short List of Events New Yorkers Will Pause For
— someone has collapsed on the sidewalk
— free samples

- accident involving a mangled bicycle or bent traffic light
- movie filming with an A-list celeb
- a natural disaster (if it's horrific enough)

This boy is a lot younger than most of the other street performers I've seen. Back home, artists like to do their thing around the Santa Monica Pier. They're typically dudes in their thirties or forties, sometimes even older. This boy looks like he's my age. With his blue eyes, blond hair, and athletic build, he's got that surfer boy look I've been crushing on since I was twelve. Along with the clearly entertained crowd of people watching him, I am transfixed. I can't help myself. Surfer Boy is bringing me right back to when I first started liking boys, wishing my first boy adventure would hurry up and happen already. Watching him feels the same way watching boys I liked back then felt. Same racing pulse. Same damp palms. Same hint of vertigo. What can I tell you? This boy is already rocking my world and I don't even know his name.

I watch his act. He's a magician, but not in a corny way where rabbits get yanked out of musty hats. His way is funny, sharp, and engaging. He's very good at making the crowd feel like they're in on the joke. Little kids laugh and their parents smile. Quirky cerebral humor rules. This boy has natural talent. He has unique tricks I've never seen before that he might have invented himself. He could be some kind of master genius magician. Tricks have to originate somewhere, right? Who knows. This boy could be igniting a revolution of contemporary magic.

He finishes his act. The crowd bursts into applause. He even gets a few whistles and one, "Righteous, man!" Some people put money in his collection bucket. The crowd scatters while he takes a break. A few people go up to him.

I wander over. He shoots me a smile while he's talking to the last person left. Then he approaches me.

"Please tell me I was even remotely entertaining," he says.

I eye him up and down like a guy. Now it's my turn to take control. I'm in charge. I'm the one with the power over boys' emotions.

"Oh yeah," I drawl. "I'm entertained."

He actually blushes a little. I bet he's never had a girl be this forward before.

"So how's the summer solstice treating you?" he says.

"You can tell it's summer. Things just got hotter."

"Are you flirting with me?"

"Is it obvious?"

"Only about as obvious as a ton of bricks. Wait, wouldn't the bricks have to fall or something to be obvious? Like a pile of bricks just sitting in some vacant lot wouldn't be obvious."

"Flirt much?"

"Tragically, no. And it's *waaay* too obvious."

"Only about as obvious as a ton of falling bricks."

"Are you always this forward with the dudes?"

"No. You inspired me. I really liked your act."

"That makes you entitled to a magician's secret."

"Sweet. I love secrets."

"You can't tell anyone. Magician's code."

I cross my heart. "Promise."

He comes up close to me. His eyes pierce mine.

"Distraction," he whispers.

"Care to elaborate?" I whisper back.

"The key to magic is distracting the audience. You want them to focus on something else while you're working the trick."

"How did you pull off that orange flag thing?"

"Sorry, that's classified information."

"Do I have to be a magician to find out?"

"No, but you might have to come out and see me again."

Again with the piercing blue eyes. My heart skips a beat.

"That's a definite possibility," I say.

"How can we make it definitely definite?"

"Promise to tell me another secret next time."

"Deal. I can also promise more witty repartee."

"Then I'll definitely be back." I could totally hang with him all day. But it's time to meet Rosanna at the arch. "Catch you later."

"Looking forward to it."

As I walk away, he reaches out to me. His hand brushes my arm for a second. A shiver goes down my spine.

"I'm Jude, by the way."

"Darcy. Awesome meeting you."

"It was awesome meeting *you*, Darcy."

Jude is a good guy. He's warm, outgoing, funny, and sharp

as a tack. The kind of boy I'd fall in love with if I were still that kind of girl.

I'm proud of myself for laying some sweet game on him. There's no reason boys should get to call all the shots.

TWELVE
ROSANNA

D CALLED ME FIVE MINUTES after I left the party last night.

Me: Hello?

D: Miss me yet?

Me: Who is this?

D: Donovan. D. The guy you were having a scintillating discussion about weirdos with?

Me: Oh yeah. That guy.

D: I wanted to make sure you're getting home okay.

Me: Um, sure. My apartment is only a few blocks away.

D: Just watch out for weirdos.

Me: Will do.

D: So have you given any more thought to having dinner with me?

Me: You mean . . . in the last five minutes?

D: Specifically within that time frame, yes.

Me: I don't know. . . .

D: Sounds like you might need some convincing.

Me: Convincing of what?

D: That you want to have dinner with me. I think you know you do deep down. But sometimes awareness has to be coaxed to the surface. Also, I'm not taking no for an answer.

Me:

D: Okay, why do I keep coming off as a creeper when I'm trying to be smooth? All I'm saying is this: I had fun talking with you and I'd love to see you again.

Me: Thanks. That's . . .

D: Do you have plans tomorrow night?

Me: No.

D: Then you'll have dinner with me?

Me: Yes.

So we're going out tonight. I'm still not sure how it happened. One minute I was all prepared to let him down easy. The next I was too shocked to invent fictional plans.

I didn't want to be flattered. But I was totally flattered.

On the way to dinner, I stop at an ATM for emergency cash. I really have to set up a new account at one of the major New York banking chains. One of them had a sign in the window offering a special promotion for signing up. I'll go check that out tomorrow morning. There's no way I'm going to keep getting slammed with withdrawal fees. Doing a mental calculation of grocery money for the weekend, I decide to take out twenty dollars. I tap in the amount and wait while the ATM whirrs. It spits out a twenty. I fold it into my busted wallet, then take my receipt.

The receipt says I have seventy-three cents left in my account.

Um. That's impossible. I can't have seventy-three cents left. All the money I have saved is in this account.

But that's what the receipt says.

I moved to New York determined to make it work. Despite crunching the numbers before I moved and discovering that my camp salary would cover housing and not much else, I convinced myself that being frugal would prevail. I moved here refusing to be afraid. Of course I was still afraid. But I squashed that fear under the hope of creating a better life. Or I thought I did. Now I realize that I'm still afraid. Really afraid. New York City without money is a scary place.

Seventy-three cents.

This is happening.

Frozen in front of the ATM, I hastily wipe away tears. I'm mortified even though no one can see how much money I have left.

Breathe. You can do this. You're getting paid tomorrow. Everything will work out.

Reminding myself that failure is not an option is all it takes to get it together. I fold the receipt into a tiny square and stash it deep in my bag.

D said we're having dinner at the Waverly Inn. We're supposed to meet at the bar in ten minutes. My stomach is in knots as I walk down Bank Street. When I researched the Waverly Inn, I found out it's one of those überschmancy places that's impossible to get into. Otherwise known as the polar opposite of my scene. The place will be packed with trendy hipsters. Probably even celebs. My wardrobe is not ready for this. I'm teetering awkwardly in the only remotely nice pair of shoes I have, which are sporting a loose right heel for this evening's excursion. And of course my only decent top was ruined by Nasty Girl last night. I don't own any dresses. Whenever I needed a dress back home, Mom would let me borrow one of hers. So I'm wearing my second-best top, which is so far below my best top in both quality and appearance that I'm embarrassed for D to see it. Maybe I should have taken Darcy up on her offer to enhance my wardrobe this afternoon. She wanted to buy me new clothes, but there's no way I could have let her do that. We just window shopped in Soho instead. Picking out things I liked and pretending I could buy them if I wanted to was actually fun.

The Waverly Inn is adorable from the outside. It sits nestled on a quaint West Village corner, tastefully surrounded by ivy and tiny white lights. A ripple of anxiety shoots through me. How can I even go in there? The second I open that door, I will immediately be exposed as an impostor. I can already see everyone turning to gawk at me when I walk in. They'll be wondering why such a scruffy girl dared to venture into the Land of the Privileged.

Calm down. You can do this.

Part of me wants to stay out here a little longer until I get myself together. But it's already eight. I take a deep breath. Then I open the door.

D is sitting at the end of the bar. He's wearing a pale blue polo shirt and dark jeans that look brand new. His black shoes are very shiny. I wobble on my discount heels. The right one will probably fall off any second now.

D takes a sip of his drink. He's having some tan whiskey in a short, fat glass with ice. He looks so good sitting at the bar in his fancy clothes with his fancy drink. My breath catches in my throat. He glances toward the door, smiling when he sees me. Then he gets up and comes over.

"Good to see you," D says. He kisses me on the cheek. His hands are cool on my arms. I hope I don't start sweating. It took all of my willpower to stay calm and collected on the walk over. Not that I'm anywhere near calm and collected.

"This place is gorgeous." Bronze fixtures around the bar glow in the dim light. A glimpse of the main dining area reveals a boisterous cluster of tables where sophisticated couples and groups are clearly enjoying themselves. The waiters are wearing dress shirts and ties with crisp white aprons tied around their waists.

"So are you," D says.

A wave of nausea crashes into me. How can I eat when I'm this nervous?

"Would you like a drink at the bar?" D asks. "Or should we go to our table?"

"The table is fine." Would he think it's lame that I don't drink? He has to find out eventually. But he's three years older than me. This won't be the only time I'm not doing something he does. Alcohol isn't something I'm dying to try again. I tried some vodka my parents' friends brought when they came over for dinner last year. It tasted like fire. Not an experience I want to repeat. It's not even legal for me to drink, anyway.

D approaches the hostess at her podium. She could be a supermodel. I feel even more awkward in my ramshackle outfit.

"Reservation for Clark at eight?" D says.

She checks her screen and gives D a bright smile. "Right this way, Mr. Clark."

D steps aside so I can walk in front of him. He puts his hand on my lower back, guiding me forward. I focus on not tripping while I follow the hostess. Why oh *why* does my heel have to be loose the first time I'm at a fancy restaurant? I steal glimpses of people at their tables as we pass by. Most of them are impeccably dressed. Even a table of guys in fitted tees and jeans are all extremely polished. How are they pulling that off? If I showed up tonight in a tee and jeans, I'm sure the hostess would have conveniently "lost" D's reservation.

When we get to our table and the hostess pulls out my chair, I try to play it off like chairs are pulled out for me every day. But when she drapes a heavy white napkin over my lap, I freak out inside all over again. This dinner is not just a date. It's a test of endurance.

"Thank you," I tell the hostess as D sits down across from

me. Maybe I can hide behind my menu for a few minutes until I get my bearings. Then I notice the prices. I knew this place would be expensive. But these prices are outrageous. I didn't even know you could charge this much for food. There's truffle mac and cheese for ninety-five dollars. That must be a typo. How can mac and cheese be ninety-five dollars?

"Sorry, but um . . ." I lean in toward D. He leans in, too.

"Celeb sighting?" he asks.

"Actually, I was wondering how mac and cheese could be ninety-five dollars."

He laughs. "Ridiculous, right? But wait until you taste it. You won't know what hit you."

"Wait, you're ordering it?"

"Why not? It's insanely delicious. The plate is supposed to be for a larger table, but you could always take the rest home."

The concept of a ninety-five-dollar takeout container of mac and cheese is beyond me.

"Oprah was at the table next to mine the last time I was here. She ordered the mac and cheese for her table. If it's good enough for Oprah, it's good enough for us. Am I right?"

I nod in a haze. He was sitting next to Oprah? I freaking *love* Oprah. She is a true humanitarian. She spreads the love and the wealth and wants to educate the world. And D was sitting next to her? I am totally counting that as being one degree from Oprah.

"Are you okay?" D asks.

"Yeah, I'm just processing. I kind of love Oprah."

"Celebs are always here. We'll definitely see someone you know."

We survey the other diners surreptitiously.

"See anyone famous?" I ask.

"No. You?"

"No."

"No worries. It's still on the early side. This was the best reservation I could get on short notice."

Even I know that eight is prime time for dinner reservations in New York. Finding out how D got this reservation only one day in advance would probably infuriate me. Inhabitants of the Land of the Privileged are gifted with a wide array of perks. The Waverly Inn menu is a good example. Do these people realize how lucky they are to be able to have dinner here whenever they want? True, I might not be the only person being treated tonight. Other guys on dates might have saved up for a long time to be able to take their girlfriends here. But for the most part, the kind of people who eat at the Waverly Inn are the kind of people who consider dropping a few hundred dollars for dinner just another Thursday night out. The menu blows my mind. Everything is so outrageously overpriced. Thirty dollars for pasta? Really? This is how investment bankers impress the ladies? What kind of materialistic airhead would be charmed by this charade?

The truffle mac and cheese arrives with a flourish. It smells amazing. It looks amazing. D motions for me to pick up my side plate. I hold it out for him to serve me some mac and cheese decadence. Not sure of which fork I should use, I decide to go for the one farthest to the outside. I sink my fork into the gooey cheese delight. The scent of truffle oil tickles my nose. D watches while I take my first bite.

"Oh. My. God," I say. This is the most incredible thing I've ever tasted. In my whole entire life.

"There's more where that came from."

"You have to stop me from eating the whole plate. I could eat this every day and never get tired of it."

D leans back in his chair, sipping the glass of red wine he ordered with dinner. He gives me a contemplative smile.

"What?" I press my napkin against my lips. "Do I have cheese on my face?"

"I love that you appreciate this so much."

I can't deny it. He got me. He got me with the fancy restaurant and the one degree of Oprah and the most decadent truffle mac and cheese deliciousness I've ever tasted in my life. Remaining unimpressed would be futile.

"Thank you for bringing me here," I say.

"Why do you sound like it's the end of the night? It's only the beginning."

"No, I just . . . wanted you to know how much I appreciate it. I've never been to a restaurant like this."

"Like I said. It's only the beginning."

D may be a materialistic manwhore, but he's also very fortunate. Money gives him the ability to do things I will probably never be able to.

"What's it like being a grownup?" I ask.

D laughs. "It definitely doesn't suck. Having the freedom to do whatever I want, whenever I want is awesome. Growing up on the Upper West was cool, but I couldn't wait to have my own place."

"You said your apartment needs work?"

"My loft, yeah. We renovated, but there are still some things I want to do." His eyes sparkle at me in the candlelight. "So what about you? What do you want to do with your life?"

"I want to be a social worker."

"Admirable profession. Do you plan on staying in New York?"

"Definitely. I've always wanted to live here."

"You'll have a tough time on a social worker's salary in Manhattan. Rents are insane."

"I don't care. I just want to do what I'm passionate about and help make the world a better place while I'm doing it."

"What makes you so passionate about social work?"

The main reason is something I could never tell D. Or anyone. When people ask why I want to go into social work, I focus on our society's abysmal moral standards instead of revealing my darkest secret.

"Watching people interact with each other," I say. "Seeing how much people lack compassion. Most people don't realize the effect they have on the people around them. Or the effect they have on the whole world. They just don't get it. Yesterday I was at the 7-Eleven and I saw a dad with his son who looked like he was seven or eight. His son was hungry. He wanted a hot dog. When he reached for one of the hot dogs in the warmer, his dad slapped his hand away. Not a light tap. A full-on, hard slap. His dad yelled at him for how he's always doing stupid stuff like that. He was like, 'What's wrong with you?! Why are you so stupid?' But that wasn't the most surprising part. Parents mistreating their kids is unfortunately a lot more common than we realize. What struck me the most was that the boy didn't cry. At first I couldn't understand that. How could he take his father physically and verbally abusing him without a trace of emotion on his face? Then I realized that the boy was hardening himself against feeling emotion. You could tell his dad yells at him like that all the time. And if he slaps the boy like that in public, what happens at home must be way worse. That little boy has programmed himself to avoid crying when his dad treats him like dirt. He's eight years old and already cold as ice."

I take a shaky sip of water. I'm getting way too worked up for a first date. But I can't help it. Kids being mistreated in any way makes me so angry. My heart aches for all the pain and suffering that boy has to endure for many years to come.

"That's how boys grow up to be assholes," D says. "He probably used to cry when he was younger and his dad made fun of him for being weak. As if being in touch with your emotions is a bad thing."

"Now there's a generation of emotionally immature guys who are unable to open up in a relationship. Men like that douche are raising the next generation of detached, unfeeling pricks. I couldn't stand watching him. It was horrible."

"Did you say anything?"

"I wanted to. I was about to go up and ask him to please stop abusing his son or I'd call the police. But he would have just laughed at me. Nothing I could have said would have changed him. And I was afraid he'd take it out on the boy. His anger at me would have come out later that night, or the next day, or the next week. And it would have been my fault. So I stayed quiet even though it was killing me to not say anything."

"You did the right thing. That guy was deranged. He might have hit you. Better to stay out of it."

"I disagree. I hate myself for not saying anything. If no one speaks up when they see someone being mistreated, these cycles of abuse will continue. We all need to take a stand. Why do people have to be so disappointing? We're better than this. As a democratic society, we are better than this. I need to have more courage next time."

D leans back in his chair. "Your idealism is sweet. It's refreshing to be with a woman who has strong opinions for a change. With other girls I've dated it was like, have an original thought, you know?"

Um. Is he seriously talking about other girls he's dated? On his first date with me? How tacky is that? The date takes an even sharper turn when I ask D about his internship. He reminds me of how disgusting his career choice is.

"My supervisor has this one client who won't stop yelling at him. The client has only made fifty million this year. He thinks it should be double by now. No matter how many times my supervisor explains that this is the best we can do in a crappy market, he's never satisfied."

"How much money does he need?"

"That's beside the point. He has more money than he could ever spend. The guy is worth billions, but it's never enough for him. He just wants to make as much as possible."

"Why?"

"Because he can."

"But he already has more than enough."

"It doesn't matter. One of the excellent things about this country is that there's essentially no limit to how much you can achieve. If you work hard, you'll achieve greatness."

"Not necessarily. There are people who work hard their whole lives and never pull themselves out of poverty. Plenty of single mothers are working two or three jobs and can barely put food on the table. No matter how hard they work, they'll always be stuck. And their kids will probably grow up to perpetuate the same cycle of poverty."

"What do you think should be done to help them?"

"More extensive educational outreach. More affordable housing. More charitable contributions."

"The client I was telling you about contributes millions to charities every year."

"We should raise taxes for millionaires. Then more government money could go toward services in low-income areas."

"That might happen. But there will always be a huge

discrepancy between low-income earners and the wealthiest Americans."

"The inequality shouldn't be so extreme."

"So you're saying there should be a limit to what people can earn? What if you became a millionaire? Would you want the government limiting the amount of success you're entitled to?"

"No, but . . . I just think it's unfair that so many people are living in poverty while others have far more money than they could ever spend. It's not right."

"Your opinion would be different if you had money."

"Is that why you want to be an investment banker? To make a lot of money?"

"Working in finance gives you the freedom to live exactly the way you want. My parents have created a comfortable, amazing life for themselves and their kids. They can afford to experience the best this city has to offer. They can travel anywhere in the world. Money is just a tool to accomplish those goals. You have to admit, life is a lot less stressful when you don't have to worry about paying the rent or putting food on the table."

Okay, he has a point. Not that I'm about to admit it out loud. Money does make life easier to some extent. But D is wrong about money allowing you to live exactly the way you want. The most important things in life can't be purchased. Love. Happiness. Purpose. Will D feel as fulfilled as he thinks he will?

Dessert menus suddenly appear. I can't believe we've already had dinner. The whole debate with D went by in a flash. Does he really think it's okay that so many people who work hard are barely scraping by? That's like saying it's okay that kids go to bed hungry every night, or spend winters with no heat or hot water, or don't even have a home to live in. How is any of that okay?

When it's time to go, I take a last look around. This will probably be my one and only time at an upscale restaurant. My life will be dedicated to working hard and helping people in need. The combination of those two goals doesn't tend to result in big paychecks.

D pulls out my chair for me. We walk to the door in silence. Out in front of the elaborate ivy, we stand off to the side so other people can get by. Thursday is apparently the big night to go out in New York. People pass by us in couples or groups. It's amazing how many people are out at ten on a weeknight.

"This was fun," D says. "We should do it again."

I really don't see that happening. But I smile and nod a little to be polite.

D hugs me. He feels really good. I can't help noticing that we fit together like puzzle pieces.

He pulls back, says he'll see me soon, and we part ways. He hails a cab at the corner. I could never afford to take cabs. They're crazy expensive. D told me he takes them every day. He takes cabs the way most people take the subway. He'll take a cab even if the subway is right there. I forget what he said exactly . . . something about how money is a tool to make his life easier. If I were him, I'd take the subway and save as much as I could. How much of a relief would it be to have money saved? I wouldn't have to worry all the time. I wouldn't feel the need for a Plan D.

Walking home, I think about D. His glossy charm and smooth ways don't impress me. I'm a long-term-relationship kind of girl. Not that I've had a long-term relationship yet. But when I do have a relationship, I want it to be serious. I could never date around casually like Darcy. I want to fall in love with a boy I can share my life with in a real way. Isn't that the point of a relationship? To really share your life with someone? And if you're sharing your life with someone, shouldn't that person share the same morals and values as you?

D could never understand me. He can't relate to my background at all. His parents are paying for everything. He has no idea what it's like to constantly worry about money every day. He doesn't need a Plan D. He has, and always will have, everything he needs. I have seventy-three cents.

I want to stop thinking about the date.

I want to stop thinking about D.

But I can't.

Yeah, he's appalling. But he's also kind. And smart. And every time he complimented me, he seemed genuine. As much as I hate to admit it, I felt a real connection. And there's the way he makes me feel. The way he looks at me, the way he touches me. Underneath the stuff that bothers me, I can't help feeling attracted to him.

Not that it matters. I could never get serious about someone like him.

THIRTEEN
SADIE

WE'RE GOING TO PAPER LOWER Manhattan with warm fuzzies.

This just might be the best idea my Random Acts of Kindness group has ever had. Our objective is to make the world a better place by doing good things for everyone. Random acts are all about being aware of your surroundings and taking an active role in improving other people's lives. A random act of kindness could be helping a senior in the grocery store reach a can on the top shelf. Or complimenting someone on her beautiful necklace. Or even just smiling at the bus driver and saying hi. These might seem like small things to you, but they could be huge to someone else. Everyone appreciates help. Everyone likes compliments. Well, almost everyone. We occasionally encounter antisocial people who don't want human contact for whatever reason. That's okay. The point is to keep reaching out.

That's why we're going to paper lower Manhattan with warm fuzzies. Most of us live downtown. We're going to break off into our respective neighborhoods of the West Village, East Village, Tribeca, Gramercy, Battery Park, the Lower East Side, and the Financial District. Each of us will make twenty-five warm fuzzies. Then we're going to leave them around for people to find. Why? The best reason for random acts of kindness. Just because.

The warm fuzzies will feature motivational quotes and uplifting encouragements like "Be the change you want to see in the world," "Go confidently in the direction of your dreams! Live the life you've imagined," and "Imagine all the people living life in peace." We've been brainstorming places to leave the warm fuzzies that are easy to find. The list in my notebook looks like this:

- Next to a coffee cup at a café
- Tucked under a string of lights in a tree outside a restaurant
- Between two books at a library
- Taped to a parking meter
- Stuffed into the takeout-menu box at a deli
- Left on a subway seat
- Sticking out of a dryer at a Laundromat

It makes me so happy to think about people finding our warm fuzzies like little treasures. Each one is unique. My rules about making warm fuzzies are strict. You can't whip out a raggedy pen, write a note on some old discolored loose-leaf, and proclaim that to be a warm fuzzy. Boring pen plus generic paper does not a warm fuzzy make. You must use fun paper. Construction paper is fine. Better if you cut the edges with patterned scissors. Pretty stationery is the best. To create the most important warm fuzzies, I use the heavy cotton stationery made with pressed flowers that Brooke gave me for my birthday. And I always use Gelly Roll pens. The glitter ones and the lightning ones are the best. Using a quality pen is just as important as using quality paper. It's a yin-yang dynamic. Warm fuzzies must also include some sort of design element. Whether it's drawn, painted, glued, or otherwise attached, artwork adds pizzazz. Additional bedazzlement involving sequins, stickers, or rhinestones is always welcome.

Making twenty-five warm fuzzies will take a while. But that's the kind of time commitment I love. Hopefully the warm fuzzies will bring a ray of happiness to everyone who finds them. Maybe their finders will be motivated to pay it forward and do something nice for someone else.

My stomach has been fluttering with butterflies the whole meeting. These meetings usually go by so fast I can't believe it when they're over. But tonight is different. Tonight I'm going to a party with a boy I like. A boy I really, really like. And he's picking me up in five minutes. Maybe he's already out front waiting for me. The thought of Austin waiting for me in his car to take me to a party for our second date, which will probably end with kissing, makes the butterflies flap like crazy.

It's time to go. I make sure I have everything. This takes a minute. Carrying around a ginormous bag is kind of my thing. Ginormous bags can be a hassle, but I like to be prepared for anything. Like for this party with Austin. What if my lips got dry and I didn't have gloss? Or it was humid and my hair spazzed and I didn't have clips? Or I desperately needed a mint? After making sure I'm not leaving anything behind, I say a quick collective goodbye and dash to the elevator. The butterflies are flapping harder than ever. They really, really like this boy, too.

Austin is in front of the community center, leaning back against a white SUV. Or one of those cars that's bigger than a regular car but smaller than an SUV. I have no idea what anything is called when it comes to cars.

"Hey," he says. "How was the meeting?"

"Awesome. We're papering downtown with warm fuzzies."

"Warm what now?"

"Warm fuzzies."

"Define."

"You know . . . encouraging notes that make people feel better? A warm fuzzy is just a way to spread the love."

"Oh. I thought it was more like a feeling." Austin pushes off the side of his car and comes over to me. "You know. As in, *You make me feel warm and fuzzy.*"

"You have so much to learn."

"I can't wait for you to teach me." Sunlight glints off his eyes. I bask in their blue glimmer. His eyes have sparkles of silver I didn't notice before. They probably only come out in the sunlight.

I can't believe how gorgeous he is. I can't believe this gorgeous boy wants to be with me.

Where are we going again? Oh yeah. The party.

Austin opens the passenger door for me. He's such a gentleman. I love how mature he is. As he's walking around to the driver's side, I resist the urge to check my hair in the rearview mirror. I covertly touch a few clips to make sure they're still in place.

He gets in and starts the car. This is so weird. Austin seems like an actual grownup.

"Thanks for driving me," I say. "Attempting to navigate the wilds of Brooklyn by myself would be an epic fail."

"You'd do fine. But I'm more than happy to drive you. It means we can spend more time together."

I glance in the back. "You have a lot of room."

"Perfect for those shopping sprees at Costco."

"Seriously?"

"No." He laughs. "I just like having the extra space. The Rodeo's good for getting out of town with friends and stuff."

"What rodeo?"

"My car. It's an Isuzu Rodeo."

"Oh."

"Much better than the Focus I had before."

I give him a blank look.

"You don't know much about cars, do you?"

"The only car names I know are Porsche and BMW. Not that I'd be able to recognize either of them."

"Classic city girl. When's the last time you rode in a car?"

"Um . . . like . . . two years ago?" Riding around in Austin's car is a whole different experience than those family road trips. Door-to-door service in New York City is so luxurious. Avoiding the sweltering subway stations. Arriving at your destination without being all sweaty from trekking in the summer heat. Being able to wear heels without having to change in and out of flip-flops. This is the life.

"Sorry about the mess." There are a few takeout bags and papers on the passenger-side floor. "I didn't have a chance to clean up."

"Are you kidding? This is better than a private car service. You're making me feel like a princess."

Austin smiles. "I'll do my best to keep it up."

To be honest, I wasn't expecting anything in Brooklyn to impress me. But Trey's rooftop garden is unreal. As a rooftop garden enthusiast growing up in the West Village, I've seen quite a few gorgeous ones. This one is exceptional. Flowers in all shapes, sizes, and colors are everywhere. Jelly jars with flowers are on each of the patio tables gathered in the center. An herb garden is flourishing in one corner. Another corner has tomatoes and lettuce growing. There are even some couches up here.

"How does Trey have all this?" I ask Austin.

"He doesn't. This is his parents' place. He lives with them."

"I thought you graduated from high school together."

"We did. If Trey knew what he wanted to do with his life, he'd probably have his own place by now."

Austin goes to get us drinks while I wait by myself. Whether or not I know anyone at a party isn't usually an issue. Meeting new people is super fun. I believe everyone has goodness in them and I like finding out what that goodness is. But sometimes the darkness creeps in. The darkness makes me forget that people are inherently good. So doing things like random acts of kindness and striking up conversations with people in line and going to parties where I don't know anyone reminds me of what I don't want to forget. But this party isn't inspiring me to be social. All I want to do is sneak off to a corner of the roof with Austin. No one else is anywhere near as interesting as he is.

Austin brings our drinks. "Is it wrong that I only want to talk to you?" he says.

"I was just thinking that!"

"Then I guess it's not."

"If only talking to you is wrong, I don't want to be right."

"We already said hi to Trey. I don't really know anyone else here. Wait, do I know that guy?" Austin squints at someone across the roof. "Nope, don't know him. Looks like we're forced to appropriate this crazy-comfortable-looking couch with the sick view of the river."

"You mean the couch that's going to be the best place to watch the sunset?"

"That's the one." Austin sits at the far corner of the couch. He looks up at me expectantly. Do I sit right next to him? Or should I leave some space between us? I don't want to leave any space between us. What if I leave space between us and I never see Austin again and I regret it for the rest of my life? But it doesn't feel like I'll never see him again. It feels like the beginning of something real.

I sit down right next to him, one leg bent against the couch so my knee is touching his thigh. When did I get so fearless? Lacking boy confidence was one of my biggest flaws in high school. Now it's like I'm a whole different girl.

The conversation flows easily from one subject to another: which quotes I'm going to use for the warm fuzzies I'm making, his case for why I need to get into *Monty Python*, my obsession with *How I Met Your Mother*, his obsession with *Breaking Bad*, my ongoing search for the perfect veggie burger and chocolate chip cookie, his favorite restaurant in Jersey City.

"Razza," he proclaims, "has the best food and atmosphere anywhere. You would not believe how good their homemade bread and butter is. They make these artisanal pizzas that take pizza to a whole other level. But I could seriously just eat their bread and butter."

"You sound like a food critic."

"I kind of am. Unofficially, of course. But yeah. I love that place."

"Maybe we can go sometime."

Austin juts his chin toward the river. "Presunset."

We kick back to watch the sunset. Everyone else has left us alone. We're giving off that unmistakable vibe of two people falling in love who do not want to interact with anyone else. A neon sign flashing DO NOT DISTURB over our heads would be less obvious.

Just as the sun touches the Manhattan skyline, Austin wraps his hand around mine.

"Being with you makes me so happy," he says. "I could stay here with you all night."

"Same here."

Austin looks at me. His look lingers. Like he likes what he sees. This is the beginning of something incredible. I have a Knowing that my life is about to change forever. Does he feel it, too?

"I know we just met," he says. "I know you're not supposed to say these things this early. But I feel like I've known you for a long time."

"Me, too."

Austin puts his arm around me and pulls me close. I lean my head against his shoulder, watching the sky bleed from blue into purple.

Austin opens the passenger door for me. "Your chariot awaits, princess," he says, waving me inside.

Instead of dropping me off at my place, Austin parks on West 11th Street. We get out and start walking slowly. Slowly is the opposite of how I usually like to walk. Hardcore New Yorkers aren't only fast walkers, we're strategic walkers. There's a certain pattern I like to follow in familiar places. But being with Austin is a whole different experience. I'm a better person when I'm with him. The most adventurous, romantic parts of me are accentuated. We're walking like we have nowhere to be. It's the best feeling ever.

"Have you ever had an epic feeling?" I ask him. "Like, a feeling that was so monumental it was impossible to describe in words?"

"Kind of like a . . . transcendental experience?"

"Exactly! You're completely transported to another realm of existence. It's more intense than any other feeling."

"I know what you mean. But I have to say . . . being with you is pretty intense." Austin reaches for my hand. And then we're walking down one of my favorite streets, holding hands on a perfect summer night.

I look up into the lit-up windows we're passing. I'm chasing that epic feeling I had a few nights ago. Would Austin think I'm strange for looking in people's windows? Or maybe he likes looking in people's windows too, like with the colored doors thing. We pass a New School student lounge. A study group is gathered in a circle of chairs with laptops and notebooks, deep in discussion. In a second-floor window of an apartment building, a guy is working at his desk in front of the window, his face illuminated by the blue light of his computer screen. Big windows a few buildings down show an open-concept office on the third floor. Large sheets of paper are spread out over a counter.

A few people are gathered around the counter, bending over the sheets and making expansive gestures.

"You got quiet," Austin says.

"I was thinking about creative energy. It's amazing how the words and art and film that inspire the world are being produced right here, right now. Tons of the most creative people in the world are here in New York. They're so passionate about their work they can't go home or even stop for dinner. We just passed a bunch of people still working, but they didn't seem to mind. That's how I feel about design."

"I feel the same way. Wouldn't it be awesome if we could skip the college and grad school parts and go straight to doing what we really want?"

"Yeah, but . . . it would be kind of helpful to actually know what we're doing."

"Oh, right. Knowledge."

"Minor detail."

I want Austin to kiss me so bad it hurts. Will he do it tonight? If he's doing it tonight, could it happen at any time or will he wait until we say goodbye? We've already been holding hands like it's a familiar habit. I'm positive he's going to kiss me. The butterflies flap spastically in agreement.

Austin doesn't go back to his car when it's time for him to leave. Being the gentleman he is, he wants to walk me home. I tell him it's okay to say goodbye at his car. But he insists on walking me home. When we get to my building, we hesitate awkwardly by the stoop again, the same way we did before.

It's weird because it's way too early to be feeling the way I feel about him. Does he feel the same way? Like there's no reason to hesitate? Like there's no reason to take it slow? When you meet the right person, there's no doubt in your heart that it was meant to be.

"What did you think of me when you first saw me?" I ask.

"You were so gorgeous I couldn't take my eyes off you," Austin says. No uncertainty. Only clarity.

"Really?"

"Absolutely. You're amazing."

I smile so big I cover my mouth to hide it. Not that I could ever hide this much happiness.

"What did you think of me?" he asks.

"I hoped we would run into each other again. And we did." Holy crap. We're doing that thing where enough time has passed that you can finally find out what he thought of you when you first met. Except we first saw each other two days ago. It's all happening so fast.

Right around the corner . . .

Austin puts his hands on my waist, moving closer to me. I look up at him. His eyes are a different blue in the glow of the streetlights. Almost like he's a different person.

"Do I get to see you again?" he asks.

"Of course. Why wouldn't you?"

"Just making sure." He brushes a wisp of hair behind my ear. "I miss you already."

"I miss you already, too."

"I can't wait to see you again."

These lines don't have to be written in Gelly Roll pen on special stationery to be the best warm fuzzies I've ever gotten.

"I have to kiss you," Austin says.

And then he does. A perfect kiss from a perfect boy on a perfect summer night.

It doesn't get any better than this.

FOURTEEN
DARCY

NEW YORKERS CRACK ME UP. They're such characters. This city has a local flavor you can't taste anywhere else. I've only been here three days and I've already seen two old guys toting exotic animals around like it constitutes normal behavior. There's the guy with the parrot on his head. That's how he walks down the street—with a freaking parrot on his head. At first I didn't think I was seeing that right. I had a moment of awesomeness when I realized I was. Tourists flocked around him to take pictures. He didn't look bothered at all. Then there's the big guy with the snake. This ginormous snake was wrapped around his neck like a scarf. I heard he's another Village regular. I also heard there's a guy who walks his cat on a leash.

Only in New York. I love it.

These wildlife encounters have sparked some questions. When did those guys decide their lives would be defined by specific pets? What inspired them to let their faunal freak flags fly? You can be as anonymous here as you want. You can walk down the street passing thousands of people and never be seen. Even when you are seen, no one cares how crazy you are. But these guys decided that people were going to take note. The parrot guy can't even go get a coffee without a swarm of tourists flocking him. How incredible is it that you can choose to live your life any way you want? And if the way you want is by proudly flapping your freak flag, you instantly become a neighborhood institution. Yeah, you stand out, but not in the way you would most other places. People smile when they see you. They respect your originality. You're different and you have no desire to fit in and that's badass.

From my window table at Chat 'n Chew, I can watch a steady stream of people walking by. People watching never ceases to amaze me. Especially here. Everyone in New York is so well-dressed. All I have to do is walk out the door to be inspired by tons of original styles and fun DIY spins. Now that I've discovered accessorizing with exotic animals is a thing, I'm on the lookout for more. Come on, eccentric old lady rocking a muskrat as a belt. I know you're out there.

Sadie rushes over and plunges into the chair across from me. "Sorry I'm late! We were in the zone finishing up a group project. I didn't want to break our stride."

"No worries at all. I'm on the lookout for a muskrat belt, anyway."

"Huh?" Sadie gulps down her water.

"Hey, really. It's no big deal. Breathe."

Sadie exhales. "I hate being late."

"Aren't New Yorkers notoriously fifteen minutes late for everything?"

"Not this New Yorker. I don't like keeping people waiting."

"Well, I enjoyed my chill time. Kicking back for a few minutes has therapeutic benefits."

Sadie passes me one of the menus that were on the table. "You're going to love this place," she says. "It's good and cheap. That's why it's been here forever."

"You're getting your usual?"

"Grilled cheese with sweet potato fries. Seriously, you have to try these fries. They're *so* good."

"On it." I quickly decide what I want and slam the menu shut.

"How sweet is it that we have the same lunch break?"

"I know, right? I'm not a big lunch person. Scarfing down a soft pretzel between classes works for me. But sitting down to lunch with you is fun."

"Doing lunch like grownups."

"Oh god, please tell me we don't have to be grownups. How boring."

"Seriously? I am completely down with my grown-up status. Freedom couldn't come fast enough."

"I hear you on the freedom. But if I ever assimilate to a typical adult lifestyle and box myself into mind-numbing suburban hell, you have my permission to kill me."

"Yeah, I don't see you as a suburban soccer mom."

"What about you?"

"New York will always be my home. This is the greatest city in the world. Why would I want to live anywhere else?"

"Testify." I'm absorbing Sadie's positive energy like a sponge. She is so full of life and kindness and joy. She's the kind of New Yorker who feeds off the vibrant dynamic of the city. Being an eternal optimist, Sadie could move away and be happy. But she wouldn't shine with the same brightness. I can't imagine her being as happy anywhere else.

"Yesterday was crazy," Sadie says. "Did I even see you?"

"I don't think so."

"How was your hot date Wednesday night? Who is he? What did you guys do? When are you seeing him again? Tell me everything."

"Excuse me, but I'm pretty sure you were the one on our stoop with the cutest boy ever. Who is *he*?"

Sadie's smile radiates so much happiness the people at the next table are probably getting a contact high. Her eyes are sparkling with joy. Even her gold highlights look brighter. She is absolutely glowing.

"Austin," she gushes.

"Tell me about him. Other than his indisputable hotness factor."

"He's . . . how much time do we have?"

"Enough."

"He's amazing. Beyond amazing. He's the kind of boy I've always wanted to be with."

"How long have you guys been together?"

"We just met this week. When you saw us, he was walking me home from our first date."

"Seriously? It seemed like you'd been together for a while."

"I know! That's exactly how it feels. Like we've known each other for so long."

"How did you meet?"

As Sadie fills me in on her whirlwind romance, it's obvious that Austin is all she can think about. So of course he's all she wants to talk about. Fine by me. I am totally down with indulging her. I remember what it was like when I first started going out with the ex. I couldn't think about anything else. I didn't want to talk about anything else. I listen as our lunches are placed in front of us and Sadie ignores her food. She can't stop talking long enough to even taste the fries she was raving about. Been there. I remember having no appetite when I was falling in love.

"Then he said, 'I have to kiss you.' How romantic is that?"

"How was the kiss?"

"Perfect. Just like I knew it would be."

Sadie is clearly a diehard romantic. That was apparent from day one. I'm happy for her. I really am. Austin is taking her for the ride of her life. The thing is, I'm worried about when their relationship or whatever will come to an end, because relationships always end. Sadie is going to crash and burn hard. But I'm happy that she's happy right now. She's living in the moment like the wild and free girl I want each of us to be this summer.

"That all sounds fantastic," I say.

"It really is. So what about you? Who did you go out with?"

"No one I'll see again."

"Why not?"

"Oh, did you not get the memo? New York City is my official summer playground. Getting tied down to any one boy in particular is prohibited."

"By who?"

"By me. The one who's making the rules. This summer is all about boy adventures. That's why I'm so happy for you. You're having the time of your life and summer just started."

"But I want to be tied down to one boy. Not tied down. Permanently connected."

"And that's awesome. If it's making you happy, go for it. What's making me happy is having the freedom to hook up with any boy I want. How exciting is it to be in a city with millions of men? Anything could happen. Doing the free agent thing means I can take advantage of any opportunity that presents itself. Basically, I'm taking ownership of what men have been getting away with forever. I'm the one in control. And let me just say it is the shiznit."

"Could your boy confidence be more impressive?"

"Not so much, no."

"Have you ever been in love?"

Memory clips flash behind my eyes. The ex telling me it's over. Throwing that drink in his face. Ripping up pictures of us as I packed for New York. None of this is anything I want to talk about. Telling Sadie about the ex would expose the raw nerves I want to keep covered so they'll heal faster. All she needs to know is who I am now. Not who I was then.

"Yeah," I admit, "but it's in the past. Looking back isn't my thing. Right now I'm focused on having the best summer ever. The other night was fun, but it's already in the past."

"You're so adventurous. I wish I could be more like you."

"You're a long-term-relationship kind of girl. Am I right?"

"Totally. I'm in love with love."

"Austin is a lucky guy."

"So are all the guys you'll be hooking up with this summer!"

"I don't know about that. But there was this cute street performer yesterday. . . ."

"Spill."

As I tell Sadie about flirting with Jude, she smiles and laughs and encourages me to share more. But I can tell she's internally judging me. That's okay. Sadie will understand why I'm this way when Austin leaves her in the dust.

FIFTEEN
ROSANNA

WHY IS THERE ALWAYS A crazy-long line at the post office no matter what time you go? That's what Sadie told me. She said that every time she goes to the post office, she has to wait in line forever. Ten in the morning. Three in the afternoon. It doesn't matter when you go. There have been times she's even waited for almost an hour. Almost an hour to mail a freaking package. The long lines are indicative of the whole postal system downgrade. Take right now, for example. There are only two people working when all six windows should be open. The other four people were probably laid off.

The lady in front of me lets out an exasperated sigh. She makes sure to direct her sigh toward the two open windows so the employees can hear how exasperated she is, as if she's the first person in one of these excruciatingly long lines to ever be exasperated. Does she think the employees don't know how disgruntled people get in their long lines? Especially New Yorkers. Waiting three minutes in a New York City line is like waiting an hour anywhere else.

Our postal system probably won't even exist ten years from now. Everything is changing so quickly. No one had the internet when my parents were teens. The entire online universe just . . . wasn't. My dad didn't even have a computer until after grad school. How crazy is that? How can you even graduate without a computer? They didn't have cell phones. Okay, I don't have a cell phone, but that's only because I can't afford one. They couldn't listen to music or watch videos online. Online shopping wasn't an option. If they wanted to buy something, they had to go to the store. What was life like without email or social media or texting? How did people communicate? The whole thing is bizarre. When I think about how much the world has changed in the past ten years, it makes me wonder what else won't be around ten years from now. And all of the inventions to come that are currently only concepts. My kids will wonder how I survived without those essentials just like I'm wondering how my parents survived.

"They should open more windows," the lady in front of me huffs. "Only two windows open? Whoever heard of such a thing?"

Does she want one of us to answer her? Or is this more of a rhetorical huffing? Several people in line watch her. Mainly because there's nothing else to do, but also to see if she freaks out. I remember what D told me about weirdos. They could be anywhere. One second they're blending in. Then all of a sudden something triggers their damage and *bam!* A freakout ensues.

A thirtysomething woman in a pretty sundress walks into the post office, takes one look at the crazy-long line, turns right back around, and leaves. Why wasn't I that smart? I've already invested so much time in waiting that walking out now would be cheating myself. Plus, I'm almost to the front of the line. Four more people to go. Does D stand in post office lines? Or any lines, ever? I'm sure his life is so refined that lines don't factor into it at all. He probably has everything delivered.

Fabulous. Now I can't stop thinking about D. That's the way it's been for the past two days. Something reminds me of him and I can't get him out of my head. I don't want to think about him. I definitely don't want to call him. But there are forces greater than me at work.

D represents everything I revile about society. I want to be with someone more on my level. Someone who is passionate about making the world a better place. Someone who understands that it's better to be poor and happy than rich and miserable.

A tourist couple is attempting to mail a humongous box home to France. They had to fill out miles of paperwork. Then they got yelled at for putting tape in the wrong place. After the tape is ripped off and applied properly, there's a huge discussion about mailing options and postage and insurance. This international drama has monopolized one window for the past ten minutes. The lady in front of me is about to lose it.

"What's the problem?" she shrieks at them. "Why are you taking so long? Move aside and figure it out so the rest of us can have our turn." She shakes her head at me, scandalized by the injustice. "Can you believe them?"

I give her a sympathetic look. Of course she wants to get out of this endless line like the rest of us. More importantly, she wants to be heard. I can hear her loneliness under the anger.

The guy at the other window finally finishes up. The line shifts a tiny bit forward. As he's heading toward the door, he drops something that looks like a receipt. He keeps walking.

Sadie was so confident when she ran over to open the door for that old lady. She didn't even think about it. I wish I had the confidence to go up to strangers like Sadie does. I know I need to be part of the solution. I can visualize what I want to do when someone needs help. Right now I can see myself running over to pick up that guy's receipt. But there's a chance he was intentionally littering, so I'd seem like an idiot going up to him. Then everyone would be staring at me. And I'd have to leave the line and might lose my place.

But my biggest obstacle is that I'm shy about approaching strangers. What if the person yells at me for interfering? Or thinks I'm being condescending for doing something they're more than capable of doing on their own? That happened a few times at my volunteer job back home. I volunteered at a low-income senior-citizen housing complex. For three years starting when I was fifteen, I'd go there after school two days a week and almost every day over the summer. One time a guy who had just gotten his mail was shuffling along holding the handrail that ran along the hallway wall when his mail cascaded to the floor. He went ballistic when I bent down to pick it up.

"Young lady!" he boomed. "I am more than capable of picking up my own mail!"

I was mortified. Getting yelled at bothered me for weeks. I still feel bad when I think about it.

Then there was the time in the lounge when a lady spilled coffee all over a side table. The coffee was seeping into a pile of magazines. I ran over with paper towels, but she stopped me.

"Here." She gestured for the paper towels. "I can do it."

"Oh, it's no problem—"

She shook her head, wildly waving her hands for the paper towels. "I don't need to be cleaned up after. I'm not a child." She was so exasperated with me I almost burst out crying. And that was in a confined environment. These are the streets of New York City, rampant with weirdos. What if I try to help an old lady open a door or a blind person cross the street who's bothered by people approaching them all the time when they just want to be left alone?

There has to be a way to help without worrying about possibly annoying people. Most people want help. A few people going ballistic on me will be worth helping hundreds of others. I also want to do more volunteer work here. There are tons of opportunities in this city. I scoped out some possibilities on Do Something before I moved. But for now, I can pick up this guy's receipt.

"Would you hold my place?" I ask the lady in line behind me. She nods. I run over and pick up the receipt, then tap the guy on the back right before he reaches the door. "Excuse me. I think you dropped this."

He turns around, clearly surprised that someone cared enough to run after him with what might have been trash.

"Thanks," he says. He takes the receipt and leaves. It's impossible to tell if he meant to drop it. But at least he has it now in case it was important.

Everyone stares at me as I walk back to the line. My face flushes with the unwanted attention and a rush of adrenaline from helping him. Let them stare. I'm the one who actually cared enough to take action.

By the time I leave the post office and dart down to the Come Out and Play Festival, Mica is already waiting for me. Come Out and Play is an annual festival of original large-scale games that takes place in a few different locations around the city. Tonight is the After Dark part of the festival at South Street Seaport. When I apologize for being late, Mica brushes me off.

"Don't even worry about it," she says. "It's like at that camp party when I wanted to come over and say hi but those yammering girls were holding me hostage. Sometimes breaking away is impossible."

"Thanks for inviting me to this. It sounds super fun."

"Welcome to New York, where you can be into the most obscure activity and find a group just as obsessed as you are."

"I didn't even know groups like this were real."

"Oh, we're real. We're very real."

"You guys are definitely making up for that heinous post office line."

"You should join Improv Everywhere. Have you heard of them?"

"They sound familiar."

"They're an improv group that organizes flash mobs and hilarious pranks. One time a group went into Best Buy all wearing blue polo shirts and khaki pants like the employees wear. The manager called the police and everything. Or they'll do smaller skits like re-creating *Back to the Future* near the MetLife clock tower."

"Have you done any of them?"

"Only two so far. About two hundred of us busted out choreo in Union Square."

"Do you get together to practice before?"

"No, the instructional video is posted a week before the event. You have to practice yourself. Which makes the flash mob even cooler because you get to see it all come together for the first and only time. Before that we did Grand Central Station. There were a bunch of us spread out in the crowd. We blended in with everyone else, doing what they were doing. And then on cue we all froze for thirty-second intervals. It was brilliant. You should check out the video."

New York is now officially even cooler. Where else could you find all these groups of stone-cold weirdos doing their thing? These kinds of weirdos are my people. Not like the weirdos D warned me about.

Aaaaand he's in my head again.

Get out of my head, Wall Street Guy. You're not wanted here.

The game descriptions for Come Out and Play are listed on a big standing chalkboard. Mica and I peruse our options. There's Super Bacon Grab 2: Return of the Bacon. Which actually has nothing to do with bacon. It's an apocalyptic survival game. As Mica and I are not fans of dystopian role playing, we rule that one out. Night Games sounds really interesting. It's an immersive sound and light environment created by the players. As players move in a group, the 3D sound changes to create micro-environments based on their interaction. You can invent your own game or just have fun influencing the sound and light. Mica and I decide to start with the large-scale Frogger game. Each player holds a sign printed with one graphic from the original Frogger. Whoever is playing the frog has to latch onto safe graphics, jumping across four rows of moving players until they reach the other side of the river. These games aren't so much about winning. They're more about having fun. Which is why I'm already in love with Come Out and Play.

Mica and I get in line for the next Frogger game. We both choose to be logs so we can help whoever's the frog get across the river. While we're watching the group currently in play, a girl who looks like she's in middle school trips and falls, going down hard on her knee.

"Oooh!" Mica grabs at her own knee. "Is she okay?"

Someone helps the girl up. She's putting on a brave smile, but you can tell she's in pain.

"That's gotta hurt," Mica says. "Poor thing."

We line up with our logs in the second row. When the game begins, our line moves to the right while the lines on either side of us move to the left. The frog is making her way across the river. She latches onto a log in the first row. Then she jumps to the back of a turtle. I try to align with her so she can latch onto me next, but she's too afraid to leap. She slides out of bounds and loses her life. Each frog gets three lives, so she starts again. This time she manages to latch onto Mica. But when she jumps to the third row, a crocodile nabs her. She's out again. One more life left.

As we're playing her third round, a strong hand grabs my shoulder from behind. I'm so petrified I almost scream. Then I whip around to see who grabbed me. A guy who chose to be a snake is like, "Sorry. Didn't mean to scare you."

Of course he scared me. He grabbed me in the same way I used to be grabbed.

But that's not something I think about. Ever.

SIXTEEN
SADIE

"WHAT TIME IS IT?" AUSTIN asks me on the phone.

I check. "Almost seven."

"Damn. I have to go."

We've been on the phone for over two hours. I swear I could talk to him all night and still have tons more to say.

"So soon?" I joke.

"I have plans with a friend."

"Where are you going?"

"Um . . . just this bar. You wouldn't know it. It's in Jersey City."

Why does Austin sound distant all of a sudden? We were having the best conversation up until now. I've never met anyone I clicked with so strongly. But now it's like he flipped the switch with no advance warning.

"When do I get to see Jersey City?" I ask.

"You can see it all the time from your side of the river." Sounds of shuffling muffle Austin's voice. He's probably getting ready to leave.

"No, I mean . . . I want to come over. To your place."

"You will."

That's it. That's all he says. I wanted him to ask when I could come over. We'd walk around his neighborhood and he'd show me where he hangs out. Then we'd have dinner at one of his favorite restaurants.

There's just silence on his end. No mention of when we're going to see each other again. I haven't seen him for two days. It feels like two years. The weekend is this gaping void without him instead of the fun free time it should be.

"You still there?" he says.

"Yeah."

"I'm late. Talk to you tomorrow?"

"Okay."

But it's not okay. My heart sinks as he hangs up. I have a horrible feeling something's wrong. Why did I have to push him like that? He obviously thinks it's too soon for me to come over. I'm nauseous with that gross feeling you get when you think things are going one way and you suddenly realize they're not.

My lack of boy confidence comes rushing back. I might burst into tears any second. Why did I bring up coming over so soon? I wasn't even saying it to imply we'd make out or anything. It was just something I was looking forward to. Of course Austin didn't ask me if I wanted to come over. We just met like three seconds ago. What's wrong with me? Why couldn't I wait and be patient like a normal person?

My relationship fail has left me emotionally exhausted. I make an executive decision to haul my drained self to my knitting circle. Otherwise I'll be mad at myself all night. I grab my knitting bag and run.

Coming to my knitting circle was the right decision. The ladies here are always so friendly. The *click-clacking* of needles enveloping me as I knit two, purl two, soothes me enough to loosen the knots in my stomach. It's like being immersed in a giant warm fuzzy instead of Mrs. Williamson's living room. At one point I even stop thinking about the whole Austin drama for a few minutes. Mrs. Williamson is dealing with much bigger issues than mine. Her son is fighting cancer. He's been really sick for the past few weeks. Even though she's doing her best to make everyone feel comfortable, she's clearly exhausted. She bends down slowly as she reaches into her knitting bag, then puts her other hand on her thigh for support as she bends back up.

When Mrs. Williamson gets up to go to the bathroom, I sneak the warm fuzzy I made for her into her knitting bag. I did the same thing for bullied kids at school. Hopefully those kids felt a little better just knowing someone was thinking about them. Hopefully Mrs. Williamson will understand that I feel her pain.

My own pain comes slamming back, tightening like an elastic around my heart. Austin probably didn't even notice anything was wrong. He has better things to do than sit around wishing he could take back things he said. Does he even like me as much as I like him? God. What is *wrong* with me? I've never been this unhinged before. The last boyfriend I had was Carlos. He worked at Rite Aid. I was super shy about approaching him at first. My extreme lack of boy confidence prevented me from even saying hi, but I finally managed to push myself. We went out until it became clear that Carlos didn't aspire to do much besides work at Rite Aid.

My relationship with Austin couldn't be more different. I'm falling so hard so fast I can't control my emotions. And controlling my emotions is something I've become an expert at over the years. I know how to compartmentalize the pain of what happened when I was seven into the one day a year in Central Park when I allow myself to feel it. But Austin is breaking down my wall. What if I like him way more than he likes me? What if this isn't going where I think it's going? Am I strong enough to put myself in a position where I'm helplessly in love with this boy a year from now . . . and he meets someone he likes better? Or he moves away? Or he leaves me for some other reason?

Click-clack. Click-clack. Click-clack.

I really need to chill. Austin seems to like me as much as I like him. He says the most amazing things to me. But I've heard of guys saying these kinds of heavier things and then vanishing overnight. From what I've heard, the disappearing-boy trick is a common one.

My yarn gets bunched up. I reach down into my knitting

bag for the ball of bright orange yarn I'm turning into a giraffe puppet. Knitting all of my Christmas gifts was a good idea, but it means I had to start early. As my needles start *click-clacking* again, I look around at the older ladies in the circle. People who knit are beyond petty worrying. They have a grasp on the inner peace I try to project but haven't actually developed yet. Maybe my chances of achieving inner peace will improve the longer I sit here and absorb their energy. And then I'll never have to care about this kind of stupid boy drama again.

SEVENTEEN
DARCY

AFTER SADIE AND I HAD lunch at Chat 'n Chew, I ran into Jude again on my way to class. He was in between acts, set up in the same spot. He saw me before I saw him. I almost said, "I was just talking about you!"

He asked me out. I said yes.

Jude's idea to meet up for coffee before he hits the park was brilliant. I'm not fully human until I've had my coffee. There are approximately one grillion places to get coffee in New York City and I intend to sample every last one of them.

The Dean & DeLuca on University Place has a light, airy atmosphere. That's why I suggested we meet up here when Jude called me to make plans. The ambience will help keep everything else light and airy.

I spot Jude the second I walk in the door. He's watching for me from a corner table. He waves even though he has to see that I'm coming over to him.

"Hey." I drop my hobo bag on the floor and pull out the wire-frame chair across from him. My bag is almost as massive as Sadie's today. After coffee I'll be doing a few errands and then camping out at the library. Slumming it at the library isn't exactly my idea of a rocking Sunday. But summer session requires you to read a horrifying amount of pages in a crazy condensed period of time. We're basically cramming an entire semester's worth of material into six weeks.

This is the first time I'm seeing Jude in regular clothes. He's wearing standard summer boy gear—board shorts, ironic tee, flip-flops—but the way he carries himself and the chill Cali vibe he gives off are making everything sexier than it should be.

"Are you from California?" I ask.

"Born and raised here in New York."

"Huh."

"Do I seem like I'm from the other coast?"

"Sort of. You have a surfer-boy look with a Cali vibe going on."

Jude laughs. "'Surfer-boy look.' That's a first."

"No one's ever told you that?"

"Not to my face." Jude stands and pats his back pocket. "What can I get you?"

"Double shot of espresso."

"Damn, girl. You're more hardcore than me."

When Jude gets back with our coffees, I dive right into what I hope will be an enlightening conversation. He's like a crystal clear ocean I can't wait to explore.

"So," I say. "Tell me about your adventures."

"Which ones?"

"The ones most interesting to tell." We reach for the sugar shaker at the same time. My hand brushes his. A shiver goes through me.

"Let's see. . . ." Jude reflects. "Most recently I met a girl."

"What's she like?"

"First off, she's smart. Like scary smart. I might be a little intimidated. And she's gorgeous . . . and inspiring. And alive."

"As opposed to all those dead girls you meet?"

"Most people aren't living in a way that makes them feel alive. They want more out of life, but they're too afraid to make any big changes." Jude picks up his mug and blows on his coffee. "You're not like that. You don't go through life like it's a series of motions. You're alive. You live out loud more impressively than anyone else I know."

Um. We just met and he's this stoked? Either the boy is playing me or he's a touch too serious.

"You already know that about me?" I ask. "Not the impressive part—sorry to disappoint on that. The alive part."

"You have an alive vibe like I have a Cali vibe."

"Do I have a Cali vibe to you?"

Jude studies me. "Actually, yeah. Are you from there?"

"Santa Monica."

"Nailed it."

"Where are you from?"

"Park Avenue. Lower Central Park."

"Isn't that supposed to be where the old money is?"

Jude puts his hands up. "You got me. But please be advised that the statements and opinions of this broadcast are in no way affiliated with Park Avenue old money."

"I hear you. My family has money, too."

"Really? You seem so down-to-earth."

"So do you."

"My parents don't approve of my lifestyle. They want me to be a doctor or a lawyer. Typical Park Avenue bullshit. Their attitude is that if a person isn't fulfilling his potential financially, he's not making the most of his life. They were furious when I deferred college. Their heads exploded when I deferred for a second year. After I graduated from high school last year and told them I was going to defer to do what I love, they cut me off financially. Way to be supportive of your kid's dreams."

"Do they know how much you love what you're doing?"

"They don't care. You'd think parents would be thrilled to hear that what their kid loves to do the most is make other people happy. Not mine."

"So . . . you're supporting yourself just from your perfor- mance art? Respect."

"Not entirely. I'm exploring some supplemental sources of income. This is far from the cheapest city."

"Where do you live?"

"On Spring Street. I'm sharing a place with three other guys. What about you?"

"We're a few blocks away. I have two roommates."

"Did you know them before you moved here?"

"No, we were placed together through UNY. They're awe-some girls. I'm psyched it worked out."

"Seriously. I didn't know what I was getting into at all with my roommates. They could have turned out to be morons."

"You didn't know them before?"

Jude shakes his head. "Answered an ad and hoped for the best."

"We got lucky."

He holds up his mug. "Cheers to our luck." I clink my tiny espresso cup against his mug, locking into his gaze. The sparkle in his eyes tells me that he's not just talking about our roommates.

Jude is the one who's impressive. He understands the beauty of going with the flow like a leaf in the wind. More than under-stands it—he's living it. He refuses to compromise. He refuses to accept less than what he wants. The boy is my new role model.

"So those supplemental sources of income you're explor-ing . . . what are we talking about?"

"Nothing sketchy. Just some side projects. One of them will hopefully take off soon. It's kind of exhausting, though. I'm always on the hustle. Constantly networking. It's weird how tiring not working can be."

"What's the project you're hoping will take off?"

"That information is classified. But I might be able to tweak its top secret status and tell you everything next time."

"What makes you so sure there will be a next time?" I tease.

"How could there not be?"

"Stranger things have happened."

"Are you saying I might never see you again?" Jude scrunches up his face. *"Incontheivable!"*

"Dude, I love *The Princess Bride*! I've seen it like three hundred times!"

"'Nonsense. You're only saying that because no one ever has.'"

"Westley to Buttercup when she says they'll never survive."

"'You keep using that word. I do not think it means what you think it means.'"

"Um, yeah. You just went up like a thousand levels of magnificent."

"By being a movie quote geek?"

"By quoting from one of my top five fave movies. How did you know?"

"Like you said." Jude smiles like summer sunshine. "We got lucky."

Some boys are so adorable I could watch them all day. Not because they're doing anything particularly interesting. Maybe there's something in the warm way they interact with people. Or in the confident but modest way they carry themselves. Or a bunch of little things like the shape of their lips, the tone of their voice, the contagious way they laugh that makes me want to get closer to them. With Jude, it's all of those things and more.

I cross my arms on the table, leaning in. I stare into Jude's eyes as he sips his coffee. I don't mean to stare. They're just the most gorgeous shade of blue I've ever seen. I notice that he has a scar above his left eye.

"How did you get that scar?" I ask.

"Bike accident when I was nine. Normal kids fall off their bikes. I flew off mine."

Jude tells the hilarious story about how he flew off his bike. I tell the not-at-all-hilarious story about how I was almost clobbered by that bike messenger. Before I know it, we have to leave. I'm surprised how quickly time flew. Jude changes into his magician gear in the bathroom while I rummage in my bag for gloss. Out in front of Dean & DeLuca, we determine that we're going in different directions.

"Thanks for getting coffee with me," Jude says.

"Thanks for treating," I say. I put my new neon yellow sunglasses on.

"Well . . . I better go. Sunday is a busy day at the park."

"Yeah, I have tons of errands. After which I get to spend all afternoon at the library!"

"Told you we were lucky."

A scraggly guy wheeling a shopping cart filled with empty cans trudges past us. He bangs into Jude with no apology.

"Don't say sorry or anything," I retort.

"No worries. Crazy guys on the subway are much worse. At least you can escape on the street."

I adjust my sunglasses, dreading the amount of reading I have to do today.

"So . . . when can I see you again?" Jude asks.

I feel bad that I have to say what I'm about to say. Jude looks so optimistic waiting for my answer. He won't see it coming. Guilt swells up inside of me. I tamp it down. If I don't protect myself, no one else will. Guilt will just have to understand.

"I don't know."

Jude's face falls. "I thought you were kidding about there not being a next time."

I know Jude is disappointed in me. So am I. I hate myself for doing this to him. But our chemistry is undeniable. He helps me forget about the ex. He makes me laugh. Plus he's someone I can look up to. Jude is the kind of boy I could fall for so hard I wouldn't know what hit me. Jude is the kind of boyfriend material girls search for.

Other girls. Not me.

"See you at the park?" I offer.

"I thought we were connecting."

"We were. This isn't about you. This is all me."

Jude gives me a vague smile. "Okay, so . . . guess I'll see you around," he says.

I walk away from him before I change my mind.

EIGHTEEN
ROSANNA

THREE DAYS.

That's how long I was able to resist calling D. Three whole days.

He called me the day after our date. I wasn't home when he called. D said in his message that he was aware he shouldn't be calling me so soon, but that he didn't want to play games. He wanted to see me again.

I didn't call him back right away.

Despite my best efforts to forget him, he's been dominating my thoughts. Constantly. I can't deny the intense attraction between us. Chemistry that strong is hard to ignore. But I should be ignoring it. I should be reminding myself that Donovan Clark is not the right guy for me. The guy I belong with isn't all about money. He hasn't had everything he's ever wanted handed to him by his parents. The right guy for me will understand the value of hard work because he will have worked hard to build a life for himself. The thing is . . . D is the kind of guy who can be with anyone he wants. Smart, gorgeous, driven, successful guys are not easy to find. What if I'm turning away from a door that should be opened? What if he meets someone else and I still can't stop thinking about him?

I broke down and called him this morning.

"Hey," D said when he picked up.

"Hey."

"I'm glad you called. I was starting to think I'd never hear from you." A car horn beeped in the background.

"Where are you?"

"Walking home from the gym. Have you been out today?"

"No."

"The heat wave has arrived. It's hot as balls."

I giggled at the balls reference.

"What are you doing tonight?" D asked.

"Um . . . staying in air-conditioning?"

"The friend I had plans with just canceled. Want to grab a drink?"

So here we are at Press Lounge, this trendy rooftop bar in Midtown. The bouncer asks for our ID.

"Here you go." D shows the bouncer his ID. Then he slips him some cash. By the way D presses the folded bills neatly into the bouncer's palm, I can tell he's done this before. Money is clearly the main tool D uses to solve his problems.

The heat wave apparently didn't get the memo that it's almost dark out. It's still broiling. The refreshing breeze I was hoping to find up on the roof isn't here. It probably stayed home in the air-conditioning.

We're seated on one of the love seats lining the perimeter of the roof. I overcome my nervousness enough to actually look around. Up until this moment it's been all about keeping it together. Trying not to look too dorky. Attempting to blend in among the beautiful people. Brushing off the awkwardness of D having to bribe my way in. I'm so nervous I didn't even notice the view. But now I do. And it takes my breath away.

You can see the whole city from up here. Press Lounge has 360-degree views. No part of Manhattan is off limits. Every neighborhood, every block, every building is within reach. I could even see my building if I looked hard enough. I take it all in. Hot summer night. Water towers illuminated with pink lights. Shimmering rooftop pool. All of New York sparkling below us. Being up here is such an amazing high I never want to leave.

"Just so you know," I say, "this rooftop is my new home."

"Nice choice."

"Thanks. I'm moving in tomorrow."

"Where will you sleep?"

"Oh, you know. . . ." I glance around at the clusters of tables, chairs, love seats, and banquettes. "Under that lounge chair is fine. I don't require much."

"A girl who's not high-maintenance. Gotta love it."

"Throw me a pillow and I'm good."

D moves a bit closer to me on the love seat. "Have I told you that you look beautiful tonight?"

My face gets hot. Why does D even like me? He is so freaking gorgeous. A gorgeous man telling me I look beautiful is not something I can get used to. Not that I'm complaining. I just wish compliments like that didn't make me feel like such an impostor. The only thing saving me from dissolving in a heap of insecurity is the new outfit I'm rocking courtesy of Darcy.

Darcy wasn't hearing it when I told her I couldn't accept her way-too-generous offer to enhance my wardrobe. She went and bought me a bunch of clothes I said I liked during our window shopping outing in Soho. How she remembered everything is beyond me. Of course I said I couldn't keep any of the beautiful clothes and accessories. But Darcy insisted I keep it all. She even went as far as cutting the tags off and destroying the receipts so returning anything would be impossible. She said I could think of the new pieces as an early Christmas/birthday present if it made me feel better. I have no idea how I'll ever repay her. But right now, sitting next to D in his polished designer ensemble among dozens of couples dressed the same way, I could not be more thankful for Darcy's generosity.

Does D expect an answer to his question? Or when guys say things like that, is it more of a compliment disguised as a question? Because he hadn't told me I looked beautiful before he asked, but I don't want him to think I'm fishing for a compliment.

I decide to go with honesty. "I don't think so," I say.

"Well, you do. That dress is perfect for you."

"Thanks." What would he say if he knew my rich roommate bought it for me?

D looks at the city stretched out behind us, absorbing the view. "I love it up here. Good place to unwind. If it wasn't for you, this week would have been unbearable."

"Why?"

"Work stress. I love my internship, but it comes with a certain amount of bullshit."

"But you love the whole Wall Street thing?"

"I really do." I must look skeptical, because D says, "What? You don't believe me?"

"No, I do. It's just . . . have you ever thought about a job that's more . . . emotionally satisfying? You might not make as much, but you could be making other people's lives better."

"I will be helping people. It *is* possible to make decent money and be happy doing it. My dad gives back to the community and I intend to do the same. He donates five percent of his income to various charities annually. Which is a lot for a seven-figure salary plus bonus." D gives me a sad smile. "Are you worried I won't be contributing enough?"

"As long as you're happy and doing something meaningful with your life, it's all good."

D gently puts his hand over mine. Until he touched me, I hadn't realized that I was snapping my thumb against my middle finger. It's this nervous tic I've been trying to stop since it suddenly started happening last year. *Get control of yourself. Stop being a weirdo.*

"You have conviction, Rosanna Tranelli," D says. "I admire you."

The air takes on a crispy-potato-skins smell. My mouth waters in retaliation against my nervous stomach.

"Sorry if I sounded harsh," I say. "But I think it's important to make a difference in this world."

"You're a better person than I am. I just want to make a decent living. And if I can help other people do the same, that's enough for me."

Um . . . yeah. D and I really are in different worlds. I'm kind of wondering why I'm even here. But then he looks at me with his intense laser focus and I instantly melt. I never expected to feel this way about a boy. My crazy lust for him is so strong it makes the stupid things he says less irritating. Maybe I could try being like Darcy tonight—wild and free and living in the Now. I could see what happens if I let myself feel everything D makes me feel. Just one night to let the fire burn.

D asks me all about camp. He asks if I found out what Nasty Girl's deal is. I'm hoping that was just a weirdo encounter I'll never have to experience again. As we talk over two rounds of drinks (some sort of seasonal beer for him, a virgin strawberry minty cocktail for me), I lose myself in the kind of chemistry I've been fantasizing about for so long. My body is reacting to him in ways I've only read about up until now. And all we're doing is sitting next to each other.

By the time D orders a third round, we're pressed up against each other on the love seat. Partly because he's been moving closer to me. Partly because I've been moving closer to him. There's like this gravitational force pulling us together. D is so close to me now I can feel his heart beating.

"I want to show you Tribeca," D says. "You're going to love it."

"Why do you love it?"

"Tons of reasons. Tribeca is known for its sick loft spaces. That's why I wanted to live there. The neighborhood has changed a lot over the years, but it still has a raw essence I appreciate. My place is a few blocks from the river. Did I tell you I run?"

"No."

"Are you a morning person or a night person?"

"Morning person."

"Me, too. I like running along the river early. It makes the whole day feel more productive if I've already worked out. What else . . . lots of my favorite restaurants are in Tribeca. I'm right near Whole Foods and Equinox. And the energy is electric. Basically, Tribeca is the quintessential New York neighborhood."

D's love for New York resonates with me. His passion is infectious. "That's how I feel about New York. This city is like a magical kingdom I can't believe I finally get to inhabit. I've been dreaming of living here since I was little."

"What do you love most about it?"

"The energy, like you said. It makes me feel alive."

D puts his hand on my arm. A jolt of electricity zips through me. "That's exactly how I feel. Why would I want to live anywhere else? The best of everything is right here. How fortunate are we that we can experience it every single day? I've lived here my whole life and I keep falling in love with this city over and over again."

D doesn't need to know that I've been constantly worrying about money. He doesn't need to know that I'll walk blocks out of my way just to save a dollar with coupons. Or that I'm planning to eat a bagel for dinner every day next week and buy a box of cereal on sale for dinners the week after. New York is a lot more expensive than I thought it would be. It's like you can't even leave your apartment without spending money. My situation is embarrassing and financial anxiety is not exactly sexy. So I keep the whole truth to myself.

"I can totally relate," I say. "I've only been here for a week, but I feel like I'm falling more in love with New York every day."

D looks at me so intensely I swear he can see into my soul.

"There's a lot to fall in love with," he says.

NINETEEN
SADIE

HEAT WAVES IN NEW YORK are not pretty. Sweaty people crammed up against you on the subway. Stenchy garbage bags on the street. Slamming into a wall of hot humidity the second you step outside. Everything slows down. I've been trying to use the lethargic pace as an opportunity to be present and look up more. But all I want to do is run to the nearest air-conditioned space.

I wipe sweat off my upper lip. Austin is late. He told me to meet him here on the corner of 11th and Bank. He didn't tell me what we're doing. It's a surprise. As much as I love surprises, if Austin doesn't get here soon his surprise will be finding me dissolved in a puddle of sweat.

One cool thing about this corner is that it was a set location for *13 Going on 30*. This is the corner Jenna rounds on her way to Matty's place when she's looking for his building. I love the plot of that movie. Jenna and Matty grow up next door to each other. He loves her. She sees him as just a friend. Seventeen years later, Jenna realizes that they belong together. They have been soul mates all along.

Two sweaty women in their twenties walk by, complaining about the heat. One of them says it's 103 degrees. The other insists it's 107. Any temperature over 80 is too extreme for me. I try not to panic that I'm going to be totally disgusting by the time Austin gets here. Even in this suffocating heat, Austin is the only thing I can think about. A few times I even catch myself making googly eyes at the streetlight. We haven't seen each other for four days. Four long, excruciating days. It will require every shred of strength I can gather to resist pouncing on him the second he pulls up.

What may or may not be Austin's car pulls up in front of me. All big white SUV-type vehicles look the same. I have to remember to memorize his license plate number so I can identify his car that way.

Austin leans over the front seat and opens the passenger door. "Sorry I'm late!" he says.

I jump in and slam the door. The air-conditioning feels so good I almost kiss the dashboard.

"Hot enough for you?" he asks.

"It could be hotter. The egg I fried on the sidewalk took a whole ten seconds to cook."

"Sorry you had to wait out there in the heat, sweetie. I promise to make it up to you."

Austin just called me *sweetie*. I love it. Even though I promised myself I wouldn't pounce, I throw my arms around him and kiss him. He kisses me back passionately.

The immense anxiety I felt after our phone awkwardness disappeared yesterday when Austin called to ask me out to dinner tonight. He said he couldn't wait to see me again. It was making him crazy that his weekend was so busy we couldn't get together. I was worried for nothing.

The only boy drama left is with Darcy and Jude. Darcy wasn't telling me everything about the Jude situation when we had lunch at Chat 'n Chew. There's more to the story than she wanted to admit. Or maybe she doesn't realize that things are more complicated than she thinks. I can't quite put my finger on what it was. I'm just not sure how believable her whole fun-and-free approach to boy adventures really is.

"Here we are." Austin pulls up in front of a small restaurant on the corner of Hudson and Jane. "Why don't you get out here and I'll find a spot? I don't want you to have to walk too far if I can't park close by."

"That's okay. I want to go with you." How sweet is it that Austin is such a gentleman?

Dinner is incredible. It's delicious and romantic and just the best dinner ever. Austin knew I would love this old-school Italian place where the chef comes right up to your table to tell you the specials. I didn't have the heart to tell him I've been here before with my parents. Piccolo Angolo is known as the best Italian place in the West Village. The atmosphere is casual but special, the kind of place I've been wanting to come to with my future boyfriend. The boyfriend who would be sophisticated enough to bring me here.

Austin could only get a reservation for six o'clock, so by the time we leave it's still before sunset.

"Want to walk the High Line?" I say.

"I was just going to ask you that!" Austin reaches for my hand. We hold hands all the way to the Gansevoort Street entrance.

The High Line is an elevated park that was built on an old railway. It extends above the street from the West Village to a bit above Chelsea. It's my favorite green space. Taking an abandoned section of the city and rebuilding it into the sweetest outdoor space ever? That's why I love urban design. I can't wait to be the one who plans spaces like this. I love that Austin is also into design. Now we can geek out together.

"It's cool how people can come together on the bleachers and the lawn, but still keep their personal space," I say as we pass the 10th Avenue Square seating steps. "And how the walkways naturally blend people together."

"I know. All these areas that invite people to sit together while still maintaining the flow of walkers. It's a brilliant design."

Since the High Line is all the way on the west side overlooking the river, the sunset views are spectacular. I hope the sunset is gorgeous tonight. One of my secret romantic fantasies is for Austin and I to come up here, cuddle on one of the lounge chairs facing the river, and watch the sunset together. Tonight will be the night that fantasy comes true. Which is why I'm not surprised that a couple gets up from what is now the only free lounge chair space when we start scoping one out. More perfect timing.

We lie back on the oversize wooden chair. Wooden lounge chairs are not the most comfortable to recline on, but they totally go with the whole minimalist, streamlined style of the High Line. I try to arrange myself in an attractive way while preventing my tailbone from ramming into the wood. Once I get relatively comfortable, I realize that we're right below John Dalton's place.

"My friend John lives there," I say, pointing to his window high above us.

"Must be an awesome view. But this view is the best." Austin isn't looking out toward the sunset. He's looking right at me.

I hold his gaze. Locking eyes with him is the ultimate test of boy confidence, especially after what he just said.

"You're so beautiful," he whispers.

We kiss in that movie love way where you're on the High Line at sunset and you're with the boy of your dreams and it's the ultimate rom-com scene. The kind of scene people say can't happen in real life. Except this is happening. And it couldn't be more real.

TWENTY
DARCY

JUDE LOVES THESE BLUE GUYS something fierce. The phosphorescent paint they poured on their drums goes flying when they start pounding. We're not in the first few rows where people are wearing rain ponchos and getting blasted with everything from masticated Cap'n Crunch to Tang. Still, a blast of electric purple paint makes me duck when it threatens to spatter my new dress.

Blue Man Group should be a rite of passage for anyone who is angling to achieve official New Yorker status. Everyone new to the city should see it within their first year. If I were in charge, I'd make it a mandatory theatrical experience. My parents brought me here over spring break in ninth grade. We stayed at the Gansevoort Hotel for five glorious days. They took me to see Blue Man Group. I was blown away then and I'm blown away now.

After our coffee two days ago, I tried really hard to convince myself to stay away from Jude. That was kind of impossible. So yesterday I decided that I could hang out with him while still keeping an emotional distance. Then I found him at the park, asked him out, and swung by the theater for Blue Man tickets.

Of course Jude has seen them before. I mean, hello, BMG are the ultimate performance artists. Any respectable artist learns from the most acclaimed ones. But he first saw them a long time ago, way before I did. Jude said he was like eight or nine when his mom took him. Watching Jude laughing as the paint flies, you wouldn't know he's seen all of this before. He was even getting excited before the show like a little kid. He reminded me of this little boy who was watching his act at the park yesterday. Same delighted expression. Same obvious joy. Same sense of wonder.

The blue men pound their drums harder. Paint zings in all directions. I love how the bright colors of the lights and paint are reflected in Jude's wide eyes. This would be an amazing experience without him. But he's making it even more amazing.

"What was your favorite part?" Jude asks me on the walk home.

"When they flung toilet paper."

"Classic. Mine was the drums."

"I could tell."

Jude gives me an amused look.

"No, I mean . . ." I backpedal. "What's not to love about paint flying everywhere?"

"The only thing better than flying paint is phosphorescent flying paint."

"That is so true."

The smell of roasted cashews wafts over from the Nuts 4 Nuts cart on the corner. Nuts 4 Nuts roasted cashews are like Auntie Anne's pretzels. Once I smell them, I must have them.

"Dude, I have to get these nuts," I say.

"Cashews?"

"How did you know?"

"You're a woman of refined taste. Peanuts just don't cut it. And walnuts are out of the question."

"Do they even have walnuts?"

"They're nuts for nuts. How could they not have walnuts?"

"They don't have walnuts."

"Wanna bet?"

I stop to look Jude in the eye. "Depends."

"On?"

"What we're betting."

"Whoever loses treats for dinner next time."

Taking this bet could be risky. Jude could see it as a romantic dinner instead of a casual dinner. But I'm positive they don't have walnuts. Almost positive. About 98% positive.

"Deal." We shake on it.

I dart to the Nuts 4 Nuts cart. Walnuts are on the menu.

"Yes!" Jude triumphantly shakes his fists above his head. "Walnuts in the hizzouse, son!"

"Preposterous," I object. "Who eats roasted walnuts? How is that even a thing?"

"Are they roasted? I thought they were candied."

"Even worse."

Jude smirks at me. "Is someone being a sore loser?"

"The only losers are the unfortunate people ordering walnuts when, as we can see from the bogus menu, several far more delicious nuts are available."

"What can I get you?" the nuts guy asks us.

"One cashews, please," I order. Then I glance at Jude. "Unless you'd like some walnuts?"

"You've been scandalized enough."

I pay for my cashews and offer some to Jude. We continue our walk home.

"Is this a good time to tell you . . ." Jude steps closer to me. He is so freaking adorable. Even the scar above his left eye is adorable. ". . . where I'd like to be taken to dinner next time?"

"Speaking of next time, you said you'd tell me what you're working on next time. This is next time."

"It's an invention. Well, more of an improvement of an existing invention. You know how you can never pump the last bit of lotion or shampoo out of the bottle?"

"And you pry off the top and bang the bottle upside down and you still can't get the rest out? *So* annoying."

"Not anymore. I've found a way to modify the pump

mechanism so the bottle empties every time. You can also hold spray bottles any way while you're spraying. They don't have to be upright for the last bit of liquid to spray out."

"Wait. You're saying I can spray Windex from any angle?"

"Too nerdy?"

"No, it's totally brill. Why didn't anyone think of that before? Why didn't *I* think of that before?"

"There are so many things I kick myself for not thinking of I can't even tell you."

"You didn't tell me you were a genius."

"A genius in disguise never tells."

The distinct sound of a harmonica approaches us from behind. I turn around to see a guy in a fedora holding a coffee cup in one hand and playing the harmonica with the other. He's trucking along like playing an instrument while walking down the street is completely normal. That's another thing I love about New York. I love how people aren't afraid to be exactly who they are. No explanations. No apologies. No pressure to conform. Just raw, honest reality in your face.

"So when can the world start benefiting from your genius invention?" I ask.

"My team is meeting with potential investors next week. We think these guys are serious. After we have financial backing, the product can be manufactured and sold to companies that will hopefully replace all of their pumps and sprays with ours."

Jude is made of way more awesome than I initially detected. It rules that he has the whole creative/going with the flow/

living outside the lines thing happening, but he's also brilliant and dedicated enough to work on a project that could potentially blow up.

"Most free spirits don't focus on any one thing long enough to finish what they started," I say. "You're different."

"Only because I want it more. Anyone could figure this stuff out if they spent enough time on it."

"But you're smarter than they are."

"I don't know about that. I just managed to wrangle investors who will probably fund me."

The certainty in his eyes makes me believe they will. He makes me believe that his invention will have a huge impact. His conviction is inspiring.

We're almost at my building when Jude flaps the front of his shirt that says MULTI-TALENTED a few times in an attempt to cool off. "My shirt is soaked."

"Feel free to take it off."

"Right here on Fifth Avenue?"

"You're allowed. I'm not."

"Actually, I think women have the right to be topless outdoors in New York."

"When's the last time you saw a topless woman walking down the street?"

"Um, I think it was"—Jude consults a phantom watch on his wrist—"half past never?"

"Because I'm pretty sure it's illegal."

"Wanna bet?"

"Oh, I'm good. You already won dinner. I couldn't handle losing again."

"So you admit I'm right."

"I admit nothing. Other than how sexy you are."

"Damn, girl. Were you born this confident or what?"

"Half born, half what." The truth is, I'm not really sure where my confidence comes from. I wasn't a shy little girl. When I was four, a lady friend of my mom's came over wearing a fabulous red dress that hugged her curves in all the right places. I remember telling her she was a sexy lady. My mom and her friend laughed hard over that.

Some boys would be intimidated by girl power. Not Jude. He seems to appreciate my spark. And I'm sure he's appreciating that I'm not pressuring him for any kind of commitment. Free spirits like Jude don't want to be tied down. This way is better for both of us. No strings attached. No hidden disappointments, strained conversations, or passive-aggressive games. Just two people enjoying being with each other and having fun. Isn't that the point?

Enjoy the freedom, dude. You're welcome.

TWENTY-ONE
ROSANNA

CAN SOMEONE PLEASE TELL ME what my upstairs neighbors are doing? Consecutive hours of high-impact cardio? Dragging furniture across the floor? Why don't they ever sit down? And why does it sound like a herd of elephants pounding on the floor every time they walk? What is this *boom boom boom* instead of normal people walking? Who walks like that?

Like no. Just stop.

The situation is entirely unacceptable. If I were a more confident person, I'd march right up there and ask them to simmer down. Perhaps they'd be interested in relaxing on the couch with a good book? Or relaxing on the couch doing anything as long as they *stop pounding on the floor please god*. I may be new to this city, but I'm pretty sure your upstairs neighbors walking around shouldn't cause your whole apartment to vibrate. For graduation my grandma sent me a framed print of Seurat's

Sunday Afternoon on the Island of La Grande Jatte, which is hanging in my room. It shouldn't shake when those meatheads pound across their floor. That's just wrong. I mean, seriously. What exactly are they doing up there?

But I'm not a more confident person. My opinions are confident. My moral standards are confident. My views regarding how society should operate are confident. Now all I have to do is find a way to be as confident on the outside as I am on the inside.

Tha-RUMP bump bump! go the elephants.

Prior to the disappointing discovery of wildlife inhabiting the apartment above ours, I was excited about the possibility of staying here freshman year. UNY lets freshmen live off-campus because the school's housing is limited. Apparently the university is facing a housing crisis where they don't have enough dorm space. They're scrambling to find places for everyone. Some subsidized apartments and shares like this one are available by lottery. Students already in summer shares have the option of keeping their apartment for the upcoming year. When I talked to Sadie and Darcy about staying, they were totally on board. We'll find out if we get to keep this place in August when the university notifies everyone of their housing situation.

What if I'm placed in a different apartment with noisy neighbors again? Or if I stay here and have to deal with these idiots upstairs all year? It's one thing during the summer when I'm only working. But what about when classes start? It will be a whole other thing when I'm trying to study and read and write papers on three hours of sleep. Which will likely be my life, considering that I'll have to work at least twenty hours a week on top of my full course load. The circus upstairs makes it impossible to concentrate on anything.

So does D.

Our date at Press Lounge was one of the top five highlights of my life. And by far the most romantic experience I've ever had. The way he looked at me when he said there's a lot to fall in love with. How I melted when he put his hand over mine. My stomach was in knots the whole way home in the cab, wondering if D was going to kiss me. When we pulled up in front of my building, D kissed me on the cheek. That's when I realized I definitely wanted more.

Seriously. What are they doing upstairs? Now it sounds like someone is doing jumping jacks. *Pound pound pound.* Is making this much noise even legal? After some quick research online, I learn about NYC Quiet Hours as specified in Local Law 113. Quiet hours are from 10:00 p.m. to 7:00 a.m. The noise code states the following:

No person shall make, continue or cause or permit to be made or continued any unreasonable noise . . . Unreasonable noise shall include but shall not be limited to sound, attributable to any device, that exceeds the following prohibited noise levels:

(1) Sound, other than impulsive sound, attributable to the source, measured at a level of 7 dB(A) or more above the ambient sound level at or after 10:00 p.m. and before 7:00 a.m., as

measured at any point within a receiving property or as measured at a distance of 15 feet or more from the source on a public
right-of-way.

So I guess filing a formal complaint would require a mea-
surement of the decibel level. Which I might be forced to take
if they don't shut up. They've pounded around every night. The
first couple nights didn't bother me. But now it's been over a
week. Every additional day of tolerating their noise is grating
on me exponentially.

Something about the unsettling effect of neighbor noise
invading my space is making me homesick. I miss my supersoft
lavender blanket my mom got on sale when I was little. Getting
under that blanket at night soothed me. I felt protected despite
all of the obstacles in my way. Maybe it was stupid to feel that
way about a blanket. But it's upsetting to be in my new bed
without my supersoft blanket, even though it's too hot to use.
Shipping it would have taken up too much box space.

Thinking about my blanket is tolerable. It's when I think
about how much I miss my family that I have to fight back tears.
I miss their comfort. Their familiarity. I miss knowing I had a
support system no matter what. My family and I have always
been really close. I knew that being so far away from them was
going to be hard, but it's harder than I expected.

My upstairs neighbors are relentless. I have to get out of
here. Hopefully Mica can meet up with me.

"Classic," she says when I call and tell her about the elephants.

"You wouldn't be having the full New York experience without noisy neighbors. I feel your pain. Neighbor noise is the worst. Even worse than traffic and construction noise put together."

"Do you have neighbor noise?" Mica still lives at home on the Lower East Side. She's in the same financially challenged boat as I am. Her plan is to live at home freshman year and save up enough at her work-study job to move out next year.

"Not anymore. This old guy used to live below us who snored so loudly I could hear him through the floor."

"You heard him *snoring*? That's insane."

"Insane doesn't even begin to describe it. Then there was my former next-door neighbor, who thumped every time he came home from work. Not like he was throwing down his shoes or something. It sounded like he dropped two concrete blocks right after he closed the door. I ran into him one time in the hall and asked him about the thumps. He had no idea what I was talking about. To this day I'm still dying to know what those thumps were."

"What happened with your downstairs neighbor who snored?"

"He died a few months ago."

Whoa. New York neighbor noise is hardcore. It's like you have to put up with the noise until your neighbor either moves out or dies.

"That's intense," I say.

"Heavy walkers are the worst. They shake your whole apartment."

"I know! What are they doing up there? Why can't they ever sit down?" I love how Mica and I understand each other. We think the same way. Usually I have to explain myself to people who never really seem like they're entirely with me. But with Mica, there's a sensation of her understanding what I mean before I even finish what I'm saying. I've never felt that kind of connection to a friend before. "Hey, I have to get out of here. Do you want to do something?"

"I have plans with some friends, but you're welcome to join us. We're meeting up at Tick Tock."

"What's that?"

"Only the best diner on the Lower East."

"No thanks, I'm okay." Tagging along with Mica's friends would feel like I'm intruding. Her friends don't want a random person showing up. "I'll probably go read at a café."

"Are you sure?"

"Yeah. Have fun. I'll see you tomorrow."

After we hang up, I consider my options. Sadie and Darcy are still out. It's just me and the herd of elephants. I could go read at a café. But D is making it impossible to concentrate on anything. I can barely read a paragraph before he infiltrates my brain. Next thing I know, I've been staring at the same page for half an hour. Or staring into space. D and I are going out tomorrow. Just thinking about the date turns me into a hot mess. I could walk around, but it's still broiling out. The heat wave is supposed to break tomorrow, taking the city down from over 100 to the low 80s.

I decide to go to bed early. I'm exhausted, anyway. The elephants are emotionally draining. My earbuds block them out when I turn my music up loud. Then I lie back on the cool sheet, close my eyes, and play fantasies of D like favorite movie scenes that always make me feel better.

TWENTY-TWO
SADIE

WHEN AUSTIN SHOWS UP AT my door with a dozen long-stemmed pink roses, I'm overcome with emotion. Not just because he brought me flowers. Or because he brought me my favorite flowers. I'm amazed that a boy I met one week ago already knows me so well.

We were obviously meant to be.

"It's like you know me better than anyone," I say. "How is that even possible?"

Austin comes in, handing me the flowers. They look fresh, their petals soft and flawless. "I missed you."

"I missed you, too."

"Not seeing you yesterday was torture." He slides his hand through my hair. Then he kisses me like he hasn't seen me for two years instead of two days.

I float to the kitchen on a cloud, breathing in the sweet

fragrance of the roses. Digging around for a vase under the sink, I uncover a rusty cooling rack and some ancient silverware way in the back. The cracked rubber band around the silverware is so old it's sticking to a knife. We really need to clean everything out if we're staying here after this summer. The thought of what other progressively disgusting treasures have yet to be unearthed is a scary one. Miraculously a chipped clear vase was stashed behind the cooling rack. I grab it without looking too hard at what else is back there.

My mom said you should trim two inches off the bottom of flower stems under running water before you put them in a vase. The flowers are supposed to last longer that way. While I'm at the sink trimming the stems, Austin comes up behind me. He rubs my shoulders in slow circles.

"You're so delicate," he whispers. "I love how fragile you are."

"Don't break me."

He leans against the counter next to me. "And I love how well I know you. Which is why I know you're going to love this old-school board gaming group."

We were talking about how no one appreciates old-school board games anymore. When Austin was younger, he used to sit for hours with his best friend playing all the classics: Sorry!, Clue, Monopoly, Parcheesi, Life. They would have gaming marathons that lasted all afternoon. A sleepover usually followed, featuring scary movies and popcorn with extra butter. Austin misses the pure joy of simple fun. So he found a board gaming group. Tonight will be his first time going. They meet at the upstairs café of the Tribeca Whole Foods. I wanted to go as soon as Austin told me about it. Their dorktastic meeting location was just icing on the cake.

I don't really know what I was prepared for. Something like a few people with board games spread out in front of them mixed together with Whole Foods shoppers eating dinner from the hot food bar. Nothing like the scene we're greeted with. The board gaming group has appropriated entire tables. We're talking long tables. They're sitting in groups of four or six or eight playing games I've never seen before. These games are beyond intricate. As Austin and I tour the tables, I notice games with so many pieces and cards it's hard to believe they all go to one game.

"How long have you been playing this game?" I ask a guy with a half sleeve of ink and horn-rims.

"Four hours," he says.

"How much longer do you have?"

"Probably another four."

This isn't just a board gaming group. This is the most hard-core board gaming group *ever*.

"Do you recognize any of these games?" Austin asks me after we've seen them all.

"None. Are they from a different planet?"

"The games or the gamers? Eight hours for one game? Do we have to do that?"

"I hope not. But at least it'll be easy to take a snack break if we do."

"Let's try to find the activity director and see what we can play. I think his name is Michael."

We track down Michael playing a game so elaborate it has two huge main boards, plus individual smaller boards. I'm surprised to see that Michael is a relatively normal-looking dude. Almost everyone else here is rocking some eccentric look. I've only seen one other girl. I don't think I've seen any other college kids. Most of these guys are probably in their late twenties/ early thirties.

"We're new," Austin explains to Michael.

"It's your first day with us?" Michael asks.

"Yeah."

"Welcome. Let's see what's starting up. There should be a Settlers group starting in about fifteen minutes."

"What if we . . . haven't played that before?" I ask.

"You've never played Settlers of Catan?" Michael is incredulous.

We shake our heads.

"How about Puerto Rico?"

We shake our heads some more.

"Asara?"

"We're not familiar with any of the games we've seen," Austin says, "but we're excited to learn."

"That's the right attitude!" Michael looks around. "Let's start you on Asara. It's a cool fantasy game where you build castles. Does that sound good?"

"That sounds awesome," Austin says. The adorable thing is,

he totally means it. I can sense younger Austin whirring with excitement under this older exterior.

Michael hooks us up with four other guys who are on board with Asara. We find a free end of a table and settle in.

"I'm Austin." He extends his hand to each of the guys. "This is my girlfriend, Sadie."

Austin just called me his girlfriend. That's the first time he's introduced me to a group of people as his girlfriend. Or to anyone as his girlfriend.

This. Is. Happening.

The guys shake my hand. The whole thing is so adult, what with the handshaking and the girlfriend calling and the chilling with fully grown men.

"A pleasure to have you, Sadie," the guy across from me says. I've already forgotten his name in my deliriously psyched state. But I'm too embarrassed to ask him what it is again.

"For reals," the guy crammed against me on the bench says. "We hardly ever get girls!"

I wonder if he means at the gaming group or in general.

Asara is super fun. You have to build castles in different colors. There are a few different ways to win points. You can win points for the highest castle. You can win points for the greatest number of castles. You can also earn points for having bling on your castles. The castle pieces are cardboard cutouts that lie flat on the board in front of you. Some pieces have gold embellishments. Others have rays of light shining from the windows. Every castle has to have a standard base and top. How many pieces and what kinds of pieces you build in between are up to you.

But the best part of playing Asara? Is pressing up against Austin on the bench. He rests his hand on my thigh. I give him a shy smile.

"Someone's winning for highest castle," the guy on the other side of me announces.

It takes me a second to realize he means me. "What can I say? White castles are my jam."

"I thought counting colored doors was your jam," Austin interjects.

"A person can have more than one jam," I clarify. "Just so everyone knows. Look how tall this white castle is. There's one, two, like thirteen pieces."

"You were clearly meant to play Asara."

And win Asara. I end up winning the first game I've ever played. Against hardcore gamers who have been beasting on Asara for years.

"Damn, Sadie," the guy across from me says. "Killing it on your first try! You are good."

"She's a natural," the guy crammed against me says. He really doesn't need to be this close. Which maybe I should have told him from the start. But I didn't want to be rude on our first day. "I should show you my castle tower adaptation."

"Sorry?"

"Game adaptations," the guy across from me jumps in. "When we think we can improve an aspect of a game that isn't working as well as it could, we invent a change. Some of us have invented entirely new games. See that guy in the gray shirt over there? He invented Climbers."

"What's that?"

"Only the coolest blocks game ever. Most of these guys would say it's not complex enough to bring. But I'll bring it next time if you want. I think you'd dig it."

"Blocks are hot."

"Right?"

When we leave three hours later, I'm floating in a happy pink bubble of Official Girlfriend Status. I can't wait to go back and be around people who know me as Austin's girlfriend. It felt so good sitting next to him the whole time. Our thighs touching as we slid closer to each other. Our arms brushing together as we played. Smiling at the inside jokes he whispered in my ear. We're a real couple now. Austin put the Official Girlfriend Status out there. No one can dispute what we are.

The heat wave broke this morning. It's such a relief to not only breathe normally outside but to have a cooler summer breeze on our skin. We take a minute outside the main doors of Whole Foods to just breathe. The air is so refreshing that we decide to walk home along the river. This is the way I've been dreaming the perfect summer night with the perfect boy would be: walking along the water in no rush to get anywhere, holding hands, laughing, talking about everything we have in common. Stopping every now and then to kiss.

Walking with Austin is exactly like that. We have to keep

stopping to make out. It's not only that we want to make out—we *have* to make out. I've always wanted to feel this kind of passion. Sometimes I see couples who are so into each other they can't contain their attraction. They do things like kiss each other the second they get up after dinner at a restaurant. I saw a couple like that when my parents took me to Mr. Chow's for my graduation dinner. They were so cute. I remember noticing them when the hostess sat us at our table. They were sitting on stools at one of the high tables, two lovers so enraptured by each other it was like the rest of us didn't even exist. They smiled at each other the whole time. They were the opposite of most couples you see at restaurants who are barely looking at each other with nothing to say. When they got up to leave, he pulled her close to him and kissed her deeply. The group of girls at the table next to ours actually sighed. Theirs was the kind of love you rarely see, but when you do it reminds you of what you're looking for. It gives you hope that what you want to find actually exists.

The same thing happens when I see couples kissing on the street. They kiss on stoops or leaning up against buildings or intertwined in the middle of the sidewalk, oblivious to the swift stream of people bending around them. I've always wanted to be those people kissing on the street. The ones you see where you want to be them so badly the longing rips into your chest and takes your breath away.

I've always wanted to be them. And now we are.

People circle around us as we kiss on the path. Runners fly

by. Moms power walk, pushing babies in strollers. An old couple picks their way by slowly, the man leaning on his cane, the woman with her arm linked through his. But the people around us hardly register. When Austin kisses me, it blocks out everything else. This is how it must have felt to be the girl whose boyfriend kissed her at Mr. Chow's. That kiss was an image I'll never forget. Maybe someone is passing by us right now thinking the same thing about us.

We start walking again. I laugh when Austin wobbles a little.

"Can't even walk straight," he says.

"How am I still standing?"

"Did I take your breath away?"

"Oh my god." I stop walking. "I was just thinking that. Sometimes I see people kissing on the street or at dinner or whatever and they're so in love it's almost painful to watch. Not painful in a bad way. Painful because I want to be them so much it hurts, you know? And now I realized that we're those people I'd always wanted to be." I wrap my arms around Austin. "We're them."

He looks at me with so much tenderness tears spring to my eyes.

"You had me at holistic wellness," I say.

"What?"

"Just kiss me."

Austin kisses me even more intensely than before. If it's possible for your brain to short-circuit from an overload of emotion, I'm pretty sure that's happening.

We walk some more until we get to the Zen garden. That's what Brooke calls it. The Zen garden is this area on the opposite side of the path from the river. It's all willowy grasses and tall sunflowers, with simple wooden benches dotted over a winding path. A series of stepping stones lines the border between the main walking path of the park and the narrow garden path. As if he's reading my mind, Austin takes my hand, angling me near the stepping stones so I can climb up. I climb the stones with him walking beside me, holding my hand the whole time. Austin would never let me fall.

Walking north again along the water, I turn around to look behind us. One World Trade shines against the purple sky. The way its colors change throughout the day is astonishing. I love how its glass reflects the clouds when you catch it midday at the right time. The glass is rose gold before sunset. Then metallic silver before twilight. You can trace the moods of the building almost as if it has a life of its own.

"What are you looking at?" Austin asks.

"One World Trade. I think its angles are really beautiful."

"And I know you dig the spire."

"The spire is awesome on its own, but I also love how it complements the Empire State Building's spire. Did you know the ESB's LED lighting system can create sixteen million colors?"

"See, this is why I love being with you. How could I have come this far and not known that?"

"Are you making fun of me?"

"Maybe a little."

"Fine, but just know that making fun goes both ways."

The Perry Street towers suddenly appear across the street. Austin's car is parked a few blocks over. This is where we're supposed to leave the park. Except I don't want to leave. I can't stand the thought of having our perfect day come to an end. We go up to the railing that traces the river's edge. Austin leans against its smooth curved wood. I lean against Austin, my cheek pressed against his chest.

"I love how you knew I would love the board gaming group," I say.

"Of course I did. You appreciate those kinds of simple things."

"How do you know everything?"

"It's like we were made for one another," he says. "That's the only way I can explain it."

We tighten our arms around each other. Austin is right. We were totally made for one another. People would probably say it's too early to know something like that. But it doesn't matter that it's only been a week. What I feel is real. And I know that Austin feels the same way.

We lean against each other, watching the New Jersey skyline. A peaceful sensation, serene and tingly, washes over me.

"I can't wait to watch the fireworks," I say.

"Fourth of July rules."

"Where do you usually watch them?"

"Hmm. My friend's roof has a decent view. Or I'll just go down to the waterfront."

"What's your view like from the other side?"

"Other side of the river?"

"Yeah."

"You can see the entire Manhattan skyline from the water-front. It's one of the most amazing views in the world."

"Take me there."

"To Jersey?"

"I want to see what you see."

"That would be extensive travel for you. You've never even been to Jersey City."

"See how overdue I am?"

"Have you been to Hoboken?"

"What do you think?"

"We'll go to the Hoboken waterfront. The view is better than Jersey City."

"When can we go?"

"When do you want to go?"

"Right now." I don't want Austin to leave. The thought of Austin getting in his car and driving away is devastating. I hate that I miss him already when he's still right here next to me. Why can't tonight last forever?

I'm expecting Austin to tell me how busy he is and that tonight won't work but we'll go another time. Instead, he surprises me by saying, "Okay. Let's go."

"Really?"

"Really."

I whoop so loud an old lady passing us picks up the little dog she's walking and scuttles to the other side of the path. I'm so excited I'm scaring old ladies.

When we get to Austin's car, he opens the passenger door for me. "We can only stay for a few minutes," he says. "Then I'll bring you back. There's some work I have to catch up on tonight. It's going to be a late one."

Austin was right about the view. The Hoboken waterfront is a bit north of where we just were in Hudson River Park. You can see everything along the Manhattan skyline from above Central Park to below One World Trade. Now I know why I never came here before. Coming to this side of the water was a first experience meant to be shared with Austin. I was meant to wait for this moment.

We sit on a bench and take in the view. Being near the water is so refreshing. I should spend more time near the river, being still like this and enjoying the Now like Darcy says. Next time I'm looking out across the water from the other side, I'll try to find our exact spot. It would have been cool to go to the Jersey City waterfront. I want to see Austin's neighborhood. I'm dying to see his apartment and where he hangs out and stuff. But I'm sure he'll show me everything next time.

A flash of light explodes over the river. It takes me a second to realize it's a firework.

"Did you see that?" we ask each other at the same time.

More fireworks explode. Not just any fireworks. These fireworks are the magnificent ones that light up the whole sky. They're like the Fourth of July ones. They're even being launched from a barge in the river where the official Fourth of July fireworks are launched.

"Dude," Austin says. "They're testing for the Fourth of July!"

"No way."

"How else would you explain this?"

He's right. The series of fireworks bursting in front of us is so dazzling it could only be testing for the big day. We're watching a preview of the fireworks that the world will be watching one week from tonight.

The same fireworks we were just talking about across the water.

No. Freaking. Way.

This has to be a non-coincidence. A non-coincidence is a phenomenal event that is too magical to be random. Non-coincidences are much bigger than that song you were just thinking about coming on the radio. Or your friend calling you when you were just about to call her. Non-coincidences are the kind of events you'd think were impossible if you read them in a book. You couldn't make this stuff up.

We were obviously meant to come here tonight. The Universe is giving me a clear sign that Austin is my destiny. How else could you explain this ginormous non-coincidence?

TWENTY-THREE
DARCY

I SWEAR I COULD LIVE at the Strand. Eighteen miles of used books is reassuring, like no matter what you're searching for you can find the answer here. The atmosphere manages to be both intellectual and laid-back. The smell of old books is intoxicating. I love perusing the skinny aisles between book-cases, running my fingers along the cracked spines. There's so much history here. So many stories behind the stories. These books have been held by thousands of people, everyone from the casual reader who grabbed a best seller at the airport to the avid reader who equates books with oxygen. If these shelves could talk . . .

The Power of Now was so enlightening that I've come in search of similar guidance. Anyone who knows me knows that my typical approach to life involves zooming head-on at an alarming speed. But ever since the ex fiasco, I've felt a need for balance. Long story short: You may currently find me shame-lessly scavenging in the self-help section.

So many choices. So much room in the big Strand bag I picked up on the way back to the shelves. It is my obligation as a New Yorker to occasionally rock a Strand bag. This orange-and-red striped one will look good in October with skinny jeans, a long sweater coat, and biker boots.

I spread my six book choices on one of the overflowing book carts. Once I read the first couple pages of each book, I can get a better sense of which ones I'm going to buy.

A boy is rummaging through books on the other side of the cart. He was bent down behind the cart when I spread out my books. I didn't even see him. But now that he's checking out the top row, I can't help noticing him. His cuteness factor is off the charts. No exaggeration. If I had to rate his cuteness on a scale of one to ten, this boy would be a sixteen. And a half.

"That's a good one," he says, gesturing at the book I'm holding.

Our eyes meet over the book cart. An immediate spark ignites between us.

"What did you like best about it?" I say, trying not to stare at his pouty lips.

"It really helped me get through a tough time," he says. "My parents had just gotten divorced. My sister and I were miserable. That book helped me see things in a different light. Highly recommended."

I nod appreciatively, flipping the book over and reading the back cover again. There's no way I'm not buying this book, but I want to make it look like I'm still considering it.

The boy wanders over to a section a few aisles down. I look through the other books, decide which ones I want, and make my way down to the aisle across from his. Except he's not there anymore. Panic hits me. He was hot. And smart. And sweet. This is one boy adventure I am definitely having.

Eventually I spy him in memoirs. Who under the age of fifty reads memoirs?

"Hey." He looks over at me. "Self-help to memoirs. Very classy."

"I try. Are you looking for something in particular?" I ask.

"Something I couldn't be less interested in. I'm researching for a class."

Obviously he's stuck in memoirs under duress. This boy is way too cute to be stuffy.

"I'm taking summer session, too," I say. "Where do you go?"

"School of the Future."

"That's like . . . a specialty college, or . . . ?"

"It's not a college. I'm in summer school."

I give him a blank look.

"Um. High school?"

"You're in high school?"

"Only on a technicality. I was supposed to graduate, but I have to make up English credits."

"Oh." This boy's cuteness factor should be rapidly dwindling given this disturbing information. Not only is he in high school, he didn't even graduate on time. Who doesn't graduate from high school on time? What excuse could he possibly have for being such a dumbass? But here's the thing. For some reason, his lack of responsibility is making him even hotter. Maybe I'm entering a bad-boy phase.

"I'm eighteen." He smiles at me. My heart speeds up. "Totally legit."

He's only one year younger than me. What's one year? Why should age even matter? Especially when two people have intense chemistry.

"Want to get out of here?" I ask before I realize what I'm saying.

The boy takes a step closer to me. I can feel his body heat. I can smell his cinnamon gum. When his eyes lock on to mine, tingles flash up my spine, making me shiver.

"What did you have in mind?" he says.

"Everything."

"Then let's go."

"Yeah, I can come back for these." I drop my books on a cart. When I walked into the Strand, the last thing I thought I'd be walking out with was a boy. Talk about finding a good deal.

We walk up to Union Square. I have no idea where we're going. We're not really talking that much. Hot desire has taken over all rational thought. It's clear that this will be a one-time hookup, like a one-night stand minus the walk of shame the next morning.

We want each other *right now*.

The boy stops us at the corner of 15th Street. He slides his hand to the back of my neck, kissing me everywhere but my lips. He kisses my cheek, my jawline, my neck, behind my ear. Shivers ripple through me again.

"What about Park Bar?" I say, pointing to it up ahead on the right.

"I can't get in."

"I can get you in. I have a fake ID. Trust me, we can get in anywhere."

He peers into the dark bar. "Happy hour. Too crowded."

We keep walking. I slip my hand into his back pocket. He puts his arm around me. This should be a lot stranger than it is. The strangest part is how not strange it feels.

"There's a Gap three blocks up," the boy says when we hit 5th Avenue. "I've been to that one before. No one checks the dressing rooms."

"Works for me."

The Gap is a perfect place for an anonymous hookup. Anyone can sneak into anyone else's dressing room. Not like at upscale boutiques where you're hyper-monitored by sales clerks asking how you're doing in there every three seconds. Sneaking into one of those dressing rooms would be a major coup. If I'm going to hook up with a random boy in a dressing room, the Gap is the place to do it.

We branch off to the opposite men's and women's sides of the store. I grab some jeans and a few tops and hit the dressing rooms. No one's monitoring the entrance. I dart to the back section of rooms and snag the big one in the corner. The boy ducks in, locking the door behind him.

"We're in," he says. He throws some tees on the bench.

I'm suddenly nervous. Flirting in a bookstore and kissing on the street is one thing. But being locked in a dressing room with a boy I met ten minutes ago is a whole other thing. Shit just got real. Then I remember that I picked him up. I wanted this. I'm in control and I can have him if I want.

I want.

He pushes me up against the wall, pulling my leg up so it bends around his body. His lips attack mine. I kiss him aggressively, scratching my nails down his back. He grabs my ass to grind against me harder.

We have to be quiet the whole time. Which makes it even hotter.

Intense chemistry is not easy to find. When you do, you have to go for it or you'll regret missing out for the rest of your life. I want my memories to be filled with amazing adventures. No regrets.

So then why, when we go our separate ways after and I'm walking home alone down 5th Avenue, am I regretting what I just did?

What went down in the dressing room was so. freaking. *hot*. It was so hot I never even got his name. But all I can think about is Jude. How could I do that to him? Picturing his face when I tell him what happened makes me feel horrible.

Only . . . do I really have to tell him? We're not exclusive.

Far from it. We just met. Jude is free to hook up with any girl he wants. He has the same freedom I do. I'm as free as a bird and flying high this summer. No one can tie me down.

Jude knows all this. Why am I even worrying?

Wandering aimlessly down Greenwich Avenue, I discover a fun retro T-shirt shop. There's a *Princess Bride* tee in the window with Inigo Montoya. He's standing there in battle stance, ready to avenge the death of his father. Above the print it says HELLO in huge, bold black letters. Only serious *Princess Bride* fans could appreciate the geeky fabulousness of that shirt.

I go in and buy it for Jude.

TWENTY-FOUR
ROSANNA

MY HEART IS POUNDING SO hard as I approach Cafe Lalo that I almost have to sit on the bench outside to avoid passing out. I convince myself to keep walking toward the stairs. D could be here already. He could be watching from the other side of this wall of windows. I want him to think I'm way more confident than I am. And way more certain that I'm doing the right thing. Should I even be here? Should I keep moving things forward, knowing we're not the best match? Or should I end it before we get hurt?

Everything shimmers at Cafe Lalo. Even the trees outside are glittery with delicate purple lights. I take a deep breath, go up the stairs, and immediately see D when I walk in the door. He looks even more adorable than he did the last time I saw him at Press Lounge. He's at a table near the front, looking at desserts in the display case. D has the kind of confidence people notice right away. Most people sitting alone would find something to distract them so they look less alone. Not D. He's just sitting there, calm and still. Completely at ease with himself. Taking in how gorgeous he looks in his lavender button-down with the sleeves rolled up and the kind of trendy jeans I could never afford makes me grateful for Darcy's generosity all over again. She bought me a beautiful, flowing silk skirt that dances around my knees when I walk. Feeling its slippery smooth material against my skin is helping me pull off a somewhat confident vibe.

D smiles when he sees me. I love how he has this intense laser focus when he smiles at me. I've seen him smile at other people and the laser focus definitely isn't there. When he smiles at me, you can totally see the difference.

D stands up and kisses me on the cheek. "It's good to see you," he says.

"You, too." Clips of the fantasies I've been imagining in bed flash behind my eyes. My face burns. I'm too embarrassed to look at D, so I fidget with my bag, then hide behind a menu. Not that there's any way he can tell what I'm thinking. Or that I've been thinking way more about him than I should. But I'm embarrassed anyway.

"Who were you in high school?" I ask D after we order and I can look at him again.

"What do you mean?"

"Were you a popular jock? A nerdy brainiac? An artistic nonconformist?"

"Who do you think I was?"

"Pretty much the same person you are now."

"How would you describe me?"

"Oh, you know. Just the typical confident, driven boy who can pull off being both intelligent and socially skilled. Who isn't that well-rounded?"

D reaches across the tiny café table. He covers my hands with his. "You're too generous. But I like it."

And I like Donovan Clark.

I can't deny my feelings anymore. I can't keep fighting our attraction. Sitting with him in this charming café, the sweet smell of brown sugar in the air, our legs touching under the table making every cell in my body hum, I can almost see my resistance breaking down in chips and shards.

I'm falling for this man and there's nothing I can do about it.

"Who were you back in Chicago?" D asks.

"The same person I am now," I say, although I'm not being entirely accurate. He doesn't need to know about the plan to reinvent myself. Part of having a fresh start comes with the opportunity to be the best version of yourself. This shiny new version of me is the only version D needs to know.

D smiles with so much warmth in his eyes my heart swells. "You mean the altruistic, brilliant girl who has no idea how beautiful she is?"

My face gets warm again. I press my lips together, trying not to smile.

"Yeah," D says. "I thought so. You went to public school?"

I nod. What a joke to think my family could afford private school. One more thing D doesn't need to know about me. A loud surge of grinding coffee beans accentuates this point.

"You're lucky," he says. "Private school can be insane. Especially in Manhattan. I went to Dalton. They don't let you get away with anything there."

"So you were a bad boy?"

"More like a typical boy. I had a problem with the amount of homework I was slammed with every night. My teachers weren't exactly sympathetic when I tried to explain that each of them assigning two hours of homework a night meant that kids had to stay up until three in the morning to get everything done. My main argument was that sleep deprivation is inhumane."

"You told your teachers that?"

"Every one of them."

"What happened?"

"Didn't make a bit of difference. They still got their panties in a bunch when I didn't do my homework."

"How did you get into Columbia if you were a slacker?"

"My grades were good. And the Ivies like extracurriculars. I ran track, I was on yearbook and in chess club and—"

"I'm sorry. Did you say you were in chess club?"

"Proud member of Pawn Stars."

"You just became a hundred times cooler."

"Nerdy equals cool in your book?"

"Definitely."

"I knew you were the right girl for me."

I shift in my chair. Does that mean he wants to get serious with me? Is that where this is going?

"Anyway," D continues. "Teachers constantly up in my business calling my mom every time I got an incomplete on homework pissed me off at the time. But now I'm thankful I had good teachers who whipped my ass into shape." He laughs. "Never thought I'd be saying that I had good teachers. Guess that's the kind of perspective you can only gain three years after graduating."

Three years. It's been three years since D was in high school.

The coffee grinder erupts again with a staccato beat. The aroma of fresh coffee beans wafts over to us. The lights dim a bit.

"Did the lights just get dimmer?" I ask.

"Some places do that as it gets later. I know a few restaurants that dim the lights in stages every hour. Way to create ambiance, right?"

"I like it."

D reaches across the table to stroke my cheek delicately. Tingles run down the back of my neck.

"I like this," he says.

"You like the Snickers cheesecake," I point out, glancing at his empty plate.

"Didn't like that at all."

"How did you find this place?"

"I used to come here all the time. My parents' brownstone is a few blocks away. We can walk past it on our way to the park if you want."

"Yeah. I want to see where you grew up."

"Done." D signals our waitress for the check. Then he whips his laser focus back to me. No one has ever looked at me with such intense laser focus before. "There's something I've been meaning to tell you. Well, apologize for, really."

"What?"

"I've been kicking myself for bringing up other girls I've dated on our first date. Old girlfriends are like the number one thing you're not supposed to talk about on a first date. Everyone knows this. Apologies for being such a douche."

"No worries."

"Your strength is a little intimidating."

"Really?" I look down at my skinny arms. I should think about lifting at some point.

D laughs. "I meant your strength of character. You just graduated from high school, but you already have your shit together. Most people don't have their shit together until they're thirty. If that. But you . . . it's like you were born this way. No one will be surprised when you take over the world."

D seems like he's been there, done that with everything. But it still sounds like he admires me, which makes me feel special. I've never really felt special before.

When the check arrives (on a little brass tray with two chocolate mints, making me fall in love with this place even more), I pick it up. "This one's on me."

D snatches the check out of my hand. "I don't think so."

I snatch it back. "I insist."

"You don't have to do that."

"I want to. You always treat. You deserve to be treated for once."

"Thanks. That's sweet of you."

As I take the check up to the register, I try not to freak out. Treating D was not my plan. It's just something I decided to do spontaneously. I try to avoid snap decisions. But I'm falling for him so hard I can't think straight. And I don't want him to think I expect him to pay for everything. Even though he has more money than he knows what to do with and he's reassured me he wants to treat, I feel like I owe him.

Standing in line, I can feel D's eyes on me. I wouldn't be surprised if I could sense his intense laser focus all the way back in Chicago. I sneak a glance at the check while pretending to admire the elegantly decorated cakes in the display case. I didn't even see how much it was. The total almost gives me a heart attack. Our dessert and coffee is basically my grocery money for the week.

Do not freak out. You will find a way to make this work.

New Yorkers don't deal well with waiting in line. Even waiting for one or two minutes seems to challenge them in perplexing ways. Is it that they always want to keep moving? Or that they're always running late? Or maybe they're just naturally restless. Their restless nature is what probably brought a lot of them here.

It's my turn to pay. My first mistake was not getting my money ready. I can never pay fast enough when there are people behind me in line. Their impatience is palpable. The lady behind me in line at a deli the other day actually pushed right up next to me and started putting her stuff down on the counter when I didn't even have my wallet out yet. Rude and rude.

The cashier repeats the total amount due. As if the image of the check isn't burned into my brain in horrifying detail. I root through the change pouch of my wallet for exact change. The cashier turns to talk to a waiter behind her. The guy behind me in line stares at my wallet. I nervously fumble for dimes. My ancient wallet is not cooperating. The coins have slipped under the lining and it's taking forever to pull them out. The guy behind me sighs impatiently. I almost rip a five in half trying to yank it from the clutches of my busted wallet. I need a new wallet. But good ones are expensive. If I buy another cheap one, it will rapidly deteriorate to a similarly pathetic condition. Maybe I can line the ripped coin pouch with a baggie.

After I pay, I can't help giving the guy behind me a harsh look. How can anyone be so disgruntled at Cafe Lalo? It could not be more wonderful here. Lalo is the kind of place you come to unwind and share a leisurely pot of tea with someone special. It is not the kind of place you come to huff at the person in line ahead of you for being slow.

D appreciates Cafe Lalo the way it was meant to be appreciated. And he wanted to share it with me. I can picture him here at various points in his life. Four years old, sitting with his parents at one of the bigger tables, chocolate frosting smeared on his face. Eleven years old, here with his mom after a Saturday afternoon soccer game. Sixteen years old, at an intimate corner table with that pretty girl from chem class. This place holds the history of D's life. These tables have heard his stories, bridged connections with friends, and charmed his girlfriends. This is where he grew up.

"Ready?" D says, waiting for me by the door.

If he only knew how ready I was.

We burst out into the warm summer night. When D told me about his idea to see an outdoor movie, I couldn't have been more thrilled. I can't wait to experience outdoor movies. I want to take advantage of everything New York has to offer. I want to do everything real New Yorkers do, the kinds of activities that will make me fall in love with this city even more.

D puts his arm around me as we walk along West 83rd Street. The delicious aroma of Lalo lingers on us. My clothes, my hair, even my skin all smell like fresh-roasted coffee. The streets are alive with weeknight activity. Cabs and trucks and bikers fly down Broadway. A bunch of high school boys zip past on skateboards. People scatter across the sidewalks, coming home from work or on their way to dinner. No matter what day or what time it is, there are always a million things going on.

"This is it," D says when we round the corner onto Central Park West. The "it" he is referring to is an impeccably maintained brownstone. I can't believe this is where he grew up.

Living in this house must have been like growing up in a fairy tale.

"It's beautiful," I say. "You must have loved living here."

"The view of the park was nice. We weren't that high, so the view was completely different than what you see from high-rises. I got to watch the seasons change in Central Park right outside my window."

A few lit windows indicate that someone's home. D's parents are probably relaxing after dinner. What would I say if D invited me in to meet them? Would it be too soon? Or should I jump at the chance to show him that what we have isn't casual?

Not that I even know what we have. All I know is how I feel when we're together. When I'm with D, it feels like the shiny new life I've been visualizing for years is finally becoming reality. I can taste the flavor of New York the most when we're together. The hope that everything will work out is always there under my anxiety. In moments of clarity, I can feel everything I've been working for my whole life come into focus. And for a bright spot of time, I can breathe again. I'm not sure why I feel the clarity mostly when I'm with D. Maybe because he's showing me the New York he loves, the New York he's lived and breathed his whole life, the true New York only someone who grew up here can share. He's reminding me of what I looked forward to about living here when New York was just a dream.

We walk down Central Park West. Fuzzy dots of lamplight glow along the paths winding inside the park. Across the street, tremendous apartment buildings with immense penthouses are stamped out on the night sky block after block, an imposing representation of the power of money. The illuminated floor-to-ceiling windows are magnetic. I keep looking into them, catching glimpses of ornate chandeliers and pianos and elaborate built-in bookshelves. I'd love to have bookshelves like those someday. But only people with money are entitled to such beautifully designed homes.

"Let's find a blanket before we go in," D says near the park entrance at 72nd Street. "I don't want your skirt to get dirty."

Normally a statement like that wouldn't make any sense. All the clothes I moved here with are pretty much falling apart. But tonight he has a point. The skirt Darcy bought me is almost too beautiful to wear. Almost.

There's a Pottery Barn a few blocks away. We go in and find the blankets section. D insists that I pick out the one I want.

"This one," I say, holding out a supersoft lavender blanket. It's like my blanket back home except nicer.

"Good choice. It matches my shirt." We take it to the register. Then I see how much the blanket is.

"Oh, this one's too expensive," I say. "Let's find something cheaper."

"It's fine," D says, taking out his credit card.

"No, there has to be—"

"Really." D puts his arms around me and hugs me close. "It's already yours."

How amazing is it that D can buy an expensive blanket on a

whim just for movie night while I'm thinking about reinforcing my wallet with a plastic bag? It blows my mind that he can just waltz into any store he wants, pick out whatever he likes without worrying about the price, and buy it like he's buying bread at Food Emporium. Like dropping all that money on something he doesn't even need is nothing. I have to admit, having money makes life a lot more convenient. Living that way must feel so free.

Sitting with D on our new blanket in the middle of the crowd while the movie plays on a gigantic screen, I almost feel like a real New Yorker.

"Here." D moves behind me, his legs bent on either side of me. "You can lean back."

I lean on D. He puts his arms around me. I am safe and adored in his arms. How much of my attraction to him is only physical? How can I even tell? What I feel for D is greater than the sum of its parts. Maybe the important thing isn't to figure out why I feel this way, but to accept that I do.

Later, when we're leaving the park, D pulls me aside to kiss me. I can't let myself feel the fireworks I imagined our first kiss would bring. Not while it's still hard for me to be intimate with a boy. But his kiss comes with a promise that things will only get better.

TWENTY-FIVE
SADIE

WHAT'S BETTER THAN BEING AT Coffee Shop with my roommates at two in the morning, eating pancakes and talking boys?

I mean, men. We're with men now.

When Darcy came here with Zander in the middle of the night, she resolved to bring me and Rosanna back for late-night pancakes. I've always loved Coffee Shop. A few times I've walked by late at night and seen tons of people in here. I wished I was cool enough to be one of them. Darcy is definitely cool enough. And now, by one degree of Darcy, so are we. As soon as we were seated in the big curvy booth, I immediately proclaimed Coffee Shop at two in the morning to be our summer ritual.

Rosanna wasn't feeling it at first. She said we should go without her.

Darcy was like, "I'm going to have to insist on your

presence. We're building memories here."

Rosanna was still reluctant. She agreed to come, but she thinks it's too late to make this into a ritual. Spoken like a classic morning person. Then the pancakes came and the conversation got good and she warmed right up to that invigorating friends high. She still doesn't get why it's more fun to come here so late. But as long as we come on a Friday or Saturday night moving forward, she's in.

The conversation has evolved into listing different types of love.

"There's the instant chemistry, can't stop thinking about the person, can't wait to see him again, burning to touch him love." Darcy.

"There's the chemistry and connection that's there from the start, that gets more intense over time and eventually turns into a deeper love." Me.

"There's the friends first that suddenly shifts when you look at him one day and see him differently." Rosanna.

"I know!" I say. "You're like, When did he get so cute? Was he always this cute and I just never noticed?"

"Or how the marginally cute guy gets cuter every time you see him," Darcy adds. "What is that? Being so desperate you'll force yourself to see something that's not there?"

"I think it's an underlying attraction that gradually builds up," Rosanna says. "He has qualities that resonate with you on a certain level, but you're not fully aware of them yet. Then suddenly things fall into place."

"Once you start considering a boy as BF material, all bets are off," Darcy says. "He could be the worst possible boy for you and you don't even see it."

"You can't see any red flags when you're in it," I say. "It doesn't matter how many friends tell you he's bad for you. They could point out his problems a thousand times and it wouldn't matter. All you can see are the good parts."

"Love is blind," Rosanna says.

"Love is crap," Darcy declares.

We look at her.

"Not crap," she says. "Just . . . not the way it should be."

"It is if you're with the right person," I say.

"But how do you know who's the right person? You think you're with the right person. You're totally in love. And then out of nowhere, everything changes. Why put all that time and energy into something that will never last? It's not worth the effort. Better to go with the flow and have fun." Darcy fidgets with the sugar caddy. Despite playing it off like she couldn't care less about love, I can tell she doesn't completely believe what she's saying.

"Relationships don't always end," I say. "Soul mates are real. True love is real. You just have to believe you'll find that kind of real love one day."

"And refuse to settle for less than you deserve," Rosanna points out.

"Does that mean you should be alone until you find your person?" Darcy asks.

"No. We learn from every relationship we have. How can we be ready for the right relationship without the experience that prepares us for it?"

"Every relationship is an opportunity to learn about ourselves," I add. "I'm constantly thinking about the kind of boy I want to be with. What's important to me. What used to be important but doesn't matter anymore. What my deal breakers are. If you have a clear idea of what you're looking for, it's easier to recognize once you find it."

"We don't only learn about ourselves from relationships," Darcy says. "Every interaction we have matters. You can have one amazing night with a boy and learn more about yourself than you would in a long-term relationship."

The three of us contemplate this in silence. We all had amazing boy adventures tonight. I went to New Jersey with Austin and had that ginormous fireworks non-coincidence. Rosanna went to Cafe Lalo and a movie in Central Park with D. Darcy hooked up with some random boy she's refusing to talk about. We're still buzzing like neon from tonight. Our boy adventure wave activity is vibrating at such a high frequency that if you captured the energy at this table, I'm sure you could supply the entire country's electrical needs for a year. When it comes to boys charging girls up, we're more powerful than a hurricane.

Rosanna breaks the silence. "Which type of love is better? Or more real? Is true love only about the immediate butterflies? Or does it qualify as true love if you feel the butterflies eventually?"

"First you have to *believe* in true love," Darcy mumbles.

"The butterflies have to be there," I say, brushing off Darcy's cynicism, "but I don't think it matters how long it takes to feel them. If you feel them right away, that's love at first sight."

"By 'butterflies,' do you mean chemistry?"

"Butterflies are more than just attraction. They're that thing where you can't eat or sleep or concentrate on anything. All you can think about is the boy. You can't wait to be with him again. And when you're with him, you feel alive in a way that you'd always hoped was possible." That's exactly the way Austin makes me feel. Alive.

"Kind of the way you feel about Austin?" Rosanna says.

"We see that smile, girl," Darcy teases. "You're glowing so bright they need to turn the lighting down up in here to maintain the ambience."

I jump at the opportunity to talk about Austin some more. "It's ridiculous how well Austin knows me already. Did I tell you he showed up tonight with pink roses?"

"Awww!" Rosanna swoons. "He's so romantic!"

"He made the board gaming group so much fun. It would not have been the same if I'd gone by myself. He makes everything way more fun than it normally is. Like walking home along the river. I can't tell you how many times I took that same walk alone, hoping to walk with Austin someday. It's like I knew him before I knew him. I imagined what it would be like to walk with him for so long that I almost couldn't believe it when he was finally right there. Walking with him was the most romantic thing ever. We were those people making out on the street. You know, those people who are so passionate about each other they have to stop in the middle of the sidewalk to kiss? We were those people I'd always wanted to be."

"That is so hot I can't even," Darcy says.

"He's perfect for me. We're totally falling in love. Is it weird that everything's happening so fast?"

"All that matters is that you're happy," Darcy says. "You love being with him. You love how you feel when you're with him. Go with it."

"You know I hung that sign over my bed for a reason. Austin is exactly who I was hoping to find. I always knew movie love was real. Now I finally get to live the dream."

"That is the most romantic thing I've ever heard," Rosanna proclaims.

"Really? Because Cafe Lalo and Central Park movie night sounds pretty romantic."

Rosanna blushes. "It really was." She gathers her long, wavy hair into a low pony. Then she twists it into the black elastic that's always on her wrist.

"What was your favorite part?" Darcy asks.

"Probably when we were sitting together on the blanket. He told me I could lean on him . . . and it felt amazing to just lean against him. He put his arm around me and rubbed my back. He made me feel safe. Which was a big deal for me. I've never felt safe with a man before."

"Why not?" Darcy asks.

Rosanna is immediately snapped out of her warm fuzzy reverie. "No reason," she says. Her tone is brittle. Whatever part of her was opening up with the memories of her romantic night has shut down. "Anyway. Enough about me. Are you going to tell us about your latest boy adventure or what?"

All Darcy said when we were walking over was that she hooked up with some guy she met at the Strand. We could tell by the way she announced her accomplishment that she was proud. Darcy thinks hooking up with random boys is hot, which I can understand in a flingy kind of way. But it's just not me. I'm not wired that way.

"There's not much to tell," Darcy says. "Unless I tell it like the kind of cheesy romance novel housewives hide under their mattress. *Our eyes locked over the towering book carts near self-improvement. He mentally undressed me from head to toe—*"

"I hate that expression, 'head to toe,'" Rosanna interjects.

"*—drinking me in like he was desperate to quench his thirst.*"

"Quench?" I say. "Really?"

"Oh, yes. *And the sweat . . .* ran *down his chest as he heaved himself over the stacks, books splaying every which way, his lust an uncontainable force to be reckoned with.*"

"Gag," Rosanna says. "I am never reading your book. No offense."

"None taken. I know I can bring the cheese when I want to."

"Way to deflect the question," I say.

"What question?"

"Hello! We're dying to know what you did tonight."

"Nothing worth mentioning. I'd rather focus on the Now. *The Power of Now* says that all we ever have is Now. Now is the most important part of our life. Essentially the Now is our entire existence. Think about it. Besides, what's funner than late-night pancakes and boy talk with my girls?"

Darcy is working hard to avoid talking about her hot fling. Of course Rosanna and I want to know what happened. But I respect Darcy's need for privacy. I know exactly how she feels. There are things I don't want to talk about, either.

"Okay," Darcy says. "We did the love thing. Now let's talk sex."

I glance at Rosanna. We don't need to have this discussion for me to know that I'm not the only virgin at the table.

"When is the right time to have sex?" Darcy asks. "I'll go first. For me, it's simple. When I want to and it feels right."

Rosanna yanks the elastic out of her hair. Then she twists it back up, staring at the table.

"When I really know the person and I'm in love with him," I say. "I have to be in love first. That's nonnegotiable."

"You don't ever see yourself going too far in the heat of the moment?" Darcy asks.

"'Heat of the moment?'" I inquire. "Are you writing more of your book?"

"It may not be a best seller, but the ladies love it." Darcy takes a sip of her coffee. She looks at Rosanna expectantly over the rim of her mug.

Snap-snap-snap go Rosanna's fingers. She is dying for a subject change.

I swoop in to save her. "Three brunettes equals girl power. We decide where, when, and with whom. That's all we need to know."

I look around to see who else goes to Coffee Shop this late. Not many people are here. Partly because it's the middle of the night. Partly because the city is dead in the summer. People start going out to their summer shares in the Hamptons or wherever right after Memorial Day. Having Manhattan all to myself in August is an annual perk I enjoy. The serenity almost offsets the gross heat/humidity combo. There's a couple in the window booth who are obviously crazy in love with each other. You can tell by the way they're looking at each other like the rest of us aren't even here.

"See that couple in the window booth?" I ask Darcy and Rosanna.

They turn to look.

"Oh," Rosanna sighs. "The way he's looking at her."

"The way he's touching her arm," Darcy says.

We stare at the enchanting couple, in awe of obvious soul mates. I wish I had stationery and a glitter pen to write them a warm fuzzy. They should know how inspiring they are.

"True love is real," I say. "That's what it looks like." That's what I've always wanted. That's what I have with Austin. Now we're the couple who inspires other people to find their own true love.

What might be around any corner in the future is irrelevant. The search is over.

TWENTY-SIX
DARCY

THERE'S NOTHING LIKE ENCOUNTERING A creeper on the subway to brighten up your day.

This one is a piece of work. A character like him—old guy, warm-weather grandpa outfit ready for an afternoon of shuffle-board and bridge at a retirement center down in Miami, tattered socks stuffed into nasty man sandals—would normally be a trip. But he's got some serious attitude adjustment to work on. He's been snarling at me for the last six stops. Just sitting across from me, snarling like I canceled the buffet spread at his regular early bird special. I do not know what his damage is.

Here's what I do know: I refuse to let some random creeper on the subway intimidate me.

These guys want to get a rise out of you. They want to see how you react to being stared at or yelled at or otherwise harassed. They get off on watching you squirm as you struggle to stay focused on your screen or page or friend, pretending not to notice the lunatic growling in your face about how your grandpappy hunted his grandpappy for sport. A couple days ago I saw a girl break down. She was being harassed by a guy who sat right next to her even though there were plenty of free seats. He proceeded to tell her all the things he wanted to do to her, as if they were filming porn instead of heading uptown on the express. She got off at the next stop. He glanced at me, but I gave him a hard glare. *Not me*, the glare said. *Don't even try it.* My sharp vibe made him move on to the next victim.

The creeper across from me continues to snarl. He can snarl all he wants. He will never get the satisfaction of watching me squirm. I'm the one in control here. He will not witness me so much as flinch.

He snarls.

I stare back defiantly.

He snarls.

I stand my ground.

He snarls.

My stop is next. I get up slowly so he doesn't think he ran me off the train. As the train slows down and I make my way to the door, he sticks two fingers up in a V-shape. At first I think he's acknowledging my victory. But then he puts his fingers on either side of his mouth and waggles his tongue at me.

I give him the finger as I walk out the door. I'm not afraid of him following me. No man will ever take advantage of me again, including perverts on the subway.

When I emerge from the muggy subway station to the street, I take a second to breathe. No one takes a second to breathe here. Everyone exists in a perpetual state of running/working/doing/shopping/freaking out. The only stationary people on the sidewalk are either waiting for someone or tourists. I revel in standing still while the city undulates around me. Physical tranquility is an excellent catalyst for mental tranquility. Mental note: Be still more often.

The Upper West Side is new territory for me. I've come in search of beach gear. Moving to New York doesn't always allow one to bring everything they own with them. Everyone knows how small the closets are here. Most of my stuff is still back home. Sadie, Rosanna, and I are talking about going to the beach over Fourth of July weekend. So my desire to find the right beach bag and towel has officially been promoted from want to need. This girl in my art history class told me about some fun shops up here she thought I'd like.

I'm not even half a block from the subway when a girl swiftly steps in front of me, blocking my way. Am I seriously about to deal with the second creeper of the day? What am I, some creeper magnet all of a sudden? But then I realize I know her. It takes me a second to figure out where I know her from.

"Darcy!" she yells. "I thought it was you!"

"Carrie! What are you—oh right, you live here!"

We hug. Carrie is this awesome girl I met while I was backpacking through Europe. She was making her way from Paris to Rome over the course of a week. We took the train from

Milan to Monaco together. Four hours of nonstop bonding over the addictive nightlife of Paris, the mellow Côte d'Azur of Nice, and the stunning architecture of Milan. Carrie and I were flying on the same unmistakable travel high. She understands the kind of freedom solo travel provides. We loved the thrill of being able to do whatever we wanted, whenever we wanted, without anyone else to drag us down. No pathetic walking tours. No standing in line for half the day. Just taking in culture at our own pace. Seeing her stirs a rush of nostalgia. Coming back from Europe wasn't easy.

"Your dress is so cute!" Carrie says. "Is it vintage?"

"ModCloth."

"I love ModCloth! Oh my god, it is so good to see you. I was just thinking about you the other day."

"Where do you live?"

"Eleventh Street at Seventh Avenue."

"Get. *Out.* I'm on Eleventh and Fifth!"

"Of course you are."

"Wait. Why aren't you surprised?"

"This is classic New York serendipity. Of course we live two blocks from each other. And of course we had to come all the way up here to find out. You wouldn't believe how many people I run into on the street that I haven't seen in forever. A lot of them don't even live here! I know it sounds crazy, but it happens all the time."

"I just moved here like a week ago and not only did I already run into you, you're my neighbor."

"Big city, small world."

Does this mean I might cross paths again with Random Boy from last night? I was kind of hoping to never see him again. Not because I'm ashamed or anything. By the time Sadie asked about the hookup at Coffee Shop, I didn't feel horrible about it anymore. There was no reason to feel horrible. Summer Fun Darcy sees what she likes and goes after him. It actually felt kind of fun giving Sadie and Rosanna a hint of what I'd done. But something still didn't feel right. If I don't understand my own feelings about something, I'm not exactly motivated to talk about it. The last thing I want to do is encounter the person who's making me feel awkward for unknown reasons.

"It's freaky how many people I've run into," Carrie continues. "One time something told me to walk down a street I never go down. One thing you'll learn about New Yorkers is that we're entrenched in our routines. We walk the same way every day without even thinking about it. Suddenly walking a different way for no logical reason is a bigger deal than it sounds. So I walked a different way and turned a corner and there he was. The boy I liked in ninth grade. This other time I was on the N train—which I never take—and an old friend of my mom's I hadn't seen in ten years got on. Not only on the train I never take at a time when I'm never on the subway, but the exact same car. There's no way that was a coincidence."

"It's a non-coincidence. That's what my roommate Sadie calls those kinds of things."

"Non-coincidence. I like that. Did Sadie make it up?"

"No, I think she heard it somewhere."

"Everything happens for a reason, right?"

I smile and nod. But if everything happens for a reason, why did I get dumped so hard for no reason at all?

"Well, I'm happy to be a part of an exclusive New York phenomenon," I say. "I guess this means I should get ready for reunions with friends from Santa Monica."

"Totally. So what are you doing on the Upper West Side?"

"I'm on the prowl for adorable beach paraphernalia. Any suggestions?"

"Hmm. Let me think." Carrie looks across 79th Street. "I can't think of anyplace off the top of my head. I'm hitting Zabar's and Fairway."

"Is Zabar's that place with the good cheese?"

"Zabar's has the good everything. Fairway is ridiculous. You won't even believe it. Are you into cooking?"

"That would be a no."

Carrie laughs. "I'll have you over for dinner sometime. You'd be surprised how easy it is to make a good meal."

"Oh, I'm good with the million best restaurants ever right outside my door. Trust me, you would not want to eat anything I cooked. Except for toast. I can usually manage not to burn toast."

"How about cereal?"

"Never burned cereal, either. No one makes cereal like I do.

My cereal is so delightful it can almost be classified as a work of art."

"Then maybe you should have *me* over for dinner sometime. Breakfast for dinner is always a good thing."

"Get ready for the best cereal and toast of your life. Just don't ask me to do anything complicated like eggs."

An ice cream truck rolls by, its signature music tinkling in the afternoon sunlight.

"I also make good ice cream," I add. "And by 'make,' I mean 'scoop.'"

"Do you put it in a bowl and everything?"

"Not just any bowl. We have a matching set of bowls from Target."

"How adult of you. Speaking of cooking . . . I have to go. Fairway at rush hour is a scary place."

As we exchange contact info and make promises to get together soon, I can't help feeling like something's off. We were so close on the train in Italy. We even spent the rest of the day exploring Monaco together. But then Carrie had to leave and we went our separate ways and we haven't talked since. It was super fun running into her, but there's a new awkwardness between us I can't quite identify. Maybe certain friendships are more dependent on past experiences than present ones.

"Are you good with getting around?" Carrie asks. "The subways are usually reliable, but they can be a nightmare if you're not sure where you're going."

"The subway is already a nightmare. I just had a disgusting

encounter I'm pretty sure is only the first in a long chain of repulsiveness."

"What happened?"

I tell Carrie about the lewd creeper.

"He reminds me of my ex," Carrie says.

"Was your ex a creeper, too?"

"He was the worst kind of creeper. You know, the kind that likes scamming on other girls behind your back?"

"Uck. I'm sorry."

"Don't be. It was better that I found out earlier than later. I can't tell you how many girls I know who are stuck in miserable relationships because they've invested so much time in them already. I'm like, This isn't about time. It's about being happy. If you're not happy with your boyfriend, what's the point?"

"Exactly." A stray breeze sweeps down Broadway, providing some momentary relief from the oppressive humidity. Temperature extremes usually don't bother me. But I'm suddenly overheated.

"Are you single?" Carrie asks.

"Yes and I am loving it, thank you."

"That's a great outlook. I wish I felt as positive as you. I've been single for three years. And I'm only twenty-three. What a waste."

"What do you mean?"

"This is when I should be in a relationship. When I'm young and we can do whatever we want. But it's more than that. I want a boyfriend."

"Why?"

"I guess I want the sense of security a long-term relationship will bring."

"But isn't it fun to be single and date around?"

"I think it's awesome that you're having fun. I'm just in a different place. Dating around was fun for a while, but freedom is overrated. I want to have someone I can count on. Someone to go out with on Saturday nights and be my plus-one at events. Someone who wants to share his life with me. I just want to find my person and know that he will always be there for me, no matter what."

This is not the Carrie I know. The Carrie I know would never say that freedom is overrated. She'd love the potential adventure an uncertain future holds. It's only been a year since Italy. She was a wild child like me back then. Now she wants stability. What happened to her?

"Sorry for the rambling," Carrie says. "I've been kind of . . . lonely. Not lonely in a friends way. My friends are amaztastic. Lonely in that way where you're tired of waiting to meet him, you know?"

I nod. I get what she's saying. We're just in very different places.

Jude is the type of guy Carrie is looking for. Devoted. Adoring. Supportive. Any girl would be lucky to have him as her person.

Including me.

I would be lucky to have Jude as my person.

What Carrie's saying clicks with a part of me that's been buried. The part of me that used to hope and dream and was certain that people are inherently good, including men.

That part of me isn't buried as deep as I thought it was. That part of me wants to feel how good it would be to hope again.

TWENTY-SEVEN
ROSANNA

OUR UPSTAIRS NEIGHBORS ARE AT it again. Moving furniture or break-dancing or whatever. I really don't need this stress right now. Getting ready to go out with D is stressful enough.

Refraining from poking my eye with the mascara wand would help.

My hand is shaking. That's how stressed I am. Last night I was stressing over paying at Coffee Shop, which is why I didn't want to go. But Darcy wasn't hearing it when I told them to go without me. My covert frugal approach was to order the least expensive thing on the menu (two eggs any style, comes with home fries and toast) and just drink water. Sadie and Darcy got pancakes. I wanted pancakes too, but they were four dollars more than the eggs. That's four bagel dinners. So I stuck with the eggs, despite their protests. I made up a lie on the spot about needing more protein. While they were ordering, I mentally calculated their shares, freaking out that we might end up splitting the bill three ways. Covering a third of their extravagant beverage and side choices (and then a third of the higher tip) would have been a problem. My share was $8.00, plus 20% of eight for the tip. About $9.50. I had a ten-dollar bill and really wanted my fifty cents back, but the girls would have thought I was even more of a freak asking for fifty cents. Fortunately Sadie took charge when the bill came. She said that everyone should pay for what they ordered.

I give myself a hard look in the mirror. My hair is frizzing out from the humidity. Why can't my hair just be normal like all the other polished women I see on the street? Better yet, why can't my hair be straight? Straightening wavy hair with various tools and products is not the same thing. Girls with straight hair are always saying how they wish they had my hair. They ooh and aah over the volume, the texture, the waves. But I am so over trying to tame my hair. Especially considering that I have to leave in ten minutes or I'll be late and I'm nowhere near ready. D cannot see me with frizzy hair.

I wipe specks of mascara from under my eye, trying not to worry about the time. Between racing against the clock, the relentless humidity despite the old air conditioner chugging away at full speed, and my dumbass upstairs neighbors, I'm a hot mess. Sweaty pits plus frizzy hair does not equal a sexy date. Seriously, what are they doing up there? Throwing each other off the couch? Every boom of the ceiling makes the walls shake and my adrenaline soar.

Boom boom boom BOOM.

Enough.

I dash to the front closet for the broom. As much as I'd like to stomp to the front closet, I reel in my frustration. Irritating my downstairs neighbors the way the elephants upstairs have irritated me would not be good karma. I'm about to attempt something I've never done before that I'm not sure will work. There's a chance it will provoke one of the elephants to pound on my door, further sabotaging my date with D. I should have left five minutes ago. But this needs to be done. If I don't take a stand, who will?

I stand on the couch, clutching the broom with the top of the broomstick close to the ceiling. When a surge of pounding erupts above me, I pound on the ceiling with the broom.

The elephants are startled into silence.

At this point I am so late that checking the time would be scarier than getting caught outside at dusk in *I Am Legend*. I can't look. All I can do is run and hope that D won't be waiting too long.

Waiting for the subway makes me even more rattled. Of course I just missed the train. The next one's not coming for seven minutes. I do not have seven minutes. Seven minutes from now I will be a sweaty, frizzy mess unsuitable for public display. I take a few deep breaths. Or what barely passes for a few deep breaths in this sweltering subway station.

When I emerge from the subway at 42nd Street a thousand years later, I blink in the bright lights of Times Square. This is my first venture into the frenetic tourist land that is Times Square. Sadie said that tourists are the only ones who really come here. D said he never comes up here, but promised that dinner at Butter would be worth it.

I plow my way through the throngs of tourists. Could tourists walk any slower? I know they're taking in the sights and snapping photos and stuff, but do they really have to take up the whole sidewalk? Not that I haven't been just as oblivious. New York moves way faster than I anticipated. I'm surprised at how quickly I'm adjusting to the rapid pace. On the other hand, I've always known I was meant to live here. When you end up where you're meant to be, everything falls into place.

Two wrong turns and a near collision with someone in a Cookie Monster costume later, I see Butter across the street. I flap my arms in a desperate attempt to air out my pits. A bike messenger zipping by at an alarming speed almost slices my arm off. Darcy warned me to stay clear of bike lanes. Too bad Sadie didn't warn me about people on the sidewalk dressed as characters for tourists to take pictures with.

When I envisioned this night, I appeared calm, cool, and collected as I breezed through the door of Butter on the dot of eight. D would turn to me from the bar and smile at how put together I looked. We would then glide to our table, turning the heads of older people who remember what it was like to be young and in love.

Here's what really happens.

I show up twenty-five minutes late. D is waiting for me

outside. He probably witnessed my embarrassing arm-flapping, bike-messenger spaz attack. But he doesn't look as mad or repulsed as I expected.

"You made it," he says.

"Oh my god, I am *so* sorry I'm late. This is unacceptable."

"No worries. These things happen."

"First my upstairs neighbors were pounding louder than ever. I actually banged a broom against the ceiling, I was so desperate. Then I just missed the subway. Then I went down the wrong street and almost ran over Cookie Monster and—"

"Rosanna." D hugs me even though I am a sweaty mess. "It's okay. You're here now. That's all that matters."

I pull away from him before he realizes the full scope of how disgusting I am. "Thanks for understanding."

"But you really should think about getting a cell phone."

"You're right." There's no way I'm about to admit that I can't afford a cell phone. D wouldn't even know how to process that information.

Butter is even more over-the-top than the Waverly Inn. I remember a scene at Butter from *Gossip Girl*. *Gossip Girl* is one of my few guilty pleasures, the kind of show obsessed with materialistic greed I'm not supposed to like but secretly do. I never imagined I'd be at one of the locations from Rich Girl World in real life. Is it wrong to be basking in the decadence?

"I'm taking you to Minetta Tavern next," D says after dinner outside Butter. "It used to be an old-school Italian joint you'd go to in the dead of winter when you craved pasta with fresh

San Marzano tomato sauce. Then it changed owners. Now it's an upscale version of what it used to be. Packed with celebs. There's even a bouncer outside."

I don't reveal that I have no clue what San Marzano tomatoes are.

"Yeah . . . I just realized how obnoxious I sound," D says. "But it really is one of the best restaurants in New York. That's why I want to take you there. I want to take you to all of my favorite places. You deserve to be treated like a princess."

A fire engine goes by, its siren wailing over *princess*. A woman passing by in gym clothes puts her fingers over her ears.

I smile at D. Could this man be any sweeter?

"So . . . ," he says. "Should we go back to my place?"

This is it. The moment when everything changes. The moment when we go from dating to something heavier.

"Sure," I say, trying for my best nonchalant tone and failing epically. "I can't wait to see your renovations."

Tribeca is beautiful. The West Village is also beautiful, but it's more historical. Where the West Village has protected brownstones and cobblestone streets and quaint courtyards you can peek in at between strands of ivy growing on their gates, Tribeca is newer construction and wider sidewalks and lots of lofts. D said he'd always wanted to own a Tribeca loft. Back in the day, Tribeca's lofts were filled with artists who preferred working in the large spaces with natural light. Now Tribeca is so expensive no one can afford to live there except Wall Street guys, doctors, lawyers, and celebs. And let's not forget the trust-fund kids like D. Thinking about the artists who were forced out makes me sad. Sadie said they all live in Brooklyn now.

D's building is unreal. The exterior looks brand-new. It has a clean, simple design. Even the street number on the awning is gorgeous, etched in a round font illuminated with a blue-purple hue.

The doorman sees us coming. He swiftly opens the door for us. "Welcome home, Mr. Clark," he says. He's wearing a fancy uniform with a hat and everything. I give him a shy smile and say thank you as I step into the expansive marble lobby. After trekking about a mile, we reach the elevators. Of course there's music in the elevator. Not tacky elevator music. The rich sounds of chamber music reminiscent of exclusive dinner parties I've never attended. Maybe I'll have the chance to attend one with D.

The elevator stops on the eleventh floor. The doors glide open smoothly. I am so nervous my body parts insist on sweating again, despite the perfectly regulated microclimate.

We walk down the pristine hallway. There's not one flaw on the textured wallpaper, not one bit of dust on the floor. The building's staff must vacuum constantly. Why am I thinking about vacuuming when I should be thinking about how to handle this situation? I feel like Darcy, going with the flow instead of making a rational decision. Yeah, it's fun, but am I ready for this? I don't even know what this is. What's going to happen when we go inside?

"After you," D says, holding his front door open for me.

When I step into his loft, I cannot believe what I'm seeing. I cannot believe I know someone who lives here. There are no words to describe this man's apartment. It could be featured in *Architectural Digest*'s urban living issue. My whole apartment could fit in his grand foyer. A large open area to the right is the kitchen. The living room is a wide-open space to the left. He has an enormous sectional sofa with one of those big coffee tables fancy people put vases of flowers and stacks of art books on. One whole wall of his living room is floor-to-ceiling windows. The city shimmers as far as I can see.

"Is it cold enough for you?" D says.

I nod. The air-conditioning feels nice coming in from the hot night. "How is it already cool in here?"

"My thermostat is programmed to turn the air conditioner on about fifteen minutes before I get home."

Of course it is.

"What can I get you to drink?" he asks. He's standing so close to me I can feel the summer night heat radiating from his body.

If I didn't know myself better, I'd think I was about to do something I'll regret for the rest of my life.

"Um," I stammer. "Just water, please."

As D opens his massive refrigerator to get our drinks together, I try not to gawk at his kitchen. Black wood cabinets run along the entire length of the longest wall with lighting underneath. The appliances are all stainless steel. There's a huge sink on the main counter and another sink on the kitchen island. Lots of counter space and drawers. He even has a dishwasher, something Sadie says is rare in Manhattan.

D hands me a glass of cold water with little ice cubes in it. "Ready for the grand tour?"

I nod. There are no words to describe the magnificence of this apartment.

After he shows me what his architect and designer did in the living room and kitchen, I notice a hallway leading back to more rooms. This is in addition to the guest room and bathroom off the living room.

"It goes all the way back?" I gasp.

"Not that far back. Just to the master bedroom and bathroom and my home office." D shows me his perfect home office. Then he steps into the bathroom from the hall and turns the light on. The bathroom is done in the same black as the kitchen with shiny silver fixtures. Starting every day in this shower must be freaking awesome. It's in a corner with glass on the side near the sink. The fourth side of the shower is open. You can walk right in. The far wall has a window to allow for convenient viewing of the city as you take your shower. It's one of those overhead rain showers you see in pictorials of famous people's homes. I've always wondered if it really feels like you're in the rain when you take a shower in one of these. Will I eventually find out? Will I be taking showers here at some point? My face gets hot just thinking about it.

D goes over to a computer screen in the shower that's flush with the wall. "You can program your settings here. Computerized shower experience, anyone?"

Was that an invitation? My face gets even hotter.

We're done with the bathroom. That leaves only one more room.

"This is my bedroom." D walks in. I tentatively follow him. The bedroom windows run along the same wall as the windows in the living room. They have that same incredible view. You could fit my room plus Sadie's and Darcy's rooms in here and still have space left over. D's bedroom is so lavish I don't even know how to act. Like all of his other furniture, the furniture in here is clearly expensive. Naturally he has a king bed with night tables on either side. Each night table has a lamp perfectly positioned on it. There's one of those plush benches I always thought would be decadent to have at the foot of the bed. His white comforter is as puffy as a cloud. D's bedroom is basically a Crate & Barrel ad. I can't believe how grown-up he is. He must have a cleaning lady. His entire apartment is immaculate. Everything is so beautiful and clean and shiny. It's like he's living in a real home with real things. Not the temporary discount stuff we have at our place. Not the kind of ratty secondhand thrift-store junk I grew up with.

"What do you think?" D asks.

"Your whole apartment is gorgeous."

"Wait until you see the best part." D touches my lower back, gently guiding me out to the living room. When I saw the living room before, I thought it only had huge windows. I didn't notice the balcony stretching along the entire length of them. Now I see the door leading out to the balcony.

"Whoa," I say. "You even have a balcony?"

"Not just any balcony." D opens the door for me. I step out and he follows me. "*The* balcony."

The view takes my breath away. I know people are usually exaggerating when they say something took their breath away. But I'm serious. The view actually makes me stop breathing. This is sort of like how the view at Press Lounge took my breath away, only more magnified. Everything that's been building up to this moment, all of my wishing and hoping and dreaming about New York, all of it comes rushing in right here and now. D's view is familiar to me in a completely illogical way. I've never been here before. This is my first time on any balcony in New York. But in my heart, I already know this view. I am connected to this exact place in a profound way. It feels like I was meant to be here. Not only here in New York. Here with Donovan Clark.

He's right about this being *the* balcony. It runs along the entire outside of the living room windows and wraps around to the other side. "This is . . . it's so beautiful." I tear my eyes away from the view to look at D. He's leaning against the balcony railing, staring at me. Something tells me he looks exactly the way I looked while I was overwhelmed by the view.

D moves closer to me. I recognize the intensity in his eyes. It's the same intensity I saw last night right before he took me aside in the park and kissed me.

He's going to kiss me again.

Of course I want him to. But if we start kissing, I'm afraid I won't want to stop. Or I'll freak out. I haven't had the chance to think this through. Do I even know what I really want? I don't know if I'm ready for this. Am I ready to be with a man? For real? This isn't high school. Donovan is twenty-one. And we're at his apartment. He's probably expecting more than just making out. I don't know how much more I can offer.

There's what I want to do. There's what I should do. And then there's what I'm afraid might happen if I let a man touch me that way. D can't know about my fear. He can't know what happened to me.

We're standing so close I can smell the hazelnut on D's breath from the drink he had with dessert. His breath catches in his throat as he leans in closer, almost touching his lips to mine.

"I should go," I say.

He pulls away. "Already? You just got here."

"I know, but . . . I can't . . . I'm sorry."

"Did I do something?"

"No! You're amazing."

"Are you sure?"

"Absolutely."

"Then what's going on?"

It would be a weight off my shoulders to tell him the truth. Tell him about what happened. Let him into my life in a real way. But I can't. I'm not ready to face it and I don't know if I ever will be. "Can we talk about it another time?"

"Whatever you want." D gives me a sad smile. "I don't want you to go."

"Can I come back soon?"

"My door is always open. I mean, not literally. You have to use a key to get in, but—what am I even saying? See how corny I get when you're leaving?"

We go back inside. Now that I've decided I have to go, I really don't want to. But I already said I should.

"Have I told you how beautiful you look tonight?" D says.

"Are you flattering me so I won't leave?"

"Yes, but also because it's true." D slides his hand down my hair. And just like that, we're back here again. The way we were out on the balcony with the heat.

I'm trying to pretend I'm not noticing the way he's looking at me. Trying to pretend I'm not forcing the same look off my face. I turn to the windows, looking out at the sparkly city, lost in a trance again.

D is behind me. I watch his reflection in the window, countless illuminated windows beyond his image, each one hiding its own secrets behind the glass. For a second I think he's going to try to kiss me again. But he stays behind me, his hands sliding down my arms. His sweet breath on the back of my neck.

How is this happening? When I was saying that I should leave a few minutes ago?

He slowly begins to unzip my dress.

"I can't do this." I pull away. "I have to go."

This time I force myself to leave. Leaving takes way more effort than it should.

TWENTY-EIGHT
SADIE

IF AUSTIN AND I WORKED on the same floor, I would be getting zero work done. Concentrating is hard enough just knowing he's two floors up. Even though I don't see him at internship most days, I love knowing that he's here in the same building. Austin is good at finding excuses to come down and see me. And we stayed late last Friday so I could go up and see his cubicle. We wanted to make out there, but Parker kept lurking.

Tonight is different. Tonight belongs to us.

After the last intern leaves, I take a folder off my desk. I do a loop around the cubicles to make sure everyone's gone. Then I head for the copy room. My heart races with anticipation. I'm as nervous and jittery as I was on our first date.

Austin is waiting for me in the copy room. He's reading notices on the bulletin board. He turns when he hears me come in.

"You showed up," he says.

"I want my prize." Darcy told me about the bet she lost to Jude and how she has to treat for dinner. That's how I got the idea for this bet. When Austin was driving me home from New Jersey last night, I bet him that I would make out with him in the copy room. We made plans to stay late tonight.

"Your floor clear?" he asks.

"Yeah. What about upstairs?"

"A few guys are still here. They probably won't come down, though."

"Probably?"

"You're not backing out, are you?"

I saunter over to the copy machine, dropping my folder on top of it with a slap. I get right up in front of Austin.

"Bring it," I dare.

He looks at me for a second. Then in one swift move, he puts his arms around me and starts kissing me hard.

This strange thing happens with time when I'm making out with Austin. What feels like five minutes could actually be an hour. Or three hours. We can never be sure exactly how much time has passed. But eventually we hear someone talking on the phone out at the cubicles.

"I thought you said everyone left," Austin whispers.

"They did," I whisper back.

We listen. Whoever it is doesn't sound like they're leaving anytime soon.

"Now what?" Austin whispers.

"We could pretend we were doing copying."

"This late? After everyone else is gone? I'm not even supposed to be down here."

The copy room opens directly to the main office floor. The second we leave this room, we'll be exposed to whoever's out there. The only reason he can't see us right now is that Austin had me pressed up against the farthest copier. Parker made it very clear during orientation that any kind of romantic entanglement between interns would lead to immediate suspension. We can't risk being exposed.

"We could sleep here," Austin whispers. "They taught us how to make bubble-wrap pillows in Boy Scouts."

A nervous giggle threatens to escape. I clamp my hand over my mouth to stop it.

Fortunately whoever was on the phone wraps it up. We hear the distant ding of the elevator as he leaves.

"Let's get out of here," I say, darting to the doorway.

"You don't want to make out some more?"

"This bet has already been won. By me. Prize time."

"You never told me you were so good at winning bets."

"There's only so much a person can disclose in one week."

"One week and one day."

Sometimes Austin will say the perfect thing or look at me a certain way and I swear I've known him forever. But it's only been one week and one day. The best one week and one day of my life. I don't know how it's possible to feel like you've known someone forever when it's only been one week and one day. I just know that it is.

"So what's my prize?" I ask when we're outside.

"Dessert at Bubby's."

"I love Bubby's!"

"Of course you do."

"How did you know?"

"It's a Sadie place. They have the best pie. How could you not love it?"

"My prize rules. I haven't been there in forever."

"Me, neither. I actually just remembered it was around here when you asked what your prize was."

"Were you planning a different prize?"

Austin lifts my hand to his mouth and kisses the back of it. "You ask a lot of questions."

"I like answers."

"Answers aren't always helpful. Sometimes the not knowing is better than the knowing."

"Like when?"

"Like when someone is trying to protect you from the truth. Would you rather hear the truth and be hurt or not know and be happy?"

"That depends. Was your original prize better than dessert at Bubby's?"

Austin laughs. He holds my hand as we cross the street. So much is happening around us on our walk to Bubby's. So much to look up at. Not anything big or even anything most people would notice. I'm all about the little things. Every nuance seems to be vibrating with positive energy tonight. The tranquil notes of wind chimes floating down to us from inside an open apartment window. A woman in a courtyard setting a table for dinner with sunflowers and brightly striped napkins. Window boxes filled with colorful flowers. The aroma of fresh-baked bread wafting from a bakery. It's a gorgeous summer night, perfect in its simplicity.

We order pie (cherry for me, blueberry for Austin, but we'll share) and coffee at Bubby's.

"Jon Stewart comes here," I say.

"Have you ever seen him?"

"Not inside. But one time I was sitting at that window table and I saw him walking by with his son."

"My friend who lives here in Tribeca says he sees Jon all the time. He doesn't even think about it when he passes Jon anymore."

"New Yorkers are so jaded. Celeb sightings don't even faze us." It's probably best not to disclose my Claire Danes stalker antics.

"Especially down here. At least three of my friends live in the same buildings as whoever's hot right now. I'm sure Jon's not the only famous regular at Bubby's."

"Do you come here a lot?"

"No, but I used to. Now I mainly hang out around campus or in Jersey City. I pretty much only come into the city for internship or class."

"But there's so much to do here!"

"Yeah, I know. It's a convenience thing. Once I'm home,

I'm usually in for the night. What can I tell you? I'm lame."

"Why do you live in Jersey City?"

"It's complicated." Austin takes a bite of pie. "Man, that's good."

"Break it down for me."

"They only use fresh blueberries. You can taste the—"

"Not the pie. The complicated."

"Oh. Well for one, rents are way cheaper in Jersey. The rents for one-bedrooms around here are so outrageous they should be illegal. And the apartments here are smaller. I don't see the point in paying more for less."

"Location."

"But I can be on campus in fifteen minutes door-to-door. I can either drive in or take the PATH or the ferry or even the bus. The city is completely accessible anytime I want."

"But if you lived here, you wouldn't have to come in. You'd already be here."

"Paying twice the rent for half the space."

"I heard the rents in Jersey City and Hoboken are almost as bad as the rents here."

"They're getting there. Especially for new construction on the waterfront. But for the most part it's considerably more affordable."

"I totally get what you're saying." I stir more sugar into my coffee. "But don't you love the energy of Manhattan? Wouldn't you rather live here?"

"Sure, as soon as I become the first urban planner to achieve millionaire status. Then I'll get right on that brownstone on Greenwich Street."

"You'll have to renovate it first."

"No doubt. Like a *boss*."

"Get ready for me to take over one of your guest rooms."

"Please do."

"Will you have a rooftop garden? I'm going to need a rooftop garden."

"You're into gardening?"

"Not yet, but I will be when you have a rooftop garden. We can grow herbs—ooh! We'll grow basil and I'll make fresh pesto all summer. Pesto is only good when basil is abundant. Of course I'll want sunflowers, daisies, lilies of the valley . . . all the good summer flowers. Daffodils in the spring. You should do window boxes for even more flowers."

"Should I get an interior designer, or do you have the whole house planned?"

"I'm down with designing everything."

"Then we're all set."

I eat my pie. Should I drop this discussion before I say too much? Of course I should. Is that going to stop me? Apparently not.

"You don't have to have millions of dollars to live here," I say. "You just need enough passion and determination to find what you're looking for."

Austin puts his fork down. He studies me. "You really are an eternal optimist. I've never met anyone like you before."

"Do you think I'm naive?"

"Not so much naive as hopeful." Austin shakes his head in amazement. "I'm so lucky I found you."

"I'm the lucky one," I say.

"We're both lucky. And I've already found what I was looking for. I found you."

I absolutely believe that Austin was looking for me just like I was looking for him. When I imagined finding my soul mate, I knew he would love me for who I am. Austin totally does.

"Can I ask you something?" I say.

"You can ask me anything."

"Would you like to spend the whole weekend together?"

"Um . . . *yes*?"

"But for real. This weekend. At my place."

Austin hesitates. "You're serious."

"What if you came over after internship tomorrow and forgot to go home until Sunday night?"

"That would be awesome. But I don't think I can swing it."

"Why not?"

Austin leans his elbows on the table, rubbing his face like he's suddenly exhausted. Crap. I shouldn't have said anything. Why did I have to rush it?

"I'd have to figure some things out, is all. Move some things around."

"You already have plans?"

"Not exactly."

"Oh." I stare at my plate. Nothing but crumbs remain.

"But . . . I think I can make it happen."

"Really?"

"Really."

I can't wait to tell Rosanna and Darcy that Austin's spending the weekend at our place. Only . . . we haven't talked about visitors yet. What if they don't want him there? I'm about to tell Austin that I have to check with my roommates, but then I decide to wait and see what they say. Even though Rosanna, Darcy, and I just met, I have a feeling they'll be in my corner when it comes to true love.

TWENTY-NINE
DARCY

SADIE AND I ARE ITCHING to start the movie when Rosanna bursts in from her date with D. If Rosanna were more like me, I would have suspected we might not see her until the walk of shame brought her home at dawn.

"Are you okay?" Sadie asks Rosanna from the armchair she's called dibs on for movie night. Which is fine by me. This couch and I have developed a close relationship.

"Yeah, I'm good." Rosanna is all flushed. Any girl on the planet could recognize her post-hookup glow.

"So was it good for you?" I prod.

"Was what—" Rosanna realizes I'm messing with her. "Just give me a second to change."

"Take your time." I stretch out on the couch and give Sadie a smirk. After Rosanna's door closes, I say, "That girl is having the time of her life."

"She can take a number," Sadie says. "I'm having the best time ever. Of anyone's life."

"What'd you guys do tonight?" I ask.

"We went to this pie place I love. Oh, so . . . Austin wants to stay here this weekend. Would that be okay with you?"

"Of course. Why are you even asking?"

"We haven't talked about the visitors thing yet."

"Visitors isn't a thing. Anyone can have over whomever they want. Isn't that part of the roommate code?"

"Totally. I mean, that's how I feel. Do you think Rosanna will be okay with it?"

"She should be. Her fancy man can't avoid this place forever. I'm predicting some reckless sleepovers in her near future."

"I wouldn't exactly describe Rosanna as reckless."

"Not yet. But you will." Don't get me wrong. I'm loving my freedom. But it's weird that Sadie and Rosanna are on the boyfriend track while I can't even figure out my feelings for Jude. The last thing I expected in this scenario was to be the one questioning how I feel about a boy while my two roommates fall in lust harder than ever.

Rosanna comes out in a matching heather-gray tee-and-shorts set that's straight out of high school gym class. The tee says PROPERTY OF LINCOLN HIGH PHYS ED. Way to be original, Lincoln High. She zooms to the kitchen in such a fit of zest I expect her to slam out a hundred jumping jacks. "Could anyone else use a snack?" she asks, yanking open the freezer door. "I'm having a Popsicle."

"Cherry for me, thanks," Sadie says.

"Grape, please!" I yell for no reason.

Rosanna brings us our Popsicles, plus a lime one for her. She plops down on the pouf I bought yesterday. It's apple green and, in my humble opinion, really ties the room together.

"Austin's bunking with us this weekend," I inform Rosanna. "It's like sleepaway camp for sexy men. How cute is that?"

Rosanna's eyes practically pop out of her head. "Oh my god, really?" She gapes at Sadie. "He's spending the night already?"

"No, we're not . . . he'll be sleeping with me, but we're not *sleeping* together."

"And you're okay with that?"

"Yeah. I know we just met, but it feels like I've known him forever. He's not some random guy. Don't worry. You can trust him."

"You trust him, so we trust him." I look at Rosanna for backup.

"I'm not worried. I'm just . . ."

"Freaking out that a man is staying with us?" I suggest.

Rosanna whips a pillow at me.

"Hey!" I yank my Popsicle out of the way in the nick of time.

"I'm not freaking out," Rosanna insists. "I'll even clean the bathroom again before he gets here."

"You don't have to do that," Sadie says.

"I kind of do. Did the people who lived here before us have a problem with cleaning? I scrubbed those tiles for an hour and they're still disgusting."

"Austin won't be judging us on cleanliness," I say. "He'll be too busy judging Sadie on her lady attributes."

"Can we watch the movie now?" Sadie says.

"Someone hit the lights," I order. Once I'm sprawled out on the couch, nothing short of a forklift can pry me up.

Our movie night selection is *Unfaithful*. It's this film about a housewife who has an affair with a book dealer in Soho. Films that are beautiful and evocative in an understated way always resonate with me. Maybe I appreciate the balance since my life-style is more of the overblown Hollywood blockbuster type.

Unfaithful is the kind of movie screenwriters watch and probably kick themselves that they didn't come up with the idea first. Connie Sumner, the main character, meets Paul Martel outside his building when they literally crash into each other during a windstorm. She scrapes her knee and it's all bloody. He invites her to his place to take care of it. While she's up there, she's admiring his massive book collection. He tells her to pull a certain book out from the shelf, turn to a page number he's memorized, and read the line he tells her. She reads, "'Be happy for this moment. This moment is your life.'"

I love that quote so much. It rings true with my wild and free summer. I've been giving advice (albeit unsolicited) to the girls from *The Power of Now*. Just tips on the importance of being in the Now and connecting with your immediate physical environment and creating meaningful interactions with others. Being in the Now helps you avoid obsessing over regrets from the past and feeling anxious about the future. Having recently wasted a bunch of time on a certain dumbass who shall remain nameless, I do not intend to waste one more second.

"Being present to fully enjoy every moment," I comment on the quote. "Where have I heard that before?"

Sadie pauses the movie. "You do realize this is the third time I've paused the movie because you keep talking."

"I can't help it if there's more to say."

"Could we say it after the movie?"

"Then I might forget."

"Or we might be up until three trying to watch this. Some of us need to go to bed."

"Oh, please. As if you two aren't jacked up on enough boy adventure adrenaline to stay awake for a week straight."

"She has a point," Rosanna says.

"Agreed," Sadie relents. "Either we'll be up all night trying to watch this in between commentaries, or you'll keep us up with your snoring anyway."

"What are you talking about?"

Rosanna and Sadie exchange a glance.

"You snore, Darcy," Rosanna blurts. "We've been wondering how to tell you."

"I do not *snore*."

"You snore."

"No, I don't. You snore."

"I think you have us confused. There was a lot of noise last night."

"You mean from when you were snoring?"

"Simmer down, kids," Sadie says. "Mommy wants to watch her movie."

We watch the rest of the movie. As a sign of courtesy, I keep my commentary to a bare minimum. My feeling is that movies are a communal experience that should be shared verbally in real time. But hey, I understand that everyone might not feel the same. I wouldn't talk over a movie in a movie theater or anything. I'm not a barbarian. But watching a movie in the privacy of your own home means you can comment on that hot sex scene as loud as you want. Oh, and PS? I don't snore. Just FYI.

The movie ends on a disturbing note. We all take a minute to gauge our reactions as the credits roll.

"Why are affairs so common?" Sadie wonders. "Do that many people marry the wrong people?"

"People settle for less than they want because they think they'll never find anyone better," Rosanna says.

"Or they get married too young," I say. "Nobody knows themselves before thirty. Your twenties are for exploring and having adventures and discovering who you are. How are you supposed to find yourself when you're permanently attached to someone else?"

"Not permanently," Rosanna corrects. "That's the problem. People take marriage too lightly. They're like, 'If it doesn't work out, I'll just get a divorce.' Like it's nothing. Marriage meant something back in the day. When our grandparents got married, that was for life. They didn't ignore the part of the vows that says 'till death do us part.'"

"I'm sure people really do feel like they'll be together forever when they get married," Sadie says. "But sometimes life gets in the way. People grow. They change in ways they can't predict. What if you're married and your husband got a job in Alaska? Would you leave your life behind to go with him?"

"You should go wherever your husband needs you to," Rosanna insists. "That's part of being married. Staying together no matter what."

"But take what happened in the movie," I say. "Connie was in love with Edward. You could tell they were attracted to each other. They probably had a hot sex life their first few years together. Then they had a kid. They got comfortable. Bogged down by routine. Her feelings for him changed. Not the best-friend feelings. The passion. That's why she's vulnerable when she meets Paul. He becomes the object of her affection. Suddenly Edward is repulsive. She doesn't want him to touch her. Was that only because she fell in love with Paul, or would she have fallen out of love with Edward anyway?"

"Are you saying that anyone who's been married for a long time is vulnerable to falling in love with someone else?" Rosanna asks.

"Anyone is vulnerable to falling in love with someone else, married or not. You can't choose who you fall in love with."

"But you *can* choose whether or not to open that door," Sadie says. "When you're married, it should be obvious that the door is closed to everyone except your husband."

"Permanently," Rosanna adds.

"If you married the right person," I say. "What about people who settle? Half of all marriages end in divorce for a reason. A lot of reasons, actually. One of the biggest reasons is that people settle. They know they're not completely happy with their relationship. But the fear of being alone or of never finding someone better for them is so powerful they convince themselves that it will work out. There's this void in their life that can only be filled by a person they'd be happier with. But they'd rather live with that emptiness than risk never finding a more compatible person."

"A soul mate," Sadie says. "If you marry a soul mate, the love of your life, the man of your dreams, you will always be happy together. Maybe not completely happy every single day. We all have our good days and bad days no matter who we're with. But if you're lucky enough to find the total package, you will always have a solid relationship. It's not even about luck. People who visualize the kind of love they want and refuse to settle for anything less will find what they're looking for."

"Agreed," Rosanna says. "You can't break up a happy relationship."

"And the only way to have a happy relationship is to be completely open," Sadie says.

"About everything?" I ask.

"Yes."

"Even negative things?"

Sadie pauses. "I guess it depends on how important they are."

"Boom!" I sit up on the couch in a burst of second wind. "Here comes the conflict. What one person thinks isn't important could be huge to the other person. So if one person's not telling the other person something and the other person finds out and they're all, 'Why didn't you tell me such and so?' and the first person's like, 'I didn't think it was important,' that's not going to fly. It's going to come off like they were trying to hide something."

"What if the negative thing could hurt the other person?" Sadie asks. "And that's why the first person was keeping it from them?"

"Yeah, that's called lying."

"People in a relationship should feel secure enough to tell each other anything," Rosanna says. "They shouldn't hold something back because they're afraid of how the other person will take it. That's not being completely honest."

I stick my fist out for a pound. Rosanna leans over from the pouf to tap me.

"All I'm saying is . . ." Sadie composes her thoughts. "If you feel like something's missing and you find a soul mate, it's like a missing piece of you has been found. Like the thing you've been longing for is suddenly right in front of you. Even if you didn't know you were longing in the first place. Or maybe you didn't realize true love was real. Maybe you thought movie love was only in the movies. But now you're in it and you've never been this certain of anything else in your life and it feels so amazing you can't resist. If that happens to someone who's already married, they should be honest about their feelings with everyone involved. Even if their marriage looks perfect from the outside."

"A picture-perfect marriage is usually far from perfect," I say.

"Not always," Rosanna says. "I know couples who have been happily married for a long time. Their marriages look perfect because they really are close to perfect."

"Like who?"

"Friends of the family back home. Neighbors. My aunt and uncle. There are just as many examples of happy marriages as there are of bad ones."

"I don't know about that. Just because people choose to stay married doesn't automatically mean they're happy." I'd rather chew my leg off than stay caught in the trap of a miserable marriage. Being uncommitted is so much better. There's no way I could ever hurt someone the way Connie hurt Edward.

THIRTY

ROSANNA

WE STAYED UP SO LATE last night I was afraid to look at the time before I went to bed. I'm paying the price today. But movie night with Sadie and Darcy was totally worth it. Not that I would have been able to go to sleep right away if we hadn't stayed up. The encounter with D at his place gave me an extreme adrenaline rush that took hours to wear off, if it ever wore off completely. My legs still feel heavy. A mild dizziness is making it impossible to operate at full speed. Every nerve in my body is like an exposed wire with frayed edges that won't stop sparking.

It would be safe to say that I'm not exactly bringing the camp counselor excellence today.

Fortunately no one seems to be noticing. Or if they are noticing, they're kind enough not to say anything. I'm relieved to be at arts and crafts this period. You get to sit down the whole time at arts and crafts, except for going over to the service window to get additional supplies. My legs were starting to feel like I was wading through quicksand.

"Does this look good?" Momo asks. She's decorating the jewelry box she made yesterday. She holds up her jewelry box for my approval. Momo seems to need a lot of validation. We bonded over our shared love of birds on the first day of camp. Campers were meeting their counselors at the pickup/drop-off station. Momo and I noticed a fat little red bird hopping on a bench at the same time. We both sort of mentally gasped at how cute the bird was. Then we looked at each other and laughed. It was one of those pure, happy moments you can only share with an eight-year-old full of wonder. Ever since our little bird connection, Momo has become increasingly attached to me. The camp director said she's never seen a camper get attached to a counselor this quickly. Apparently we will all be sobbing wrecks on the last day.

"It's beautiful," I say. "Your pink sequins are pretty."

"They're rhinestones," Momo corrects.

"Oh, sorry. They're really pretty."

"Do you have a jewelry box?"

"No."

"Why not?"

Momo doesn't need to know that almost all of the items I own are necessities. With the exception of my fabulous wardrobe expansion, thanks to Darcy. I still feel guilty about her generosity.

"I don't have that much jewelry," I tell her. "I just keep it in a container."

"Like a Tupperware container?"

"Sort of."

"Every girl should have a jewelry box," Momo proclaims.

"You're right. A lot of things should be the way they aren't."

Momo turns the jewelry box around, inspecting all sides of it. "Do you think it needs more glitter?"

"You can never have too much glitter."

"I know, right?" Momo selects the purple glitter. She looks around for glue.

"Let me get you some glue," I say. The other tables don't have any free glue. I go up to the service window on the side of the arts and crafts hut. The arts and crafts director is inside, loading metal tubs onto a shelf.

"Sorry to bother you, Shirley, but is all the glue out?"

"Good question," Shirley says. She swings around to peer out at the tables. Her long, colored feather earrings flutter around her face. "We might have some more in one of these tubs. A bunch of supplies just came in. Let me—" The metal tub Shirley was holding falls to the cement floor with a loud clang. "Yeah. There wasn't anything fragile in this one, was there?"

"Probably not."

"We'll go with definitely not. More convincing." Shirley rounds up some extra glues and passes them through the window. "I'll be out in a sec."

"Take your time. It's pretty quiet out here. Everyone's absorbed in their jewelry boxes."

"Oh good, I was hoping the girls would like them."

"What are you doing with the boys later?"

"Planes. Same as the jewelry boxes: they put them together yesterday and they're decorating them today."

"Have fun. Thanks for the glue." When I get back to our table, Momo's not there. A counselor sitting at the other end of the table points to the water fountain. I watch Momo take a sip of water. Then she just stands there, facing away from the group. She takes another sip.

The counselor comes over and whispers in my ear. "She jumped a mile when that thing fell." She looks at Momo, concerned.

I go over to the water fountain. Momo is breathing hard. She's all sweaty.

"Are you okay?" I ask.

"It scared me."

"What did?"

"That loud noise."

"That clanging noise?"

She nods.

"Shirley just dropped a supplies tub," I explain. "That's all."

Momo takes another sip of water.

"She won't drop another one," I say.

"Promise?"

"If she does, I'll be right there next to you. Okay?"

Momo glances back at the arts and crafts hut.

"Should we go back to our table now?" I ask. "We have glue. You can show me where you're going to put the purple glitter."

"I might use purple and pink," Momo says. "They're my favorite colors."

"Those are the best colors." We walk back to the table. I sit close to Momo, trying to project soothing energy. Momo debates the pros and cons of putting glitter on only the sides versus the sides and top.

"Overusing glitter is a mistake," Momo informs me. "It doesn't look good if you pile on too much. What if I do squiggly lines on the sides like this. . . ." Momo squeezes squiggly lines of glue on one side, immediately followed by careful glitter application.

"That looks really good. Very glamorous."

"Thanks." Momo sprinkles more glitter. "It's good we're making jewelry boxes."

"Because every girl should have a jewelry box?"

"Also because I used to have one, but I don't anymore."

"No? What happened to it?"

"I told my mom a secret I wasn't supposed to tell. My jewelry box was taken away as part of my punishment."

"Are you ever getting it back?"

"No." Momo touches one of the rhinestones. "But that's okay. Now I have a jewelry box I designed myself." She curls over her jewelry box protectively.

Something about her behavior is familiar. I recognize part of myself in Momo. What she said about being punished for telling a secret . . .

When I was eleven, I was molested by a family friend who lived down the street. No one would ever suspect him. He was older, like in his forties, but he never got married. He lived alone in a tiny house and worked at a meatpacking plant. He was always friendly to everyone—the kind of neighbor who would help you shovel your driveway or give your car a jump start. He took me and my little sister out for pizza and to Lincoln Park Zoo. He even took me and my brothers to a baseball game at Wrigley Field once. He was like an uncle to us and a good friend of my dad's.

One day when I was over at his house playing Scrabble, he moved his chair around to my side of the table. He grabbed the sides of my face and forced his lips against mine.

"Does that feel okay?" he asked.

I had no idea what to say to that. I made an excuse to leave and went home.

Things got worse over the next few months. He would repeatedly grab me and try to kiss me. He touched any part of me he wanted. One time at a neighbor's cookout, he trapped me on the way out of the bathroom. He pulled down the zipper of my jeans and put his hand inside my underwear. Everyone was outside having a good time. I could hear my mother laughing through the open window while he violated me on the other side of the wall. I tried to avoid being alone with him, but he told me that if I stopped coming over or if I told anyone he would hurt my little sister. Then he would attack me. So I never told my parents what was happening. When I got really scared that he was going to attack me anyway, I told my best friend at the time what was going on. She told her mom. Her mom called my mom.

My dad confronted him. Of course he denied everything. There wasn't enough evidence to convict him as a sex offender. Since he never raped me or even took my clothes off, my dad didn't have a strong enough case. But he made sure everyone in town knew what a scumbag that guy was. Eventually he moved away.

Could Momo be going through the same thing I did?

Last night when we were talking about affairs, Sadie said how people who've experienced the same type of pain gravitate toward one another. Like they have a special radar set to the tone of that particular pain. It's one of the reasons why some marriages don't work out. When you've been through trauma, you feel like no one else in the world understands how you're feeling, except for people who've been through a similar experience.

Maybe that's why Momo became attached to me right away. Maybe she recognizes part of herself in me.

THIRTY-ONE
SADIE

OUR MARATHON WEEKEND IS ON.

We immediately started making out the second Austin walked in the door. He got here right on time at six thirty. He wanted to come over at six, but I needed time to take a shower and get ready. And clean my room since that's where we'll basically be living together all weekend. I raced home after internship, took the fastest shower ever, couldn't decide what to wear, cleaned my room while simultaneously trying on eight more outfits, and then, way too soon but not soon enough, Austin rang my bell. We're still attached at the lips. We're like a dream. Except this dream actually came true.

"Hi," Austin says when we stop kissing.

"Hi."

"Can you tell I'm happy to see you?"

"Sort of. Could you be more explicit?"

Austin kisses me again. Good thing the girls are out. It's already awkward that Austin is staying here and he hasn't even met them yet. We don't need to pile on more awkwardness by having them watch us ravage each other in the doorway.

"So," Austin says, looking around for the first time. "This is where you live. It's cute."

"Thanks. We're still working on it."

"I like this . . . what's this called?"

"Pouf."

"I like your pouf. It's very you."

"Darcy bought it."

"Is she like you?"

"Not really. But we both have good taste."

"Are we alone?"

"Yeah. Darcy and Rosanna are out. My guess is that Rosanna will be back soon and Darcy will get home around two."

"Want to order a pizza?"

"You read my mind. We have Blue Bunny Birthday Party ice cream for dessert."

"Sounds delicious."

"It's a party in a carton."

"What do you like on your pizza?"

"I'm a purist. Extra cheese and roasted tomato is good."

"No pepperoni? Mushrooms? Pineapple?"

"You did not just say pineapple."

"Pretty sure I did."

"Pineapple does not go with pizza. It should be outlawed as

a pizza topping. Like as a federal law."

"Some people like it."

"Ew. Oh, wait. Did you want pineapple on your half, or . . . ?"

"Not anymore. How about one large extra cheese, half pepperoni, half roasted tomato?"

"Awesome."

Austin orders the pizza. While we wait for it, I show him around. I'm so excited that he's sleeping over. In my bed . . . where I will also be sleeping. If this is what being a grownup is like—no parents around and your own apartment where you can stay out all night and your boyfriend can come over anytime you want—then sign me up.

"Here's my room." The thing about showing a boy your room is it feels like you're saying, *Here's my bed and some other stuff.* It's like my bed activated this magnetic force the second Austin walked in. Even as I'm watching him look around at other things, I can feel the bed emanating salacious waves of subtext.

"You have a teapot," Austin says. He picks up the seafoam teapot I've had in my room since tenth grade. "I knew you were a classy girl."

"Not a nerdy girl?"

"You have nerdy undercurrents that surface now and then."

"Like what?"

"I'll let you know the next time one surfaces."

"Would you like some tea?"

"Let's save the tea for tomorrow morning." Austin puts down the teapot. He comes over and hugs me. "Or Sunday morning. I can't believe I get to wake up next to you two days in a row. How lucky am I?"

"I'm the lucky one."

"We're both lucky." Austin looks around some more. He notices the sign over my bed. "'Right around the corner.' What does that mean?"

"Do you know that soul mates are real?"

Austin laughs. "I love how you framed the question. People would usually ask something like, 'Do you believe in soul mates?'"

"But soul mates are real. It's not a matter of belief."

"Like global warming?"

"Exactly. Asking someone if they believe in global warming is like asking if they're smart. Only idiots refuse to believe reality."

"So if I don't believe in soul mates . . . sorry, if I don't know they're real, then I'm an idiot?"

"No. You would just be uninformed, which is a completely different thing. Then I would school you and you'd know."

"I guess I've always hoped soul mates were real. I'd never experienced that kind of attraction before. But now . . ." Austin's blue eyes sparkle with silver in the evening light slanting through my window. "Now I understand. I've never felt this way about anyone, Sadie."

"I've never felt this way about anyone, either."

Austin looks like he wants to say more. Instead he turns toward the sign again. "So . . . right around the corner?"

"It means that my soul mate could be anywhere. We each have more than one soul mate. This city is all about the energy bringing people together in mysterious ways. There are so many chances to meet a soul mate doing routine things. Going to work or to school, running errands, in coffeehouses, at the gym, at group meetings. Or even just walking around. I would take walks along the river and imagine meeting my soul mate there. He'd pass me and take one look at me and just know we were meant to be together. Or I'd be reading on the grass and he'd come over to talk to me because he loved that there was a girl reading in the park. Something he couldn't explain would pull him in my direction. He would be compelled to talk to me, like he didn't have a choice, even though he didn't know me. That's what the sign is about. He could literally be right around the corner."

"Wow." Austin stares at the sign, contemplating the enormity of it.

The door buzzes. I totally forgot about the pizza.

"I'm getting this." Austin takes his wallet out of his back pocket and answers the door.

After we eat, we go back to my room. Austin says he wants to see pictures from when I was little.

"You do?" I say. No one has ever wanted to see those pictures before.

"I bet you were adorable."

"Not really."

"Of course you were. Look how adorable you are now. That had to come from somewhere, right?"

"But why do you want to see them?"

Austin sits on my bed. I try not to freak out that he is sitting on my bed.

"You fascinate me," he says. "I want to learn as much about you as I can this weekend."

I open my closet door, thankful that the closet hasn't had a chance to get messy yet. I dig around until I find the box with my photo albums. My mom started making these for me when I was a baby. Every year she gave me one on my birthday, filled with photos that documented the events of the past year. I was going to leave them at home, but something told me to bring them. Now I'm happy they're here. I take the photo albums from when I was two to eight over to the bed.

"Dude," Austin says. "You have actual photo albums."

"That's how I roll. I'm old-school."

"I love that about you. No one has real photos anymore." He slides his hand over one of the textured covers.

We lie back against my pillows to look at the pictures. We get to the ones from Christmas morning when I was four. There's a light in Austin's eyes as he looks at them. He flips the pages carefully, as if they might break. I love that he's treating my albums with respect. Boys are usually oblivious to things that should be handled delicately.

The front door opens and closes. It's probably Rosanna.

Darcy loves staying out late. Usually I would go out and say hi. But not tonight. Tonight I'm busy. Tonight I'm in bed with Austin. A ripple of nervous excitement rockets through me, making me giggle.

"What?" Austin asks.

"Nothing. Just . . . I'm happy you're here."

"Not as happy as I am."

"How do you know?"

"Because you make me happier than anyone ever has." Austin puts the photo album on the bed. He wraps his arms around me so we're lying on our sides, facing each other. "I mean it, Sadie. You make me happier than I've ever been. I didn't even know it was possible to feel this way."

Soul mates, I think. That's the way it feels with a soul mate. Like a whole new world is opening up for you. Like everything you've imagined can finally become reality. Even things you didn't know to imagine. Things you wanted deep down that you didn't realize you wanted until you found them.

There's so much I want to say to Austin. I want to tell him everything I'm thinking. I want to describe everything I'm feeling until he understands exactly how much he means to me. But I don't want to scare him off. You can't overload a boy with too much too soon. Even a boy who seems to feel the same way about you.

Austin kisses me. I kiss him back. Soon I'm on top of him, kissing him harder than ever.

I hear the sounds of Rosanna going to her room and closing

the door. After the movie last night she warned me to take it slow. No offense, but her limited boy experience is showing. When you find someone who makes you feel the way you've always wanted to feel, there's no reason to take it slow. Not that I'm ready to have sex with Austin. But there's no reason for us to take things slow emotionally. Why would you hold back when you know you've found something real?

We're not having sex this weekend, but there are other things we can do.

I kiss Austin even harder. My hand slides down his chest, his stomach, the front of his jeans. I grab his zipper and start pulling it down.

"Hey," Austin whispers. He puts his hand over mine, stopping me.

"What?"

"You know I adore you, right?"

"Yeah?"

"Well, I also respect you. And if you unzip my jeans, I can't promise that I'll control myself." He strokes my arm tenderly. "I want our first time to mean something."

Austin gazes into my eyes with an intensity that permeates down to my soul. I'm having one of those epic feelings. Except this one feels bigger than anything I've ever experienced. I've never felt so connected to another person.

"Sadie," Austin whispers.

"Yeah?" I whisper back.

"I'm falling in love with you."

"I'm falling in love with you, too."

This is what every girl dreams of. To bask in adoration from the person she loves. What we have really is a dream come true.

I don't want to settle for less than what my heart desires in my fantasy life. And I definitely don't want to settle in my real life, either.

THIRTY-TWO
DARCY

YOU KNOW HOW MOST WEEKS Friday cannot come soon enough? That was especially true this week. I could not possibly have more reading to plow through or papers to write or facts to memorize. It's astonishing I have time to do things like sleep and take showers. Taking a year off has its consequences. Trying to catch up on basic requirements isn't as basic as I'd presumed.

Maybe these classes would be more interesting if they actually pertained to my future career. Not that I know what my future career is. I don't even know what I want to major in. A career that lets me flaunt my social butterfly tendencies and solid people skills would be awesome. I'm hoping enlightenment will strike at some point this summer so I can officially start college with at least some idea of where my education is going. Going with the flow is significantly less fun when

Daddy pressures me to make the big decision. He called me this morning to drill me again about where my life is going. My argument is that college is for discovering yourself and what you want to do with your life. Why should teenagers be forced to decide what the rest of their life will look like? Daddy's not feeling my argument at all. But I get that you have to start taking specialized classes sophomore year. It makes sense to take ones that will support your career.

So yeah. TGIF. My determination to whip up some serious summer fun is stronger than ever. No amount of work can prevent me from having a blast this weekend. On my way out to meet up with Jude, I swing by Sadie's room to say bye.

"Have fun with your hot boyfriend," I say.

Sadie is in a frenzy of getting ready. Clothes are scattered everywhere. I feel for her. Having Austin come over for the weekend is super exciting, but also super nerve-racking.

"Have you seen my bronzer?" she asks. "Forget it—no time!"

"Your makeup looks perfect," I reassure her. "Not many girls can pull off the natural look as flawlessly as you do."

"Oh, you are a good friend to lie. Keep them coming."

"I'm serious. Austin is a lucky boy."

"So is Jude." Sadie yanks off the top she tried on. She grabs a dress from her bed. I leave before I distract her any more from her race against the clock.

Jude and I have the whole night to do whatever we want. We just saw each other three days ago, but it feels like way longer. I haven't given him the HELLO shirt yet. Tonight is so gorgeous we decided to walk around the West Village before dinner (for which I have to treat, as per the bet I lost last time), hitting this all-ages lounge called Welcome to the Johnsons, and then seeing where the night takes us. I didn't want Jude to be carrying around a shirt the whole time.

"So what have you been up to?" Jude asks as we round the corner onto West 10th Street.

"Not much." A flash of hooking up with Random Boy at the Gap strikes me like lightning. "Classes. Hanging with my girls. Going out. What about you?"

"Working the park as much as I can. That's how I roll in the summer. Later sunset means more performance time. It's been a really good season so far. The park's been super busy. I don't remember it being as busy last year."

"That's hot. More people are discovering you."

"Not much to discover. I'm just happy to have such a fun gig."

We pass a townhouse with a silver swing in the ground-floor picture window.

"Yo, they have an entire swing in their house," Jude says. "They're like, 'We don't have a yard, but fuck that.'"

There's a woman standing outside taking pictures of the swing. I ask her for the backstory.

"It's an art installation," the woman explains. "I know the owner of the house. He has two little girls who play on the swing. They all live upstairs. He switches the piece every few months."

"How badass is that?" I say. "Can you imagine being able to showcase your own art where you live? For anyone walking by to see?"

"It's pretty amazing down here," she agrees. "I live up in Harlem. The Village is like a whole other world."

"Do you like Harlem?"

"It's affordable. That's where I'm at." She tilts her head back, gazing up at the top of the townhouse where part of a tree is visible. "Making a living as an artist *plus* having gallery space right in your own home? That's an incredible achievement anywhere, much less pulling it off in the most expensive neighborhood in Manhattan."

We say goodbye and continue down West 10th Street. Conversations like this make me thankful for my financial situation all over again. I have access to major parental financial supplementation. Not a day goes by where I'm not grateful for my luck. I could have just as easily been born into a poor family. That's why I enjoy treating my friends and spreading the wealth. Rosanna keeps protesting over the clothes and accessories I gave her. But I don't care. She can protest all she wants. There's no way I'm taking any of that stuff back. The clothes look amazing on her. She's a good person who deserves to be treated. And she needs nicer things to ride the D train. He's taking her to the most exclusive restaurants and venues. You can't do Butter rocking your best Kmart/Payless ensemble.

But yeah. I can essentially stay here after graduation for as long as I want. I can even buy a place like D's loft if I want to.

As long as I decide on a viable career, Daddy would totally be willing to help me out in the home department. The kind of home most people work for their whole lives and never get to have.

"Are you so excited for next week?" I ask Jude. He's presenting to a few potential investors. One of them will hopefully back his project.

"Either excited or terrified. I can't really tell."

"Everyone will love you. How could they not? Your invention is genius." I'm worried that Jude won't get funded, but I'm keeping that doubt to myself. He needs nothing but encouragement right now.

After I treat for dinner at ABC Kitchen, we head to the Lower East. Welcome to the Johnsons is packed by the time we get there. Jude knew I'd love this lounge. It's tricked out like some suburban family's living room circa 1985. Plastic-covered couches. Pac-Man. Pink flamingoes. The works. I'm in kitsch heaven.

We grab drinks and snag a huge recliner in the corner. There's a Hawaiian doll in a grass skirt dangling from the pleated lampshade above us.

"Classy," I say.

"I knew you'd love it."

"You know all the best places."

"Stick with me. You'll be an expert on the best holes in the wall by the end of the summer."

"How could I resist?"

"I'm hoping you can't." Jude gives me an adorable smile that makes my heart melt. Or would make my heart melt if I was on the market to have my heart melted.

"Who were you in high school?" I ask. Rosanna told me how she asked D this question. I immediately acquired it as part of my small talk repertoire.

"Other than myself?"

"I mean what kind of person were you? Were you always the laid-back, go-with-the-flow, artistic-entrepreneurial-genius type?"

"More like the geeked-out, loser, slacker type. The girls couldn't keep their hands off me."

"Who was your first crush?"

"Samantha Rutherford in fourth grade. She sat next to me. I kept getting in trouble because my teacher thought I was staring out the window, but I was actually sneaking looks at Samantha. She had the lightest blond hair I've ever seen. She looked like an angel."

"Did she like you back?"

"Circumstances would indicate not so much. But I know she's been pining for me ever since. She's probably stalking me online and strategizing how to find me in the park accidentally on purpose."

"Maybe she was waiting for you to tell her you liked her."

"You mean when I snuck a love letter in her desk at recess and she showed it to all her friends and never spoke to me again? Yeah, tried that."

"That's what you get, falling for a blonde."

"I was devastated."

"At least you told her how you felt. That was really brave."

"You'd think I'd be more cautious about revealing my feelings too soon. But, no. Here I am wearing my heart on my sleeve, transparent as ever."

"I think it's sweet. So many guys are obsessed with hiding their feelings. Or playing games. What is it with guys being emotionally unavailable? Who even came up with that? Guys think they're protecting themselves from getting hurt or hurting someone else, but they're actually preventing themselves from experiencing so much."

Jude watches some girls dancing to the next retro track in what I'm sure is a long lineup of throwback jams. "Isn't that kind of what you're doing?" he asks.

"What?"

"Protecting yourself? Or . . . preventing yourself?"

How am I supposed to answer that? The last thing I want to do is explain the catalyst for Summer Fun Darcy.

"You know when I wasn't protecting myself?" I deflect. "When I had more first crushes than I can remember. You're like, Bam! Samantha Rutherford. But I do remember the first crush I had that mortified me. There was this boy I liked in seventh grade. I doodled his name with hearts all over a practice quiz I thought we were throwing out after class. I almost died when my teacher collected them so we could switch and grade each other's quizzes. Of course his friend got mine. He saw what I wrote and caught my eye. He taunted me with these menacing snickers all through grading the quizzes. He couldn't wait to tell my crush. Mortified."

"At the time it was huge, wasn't it? I remember how everything was so much larger than life back then. Every little thing was blown out of proportion."

"I know. I can't believe I cared about half the stuff that bothered me in high school."

"I can't believe anything ever bothered you."

"Yeah, well." I lean back on the recliner. My tiny skater dress is hiked up high on my thighs. I don't pull it down. Let Jude enjoy the view. "That was then."

"And this is now, where you only focus on the present?"

"Exactly." Cathartic full-circle moments like this rule. I love how we can talk about memories from back in the day that were devastating at the time, but have now been reduced to funny stories we laugh about. There was the boy I really liked who remained elusive in seventh grade. Then there was the boy who ripped my heart to shreds before I moved here. Now there's the boy who likes me who wants to be let in. I don't know what's going to happen between us. I just know I'm not going to worry about it. Worrying about the future is pointless. All we ever have is the Now. This moment, right here, is the only thing that matters.

THIRTY-THREE
ROSANNA

SADIE'S DOOR IS CLOSED WHEN I come home from Dean & DeLuca. She's probably in her room with Austin. I don't want to disturb them, so I go to my room and close the door.

Hanging out at Dean & DeLuca should have been fun. I found a cute spot on one of the couches to read. I was doing that thing where you want to look like you're totally into your book, not caring if anyone comes over and talks to you, but you're actually half-reading/half-hoping someone will. The Dean & DeLuca excursion was the first of many to come. I'm trying to get out more in this city I loved way before I moved here. Putting myself out there is the best way to meet new people. Darcy keeps saying how all I have to do is start chilling at places I'm attracted to and I'll find people I will like. But my mind really isn't on meeting new people.

I've been struggling all day with what happened at D's last

night. I thought he would have called by now, but he hasn't. I haven't called him because I don't know how to explain my crazy behavior. Who runs out of her boyfriend's apartment when he tries to kiss her? Not that he's even my boyfriend. He probably never wants to see me again. He'd rather find a girl who can handle being intimate. The hard truth is, I'm embarrassed and depressed and I don't know how I'm going to survive the weekend if he doesn't call. Not exactly living up to my girl-power standards.

That's why I went to Dean & DeLuca. As soon as I got home from camp, I realized I'd be waiting for the phone to ring all night unless I tore myself away. So I forced myself to go out and focus on other things, which didn't work at all. All I can think about is D.

This is insane. I am not going to be that girl. The one waiting for some boy to call to make her feel better. I decide to call Mica about Momo. We didn't get a chance to talk at camp. I shouted Mica's name after her when I saw her leaving, but she didn't hear me. I also want her advice about D. She can help me put things in perspective.

Ten seconds into our conversation, it's obvious something is wrong. Mica is being weird.

"What's wrong?" I ask her.

"What makes you think something's wrong?" Mica challenges.

"You don't sound like yourself. Are you okay?"

"No. I'm not okay. Would you be okay if someone you

thought was a friend said disgusting things about you?"

"What are you talking about?"

"How could you say those things? I thought we were friends."

"What things? I didn't say anything."

"So you didn't call me a selfish bitch who hates kids?"

"Of course not!"

"Then why did I hear that you did?"

"I didn't! Who told you that?"

"Addison."

"Who's Addison? I don't even know who that is."

"Yes, you do. She knows all about you."

"I swear I don't know Addison."

"You're such a liar. I saw you talking to her at the party."

"The camp party?"

"She said you yelled at her for spilling her drink."

"Wait, you mean Nasty Girl?"

"That's what you call one of your closest friends from high school?"

"She's not my friend. How do you know her?"

"She works at the Upper East camp. I met her at the party. Her UNY housing is in my building and she recognized me last night in the hall. She asked if I knew you. When I said we were friends, she told me everything you said about me. She told me what you did to her. Do you treat all your friends like shit?"

"She was never my friend! She didn't even go to my school!"

"Why are you lying to me?"

"I'm not!"

"Addison told me all about how you used to be good friends until you made out with her boyfriend at the junior prom. Who does that?"

"That never happened!"

"You turned on her like your friendship didn't even mean anything. She warned me you'd do the same thing to me."

"I would never do that to anyone! She's lying!"

"You're the one who's lying. You swore you didn't know her. Next you're going to deny that you told her I'm a lazy charity case who has no problem living in poverty for the rest of my life because I can get by on government handouts. How dare you talk about me like that."

"Please, I would never say those things! That's horrible!"

"You know the saddest part? I thought you understood me. You were supposed to be someone who would never talk that kind of smack about me."

Fear numbs my body. My heart races. I try to speak, but the words catch in my throat.

"You totally violated my trust," Mica says. "I'll never forgive you for that."

"Addison is the one you can't trust. I've never even talked to her."

"Oh my god. I saw you talking to her at the party!"

"No, that was—I'd never even seen her before! She's had an issue with me since the party. That was the first time I'd ever seen her. I don't know what her problem is. But it was clear at the party that she hates me."

"If you don't know Addison, then why does she know so much about you?"

"Like what?"

"She knows you're from Chicago. She knows you went to Lincoln High School because that's where she went."

"She didn't—"

"She knows all about your family. Everything you already told me. She told me all the same things you did. How could she possibly know all of that if you've never even talked to her?"

What the hell is going on? Who is this Addison person? Why does she hate me so much she's spewing all these lies about me? Lies that Mica is more than willing to believe.

"I don't know Addison," I say. "You have to believe me."

"No I don't." Mica hangs up.

She doesn't pick up when I call her.

I sit on my bed in shock, trembling. How does Addison know all those things about me? And why does she hate me so much?

Nasty Girl is out there turning my friends against me. She's getting away with it. There's nothing I can do to stop her. She already took the one person I thought would become my best friend away from me. What bothers me even more than a stranger spreading lies about me is that anyone could possibly hate me so much. What could I have done to her? I don't even know her. Maybe she's a friend of someone who hates me? But no one hates me. At least, not that I know of. I rack my brain trying to think of anything I could have done to make someone mad. There's nothing. The other part that's really bothering me is that Mica believed her. Doesn't she know me well enough already to see that I'm a decent person? Couldn't she tell I wanted to be good friends with her?

This really sucks. Two days ago it seemed like all of my dreams were coming true. Things with D were amazing. Being friends with Mica was so easy, without any tension or drama. I had the best summer of my life ahead of me. Now everything is gone. What a joke to think, after years of believing the contrary, that I finally deserved to be happy.

THIRTY-FOUR
SADIE

OF COURSE I COULDN'T SLEEP last night. What girl would be able to sleep with the most adorable boy in bed right next to her?

Originally we talked about having one of those perfect New York summer days where you walk around aimlessly with no plans. But it started raining after we woke up. The dreary, gray day got to us. So we decided on a movie marathon in my room. I put my glasses on. Rassling with my contacts was not a desirable option. My eyes were burning from getting like no sleep.

While I select the second movie after the first one ends, Austin smiles at me.

"What?" I say, smiling back.

"You're too cute in those glasses. How can I concentrate on our movie marathon when you're so cute?"

Wearing your glasses in front of the boy you like is a test

to see if he's worthy. If he thinks you're cute in glasses, he's a keeper.

"You know when you told me to let you know when one of your nerdy undercurrents surfaces?" Austin asks.

"Yeah?"

"Your cat's-eye glasses are one of your nerdy undercurrents surfacing. You should wear them more often."

"But I look so dorky in glasses."

"Which is why I find you adorkable." Austin reaches out for me to lie against him again. I snuggle up the same way I did while we were watching the movie: lying on my side pressed against him, right leg bent over his, arm slung over his chest.

I'm amazed all over again by how quickly our relationship has grown. Today is June 30. We first spoke to each other ten days ago. All of this—the immediate connection, the crazy chemistry, that ginormous fireworks non-coincidence, falling in love—has happened in the space of ten days. The best ten days of my life.

If I weren't in this for real, I wouldn't believe it was possible.

"Tell me a secret," I say.

"Why?"

"I want to know something about you no one else knows."

"Okay, but then you have to tell me one."

"Deal."

Austin takes a minute to think about it. "Remember when I ran into you at internship the day after my presentation?"

"How could I ever forget?"

"I didn't run into you randomly. I made an excuse to come down to your floor to look for you."

"Weren't you looking for Parker?"

"Parker's not hard to find. I was looking for you."

"Aw."

"Was that a good secret?"

"The best."

"Now you."

I wasn't planning to tell Austin my biggest secret. I've never told anyone before. But suddenly I want to tell him. I want to get it out and I know I can trust him with anything.

"Something happened when I was seven," I say against his chest. It's better this way, where I don't have to see the pity in his eyes. "The most horrible thing that's ever happened to me, actually."

Austin rubs my arm in slow strokes.

"My mom and I were on the subway. She was pregnant with my little sister. The seats were all taken with a few people standing. Someone got up for her, but she told me to sit instead of taking the seat for herself. Someone else offered her their seat, but she said we only had two stops so she was fine standing." The memory tears into my brain. I let myself watch what happened all over again. "Two guys were standing near us. They started arguing. One of them became so enraged he shoved the other guy, who bumped into my mom really hard. Mom fell . . . and she lost the baby."

"Oh my god." Austin hugs me tight. "I'm so sorry."

"I lost the sister I never even got to have."

Part of me wants to keep talking. I want to tell him about how I turned my anger into hope for a better world. About how I channeled my energy into warm fuzzies and random acts of kindness. But some of that anger still undulates beneath my optimism. And if I start ranting, I'm afraid I will never stop.

"My parents were crazy suffocating last year," I say. "I used to have nightmares after the accident, but they eventually went away . . . until last year for some reason. I guess I woke up screaming a few times. My parents kept having these whispered worried chats and throwing me pity glances. My mom kept harassing me to go to counseling. They made it impossible to move on. I couldn't wait to move out. I even hauled a ton of dirty laundry with me, I wanted to leave so bad."

"I hear you on the suffocating thing," Austin says. "Feeling trapped is so frustrating."

"When did you feel trapped?"

Austin doesn't answer. He just goes back to rubbing my arm in slow strokes.

Eventually we need a snack. I agree to forage in the kitchen. Opening my door feels strange. It's like I forgot this whole world beyond my room existed. Austin met Rosanna on the way out of the bathroom this morning, but that's been the extent of our interaction with other people today. As I head to the kitchen, I see Rosanna on the couch in the living room. She does not look happy.

I go over and sit next to her. "What's wrong?" I ask.

Rosanna shakes her head miserably. "I don't want to bother you. How's the romantic weekend going?"

"Rosanna. What happened?"

She takes a deep breath. "Remember that girl I told you about at the camp party who hated me for no reason? The one I'd never seen before?"

"Nasty Girl?"

"Except Nasty Girl has a name now. Addison. And guess where Addison's housing is? In the same building as Mica. They ran into each other in the hall. And guess what Addison told Mica? That I've been talking all this trash about her. That I called Mica a selfish bitch who doesn't like kids and is fine with living in poverty for the rest of her life taking government handouts."

"What the *what*?"

"Yeah, no, it gets better. Addison said that we were good friends in high school and I stole her boyfriend at the junior prom. Sadie, she didn't go to my school. I'd never even seen her before the party. But she knew all this stuff about me, like where I'm from and personal things about my family. How does she know all that if I don't even know who she is? And why does she hate me so much?"

This sounds like something out of a horror movie. Those twisted ones where a deranged girl is stalking another girl and creates this whole alternate reality in her mind. Addison sounds like a lunatic. I hope Rosanna is safe.

"Are you sure you'd never seen her before the party?" I ask.

"Never! I've been racking my brain. The party was the first time I'd ever seen her."

"That's so weird. Is there a way to get in touch with her? So you can ask her what her damage is?"

"I could call the Upper East camp and get her number. They're closed until Monday, though."

"You should definitely call them. I can't believe she turned Mica against you. Why did Mica believe her?"

"Everything she said seemed believable. What motive would she have to lie? Mica just met me a few days ago. At first I was surprised she believed Addison. But then I realized that even when you click with someone right away, you don't really know them." Rosanna rubs her arms like she got a sudden chill. "No one really knows anyone."

"Excuse me, but *I* know you're a good person. And we just met. There's no way you'd say or even think those things about Mica. This girl is going down. If anyone named Addison confronts me, I will get in her face so fast she'll wish we'd never met."

"What would your Random Acts of Kindness group say?"

"They'd congratulate me for defending you against a negative, horrible person. Kindness isn't only about spreading happiness. It's also about reducing the amount of suck in the world. It's pretty clear that Addison sucks more than anyone."

My door creaks open a little. I peer over my shoulder to see Austin peeking out.

"Go back to your hot man," Rosanna says. "I'll be fine."

"Are you sure?"

"If I can stop staring at the phone. D hasn't called today."

When Rosanna told us how she ran out of D's place, I could empathize. Being in a new relationship that's moving too fast is scary. Not only that, but being with a grown and sexy man in his fancy apartment for the first time, just the two of you? That's intense. Especially if you don't have a lot of experience. Rosanna hasn't said much about her past love life, but I get the impression that the boyfriend thing is new territory for her. Of course she ran out of there. I'm proud of her for having enough courage to even go back to his place.

"Actually . . . he called last night," Rosanna says. "Right after Mica hung up on me. I didn't feel like talking to him. I was too afraid I would start crying or something. He doesn't need to be bothered by this catty high school drama. Only . . . I'm not in high school anymore. My expectation was that all of this petty nonsense would cease to exist in the real world. What a colossal disappointment to discover that's not true."

"On the bright side, D obviously cares about you. That's why he called you last night. He wants to make sure you're okay."

"Last night I was way too upset to pretend everything was okay."

"He doesn't want you to pretend. He wants you to be yourself."

"How do you know?"

"Isn't it obvious?" From everything Rosanna has told me

about D, he sounds like a good guy. The kind of guy who likes Rosanna for exactly who she is.

"Then why hasn't he—" The house phone rings, cutting Rosanna off. We look at the screen. Donovan Clark is calling.

"Oh my god, that's him!"

Rosanna just stares at the phone.

"Pick up!" I yell. "He probably wants to see you tonight!" I'm so freaking thrilled D is calling. Of course he's calling right when we were talking about him not calling. Other people's love lives are infinitely fascinating to me. I can't wait to hear what D says, but I go back to my room to give Rosanna her privacy.

Austin is beyond adorable lying on my bed. He's flipping through the book I'm currently reading.

"Everything okay?" he asks when I come in.

"Minor crisis. Nothing that can't be resolved."

"Good. Because it stopped raining and I'm taking you to dinner."

"Sweet!"

"And I have a surprise for you."

"How much do I love surprises?"

"So much."

"What is it?"

"You really want me to tell you?"

"Tell."

"You know how you've been searching for the best veggie burger in New York?"

"Yeah . . . ?"

"I found it for you at Hillstone. It's a more upscale place, so you'll probably want to wear one of those cute dresses I saw in your closet."

I jump on the bed and throw my arms around Austin. "You are the best. boyfriend. *ever.*"

Rosanna is still on the couch when we're leaving for dinner. She looks a lot happier.

"What did he say?" I ask.

"You were right. He wants to go out tonight."

"Yay! Where are you going?"

"We couldn't decide. He's calling me back."

"We're going to Hillstone if you guys want to meet up there later."

"It's a restaurant, but it has a cool bar," Austin adds. He arranges for Rosanna and D to call his cell if they decide to meet up with us.

We hold hands the whole walk to Hillstone, stopping to kiss every few blocks like we do. The night is clear and fresh. Most people we pass seem less frazzled than usual. Even the air feels lighter, as if the rain washed our collective angst away.

Austin puts our names in when we get to Hillstone. Then we sit at the bar to wait for our table. I'm loving the dim lighting, cool vibe, and smell of garlic bread.

"Have you ever tried an amaretto sour?" Austin asks.

"I don't drink."

"Why not?"

"Um, because I don't see the point?"

"The point is to have fun. Are you seriously telling me you've never been drunk?"

"I am seriously telling you that."

"You're more straight-edge than I thought."

"Thank you. But I'm actually straight-edge with a twist."

"Would you like to try one?"

"An amaretto sour?"

"You'd like it. It's really sweet. Like you."

"I'll try a sip of yours if you get one."

"Hmm. Then maybe I'll have to order two drinks for myself."

"Party on."

"Bathroom break first." Austin gets up from the bar stool just as a guy is sitting down on the other side of him. The guy bumps into Austin, shoving him against the bar.

"Sorry, man!" the guy slurs.

Austin holds up his hand like it's okay. "I'll be right back," he tells me.

I don't notice Austin's phone on his bar stool until it rings. It must have fallen out of his back pocket when the guy bumped into him. Thinking it might be Rosanna, I pick up his phone. I really hope she and D are coming. I cannot wait to meet him. How much fun will it be when the boys start becoming friends?

Rosanna is not the one calling Austin. There's some strange woman's name Austin has never mentioned before.

I'm not sure what makes me answer the call. Something just tells me I should.

"Hello?" I say.

"Hello?" she says. "Who is this?"

"Sorry, this is Austin's phone. I picked up for him."

"Put Austin on."

"He's in the bathroom. May I take a message?"

She lets out a sharp laugh. "You don't want to hear what I'm about to say."

My stomach drops.

"Who is this?" I ask.

"This is Austin's wife," the woman says. "Who's *this*?"

No.

This is not happening.

Austin cannot be married. That doesn't even make sense.

The woman claiming to be Austin's wife wants to know who I am. This probably isn't the best time to tell her I'm his soul mate.

I don't answer her. I hang up and turn his phone off.

I'm still staring at the phone in my hand when Austin comes back.

"Calling someone?" he asks, sitting down.

"Your wife called." The words sound like a lie coming out of my mouth. Like we're acting out some movie scene. But I'm pretty sure what I just said is true.

"What?"

"I did not just talk to your wife."

Austin looks at the phone. He doesn't say anything.

"Please tell me you're not married," I say.

"Sadie." Austin puts his hand on my arm.

I yank my arm away. I throw his phone down on the bar.

"Please," I say.

Austin looks at me. "I can't tell you that," he says.

My entire world crumbles. My entire world, containing every truth I've ever known, every relationship I've ever built, every experience I've ever had, crumbles to pieces around me.

"I was about to get separated before I met you," Austin says. "We got married too young. I've been regretting it. Then I found you and . . . now I know how love is supposed to feel. For the first time in my life, I understand what it feels like to really be in love."

We got married too young. Not *we* as in Austin and me. *We* as in Austin and his wife.

"I thought we had something real," I say.

"We did. We do."

"How can something real be based on a lie?"

"Everything I've told you is true."

"Except you forgot the part where you're married." Underneath the shock, I know I should leave. Just walk out and never look back. But the shock is keeping me glued to the stool.

I can't believe he's married. I can't believe this is happening.

"You don't wear a wedding ring," I point out.

"I stopped wearing it a few weeks before we met."

"But you put it back on when you go home."

Austin stays quiet.

"Right?" I press.

"Yeah."

"How could you do that to your wife? How could you do that to *me*?"

"Sadie, I—"

"What about when you told me we were made for each other?" A million unanswered questions flash through my mind all at once. None of this makes sense. "When you said we were meant to be?"

"I really do feel that way. I feel closer to you than I ever have to my wife."

My wife. Not me. Some other woman.

"Who are you?" I ask.

"Someone who adores you."

"What about last night when you told me I make you happier than anyone ever has?"

"That was true. Everything I've ever told you was true."

"Even when you told me you're married? Oh wait, you never told me that. I had to find out from your *wife*."

This is bullshit. I spring up from the stool, almost toppling it over.

"We're done," I say. "Obviously."

I walk out. Austin doesn't follow me.

I am completely shattered. I walk without realizing what I'm doing or where I'm going. When I reach Hudson River

Park, where we were those people I'd always wanted to be and the epic feeling burst open inside of me brighter than a million stars, I look out across the water. Austin lives on the other side. He doesn't live alone. He lives with his wife.

My soul mate is not who I thought he was.

Our entire relationship was a joke.

He was married the whole time.

How do you ever come back from that?

THIRTY-FIVE
DARCY

SO I MADE AN EXECUTIVE decision. But first I had to admit something to myself I really didn't want to.

I like Jude.

We were making out last night in that recliner at Welcome to the Johnsons for an astoundingly long time. Straight up, we must have broken like five different records. I couldn't wait to be alone with him. Let's just say I could tell Jude felt the same way. We went to his place after. Only one of his three roommates was home. Jude introduced us and then we disappeared into his room.

And then . . . we spent the night together.

Nothing serious happened. Unless you call making out all night serious. But I have to admit that my feelings for Jude have been upgraded. I'm in the hookup haze and feeling all types of twirly emotions. Twirly emotions have been known to get out of control.

Back to my executive decision. If Jude needs us to be all official boyfriend/girlfriend material, then I can't help him. But if Jude is into keeping things casual, I'm into keeping things casual. With potential. Sort of an exclusive casual thing. Like maybe we could try just seeing each other, but with no expectations. Our chemistry is ridiculous. We have tons of fun together. So I was thinking it might be an interesting experiment. The exclusive casual thing gives us the best of both worlds: being with a person we really like without the pressure of a heavy commitment. How could he not agree that would be a sweet deal?

Last night made me realize one thing I miss about being in a relationship. I miss the consistency of always being able to share the Now with your person. Someone who feels the same way about living in the moment as you do. Someone you can share your life with who you not only love, but love spending time with. As much as I live for adventure, part of me needs that deeper connection with another person. Connection makes the adventures more meaningful. Without me realizing it was happening, Jude has been filling that void for me.

So yeah. Jude's on his way over. I am bursting to tell him these things. He'll want to know what happened to the Darcy of fun summer flings and keeping the boys at a distance. I'll have to find a way to explain that wasn't the best solution.

The door buzzes. My heart jumps so high it nearly lifts me right off the floor. I'm secretly relieved that Sadie and Rosanna are out. They would not recognize me in my hyper boy-crazed state. I literally cannot wait to see Jude, so I run down to the front door to let him in. Buzzing him up and waiting for him to climb the stairs would be excruciating. The best part is that I didn't even ask him to come over. Before I left his place early this morning for the almost-walk-of-shame home, Jude said he was going to come by tonight to pick me up. He said he had something special planned, and that this will be a night I will never forget.

I zoom down the stairs and zip to the front door. I whip it open.

But it's not Jude.

It's my ex.

My ex who dumped me like a bag of trash in some ghetto Dumpster. Like everything he'd said to me, all the promises he made, everything we'd been through, meant nothing.

"Logan," I say. "What are you doing here?"

"I was wrong," Logan says. "I should have never let you go."

Oh.

My.

God.

How many times did I secretly hope Logan would show up at my door like this, saying these exact words? I must have pictured this scenario a thousand times my first few nights in New York. Lying in bed staring into the darkness, waiting for the light traffic noises of 5th Avenue to lull me to sleep, wishing that Logan would realize he made a mistake and come for me.

But Logan told me it was over right before I left for New

York. That was the most painful type of breakup I can imagine: when you're relying on your boyfriend during a big life transition and then—*poof!*—he's gone. Actually that was my only breakup. Logan was my first love. He was the first boy to dump me. When he told me it was over, I began extricating him from my heart. Or so I thought. Seeing him standing in front of me now, every feeling I ever had for him crashes into me like a tidal wave.

My first love is right here. Standing on my stoop. Asking for a second chance. Exactly the way I'd hoped he would. Despite my best efforts to forget him and move on, deep down I never stopped hoping. And now he's come all the way from California to get me back.

Logan puts his bag down. I try not to let his tall-lanky-dark-hair-and-eyes-sexy-sloucher thing affect me.

"We should be together, Darcy," he says. "I want to be with you. I've always wanted to be with you. I just got scared. You were the first girl I'd ever been in love with. You opened my eyes to so much. Some of it I wasn't ready to see. But I'm ready now."

"You broke my heart."

"You'll never know how sorry I am. You were right about the long-distance thing. We would have been the exception. We would have made it work. We still can."

"How are you realizing all this now? Why didn't you know this two weeks ago?"

"That would have been easier, I know. I'm so sorry I hurt

you. Guys are idiots. If you didn't know that before, it should be obvious now."

"So . . . what, you're an idiot and you realize we belong together and I should take you back?"

"Pretty much."

"And then what? We just pretend you never broke up with me?"

"No, of course not. We can talk about it as much as you want. I don't expect to be forgiven overnight. Let me prove to you that you can trust me again."

"That's . . . I mean, you can't just show up here and expect everything to go back to the way it was."

"Why not?"

Out of the corner of my eye, I see Jude down the block. Coming for me.

THIRTY-SIX
ROSANNA

WHAT A DIFFERENCE A DAY makes when you have the right support system. I'd been feeling gross all day about Mica blowing up at me. How could she believe I said those things? I just couldn't wrap my head around it. I still can't. Talking to Sadie helped. When camp is back in session on Monday, I'll call the Upper East location and get Addison's number. I'll find out what her problem is. Whatever is wrong, I'm sure we can find a solution that doesn't involve Addison spewing lies about me. I'll ask Addison to tell Mica that no part of what she said was true. Given how much she hates me, it won't be easy to convince her to own up to her lies. But people shouldn't act like monsters. If they do, they should be forced to face the consequences of their actions.

I've been told that my expectations of people are too high. The thing is, I don't think expecting someone to treat other human beings with courtesy and respect is unreasonable. The world would be a much better place if everyone treated others with kindness. It astounds me that such a basic principle is beyond the scope of comprehension for anyone.

Sadie was also right about D. He was calling to ask me out. It's true that I didn't answer the phone when he called last night because I was afraid I would burst into tears. But I was also afraid of what he might say. D breaking up with me right after Mica did would have been too much. He deserves to be with someone more experienced who can give him what he wants. When we talked tonight, it was a huge relief that he was calling to see if I was okay and to ask if I wanted to see him. At first we couldn't decide where we wanted to go, but then he called an hour later and told me to meet him at Otheroom. D said it's one of his favorite bars. Very dark and romantic.

I call Austin before I leave to let him know we won't be meeting up with them. It goes to voice mail. I hope he gets the message so they're not waiting around for us.

Walking down Perry Street toward the river, a refreshing summer breeze lifts my hair back and rustles my dress around my legs. Three cute guys turn to look at me as they pass me on the street. I smile at the orange sky.

D is waiting for me outside Otheroom. He's so gorgeous I don't even know what to do with myself. He's standing still with the same serenity he had at Lalo, confident and patient. His skin is sun-kissed and his sandy blond hair looks lighter. He sees me a few doors down and smiles. I wave at him, smiling back.

He watches me walk toward him. I try not to feel self-conscious with his eyes on me, teetering on the fancy heels Darcy insisted would go with every new ensemble she bought for me. Looking like I actually know how to walk in heels would probably help. Plus I'm nervous about seeing D again after running out like a freak. Awkward doesn't even begin to describe it.

"You look beautiful," D says.

"Thanks. I wasn't sure if this was too dressy, or . . ."

"It's perfect."

Otheroom has to be the smallest bar in New York. The front windows are wide open. A counter runs across them, jammed with people laughing and yelling over the music. We push our way up to the bar. D told me that this place has regular drinks like cherry soda and root beer, which are apparently rare finds in bars. He orders a cherry soda for me and a beer for him and we go to the back room. A couch curves around the edge of the tiny space. A couple is just leaving from a spot on the couch in the far corner as we walk in. We snag the spot.

"This place is awesome," I say. I'm not a bar person at all, but I would come back here. The two small rooms are both very dark. Candles are placed on every table and ledge, illuminating everyone and everything with a soft glow. We sip our drinks in the candlelight. D captures me with his intense laser focus.

"Remember when you were out on my balcony?" he says. "Admiring the view?"

I nod.

"Your reaction was amazing. The way you were lost in your

own world for a few minutes. It reminded me of my first week in the apartment. I would stand out there every night, mesmerized by the lights and buildings and rooftops. Every night I would notice something new. I still find new things all the time. It would be impossible to see everything there is, even if I stood out there every single night. The city is constantly changing. Growing. Improving. The energy is like this fuel I run on. When you were out on my balcony taking it all in, I could tell you felt the same way. You get a rush from just being here."

"Being here means everything to me. This was my big dream for so long."

"I'm proud of you for living your dream. Not many people have the courage to do that. People usually hold back because they're afraid. You're not like that."

My mind flashes back to running out of D's apartment. I was afraid then. But here he is, telling me that I'm not the type of person to let fear hold her back. Not only does he see the potential of what I can become, he sees those qualities as if I'm already showing them.

"I really wanted to kiss you," D says. "Why didn't you let me?"

I can't admit what happened to D. I couldn't even talk about it with my friends. He doesn't need to know, anyway. My past does not have to define me. All he needs to know is this best version of myself.

"Sorry," D says. "You said you didn't want to talk about it. I shouldn't be pushing you. Was I really that deranged creeper unzipping your dress? After you said you had to go? That was—" D rakes his hands through his hair. "That was wrong. You need to take it slow. I respect that. Don't worry, I won't push you anymore."

"It's okay."

"Can you forgive me?"

"Of course."

"I think I was just . . . overwhelmed. You've been making me feel things I haven't felt in a long time. And you've been making me feel things I've never felt before." D slides his hand over mine, putting me in a tingly trance. He's looking at me with that intense laser focus again.

This is it. The moment I've been waiting for. The moment when I know for sure that I'm doing the right thing. The doubt and fear have disintegrated. All I want is to never stop feeling this way.

My lips find his in the dim candlelight. I kiss him the way I have a million times in my fantasies. He kisses me back with the same passion. The way he's making me feel is how I've been waiting to feel for so long. I want to touch him everywhere. Kissing him this way is even hotter than I imagined.

D is wrong for me in a lot of ways. There are guys out there who would be a better match for me.

But I want him.

Someone who, despite every fiber of resistance I've been straining to keep resilient, is what my body wants. I want to start overcoming my fear of being intimate with a boy. I can't handle sex yet. I just want to feel empowered. I want to be with D the way I've imagined in my fantasies. Then I can stop being so afraid.

And then the present will become powerful enough to erase the past.

THE STORIES OF SADIE, DARCY,
AND ROSANNA WILL CONTINUE
IN BOOK TWO OF

ACKNOWLEDGMENTS

THESE SPECTACULAR POINTS OF LIGHT glitter more brightly than the Chrysler Building, the Empire State Building, and One World Trade put together:

Katherine Tegen, who welcomed me with open arms. Your editorial insight, creative vision, and overall brilliance have sculpted this book into the best version of itself. Thank you for a world of new possibilities.

Emily van Beek, who understands the importance of dreaming big. We took a leap and the net appeared, just as we had a Knowing it would. Thank you for everything.

The amazing team at HarperCollins who made this book shine, including Kelsey Horton, Kathryn Silsand, Lauren Flower, Alana Whitman, Rosanne Romanello, and Kate Morgan Jackson. And thanks to Barb Fitzsimmons, Amy Ryan, and Erin Fitzsimmons for designing a cover that takes gorgeous to a whole other level.

My friends, whose love, support, and positive energy have helped me tremendously over the years. Thank you for all the happiness you bring.

My readers, who make this life possible. You are why I write. I can't thank you enough for all of your support and enthusiasm. I have the best readers in the world and I am eternally thankful for you.

Librarians, teachers, booksellers, and bloggers who spread the love. You inspire teens to develop a lifelong love of reading. Thank you for your hard work and dedication.

Matt, who is my soul mate, the love of my life, and the man of my dreams. Even when my teen self was wondering where you were, you were always so much closer than I realized. Go karma.